DEEP HARMONY

Deep Harmony

by

Sonia Deane

Dales Large Print Books
Long Preston, North Yorkshire,
BD23 4ND, England.

British Library Cataloguing in Publication Data.

Deane, Sonia
   Deep harmony.

   A catalogue record of this book is
   available from the British Library

   ISBN   978-1-84262-456-2 pbk

First published in Great Britain by Hutchinson & Co. Ltd.

Cover illustration © Nigel Chamberlain by arrangement with
Alison Eldred

The moral right of the author has been asserted

Published in Large Print 2007 by arrangement with
The estate of Sonia Deane, care of Rupert Crew Ltd.

Dales Large Print is an imprint of Library Magna Books Ltd.

Printed and bound in Great Britain by
T.J. (International) Ltd., Cornwall, PL28 8RW

CHAPTER I

Nicholas Young came forward to greet Stephanie as the maid admitted her to his study.

'Miss Reid?' He spoke inquiringly.

'Yes.'

'What can I do for you?'

Stephanie looked at him, summing him up as she did so. Tall, dark, but not, she decided, handsome without in any way lacking charm, which emanated more from a mental and spiritual quality than any uniformity of feature. Artistic, definitely; aloof and somewhat unapproachable, forbidding; a man living very much within himself while daring any outsider to invade the secret precincts of his private world.

She came straight to the point.

'Sell me your Hepplewhite, serpentine card table and early eighteenth-century wall mirror.' She met his gaze boldly. 'I was told you were disposing of a great deal of the furniture here and I hoped these might be included.'

'Then I'm sorry to disappoint you,' he said coldly. 'They are not for sale – now or ever.'

'That would seem to settle the matter.'

'It does settle it,' he corrected her with studied politeness.

She smiled.

'Then there is no need for me to waste your time further.'

He raised his gaze as one suddenly aware of a deepening interest; as one appreciating that Stephanie was both attractive, intelligent and singularly disarming.

'It is,' he said abruptly, 'unusual to find a woman who can be so direct and will take "no" for an answer.'

She didn't avoid his eyes.

'You must have been unfortunate in your contacts with women, Mr Young.' Her lips twisted into a wry smile. 'But, then, men would seem ever to woo that which they despise.'

'Cynic?'

'No; merely a student of psychology.'

'It could,' he suggested, 'be the same thing.'

'Only it isn't – in my case.'

'You are very definite.'

'One has to be in business.'

'And you,' he said, moving to a table on which stood a decanter of sherry and some glasses, 'are in business.'

Stephanie was suddenly disconcerted by his steady gaze. It unnerved her; the cool, business-like façade faded; the feminine and capricious took possession.

'Yes,' she exclaimed. 'I am just starting in partnership with Mr Morly. Antiques. It's fun,' she added, blithely, 'collecting things.'

He nodded.

'And you hoped to "collect" my card table.'

'Yes ... we have a buyer.' It was a frank utterance. 'Or I should say, we *had,* since you are not disposed to sell.'

'You do not make the mistake of imagining I should change my mind?'

For a second they looked at each other in faint challenge, then:

'No,' she replied firmly. 'You are not the type to do that.' And she added provocatively: 'Certainly not through any feminine persuasion.'

'Immune from the wiles of your sex – eh?'

Her gaze was very level.

'No doubt you imagine yourself to be immune... If all I hear about you is true...' She stopped.

He prompted almost roughly:

'And that is–'

'Do you want the truth?' Spirit flashed into her eyes.

'Most certainly.'

'Merely that you are a hermit. I was considered brave to storm this citadel of yours,' she added.

'Really.' It was a clipped sound; he became suddenly grave.

She hastened:

'And if you are telling yourself that I listen to local gossip, you are quite wrong.' Her smile came naturally. 'Although I must confess I have always been intrigued by hermits.'

Nicholas wanted to be angry, but there was something about Stephanie's attitude that made it impossible, and he found himself saying involuntarily:

'Very well ... suppose the hermit offers you a sherry, will you accept one?'

'I'd love to.'

She watched him as he poured out the wine from the decanter, and did not attempt to deceive herself about her reactions. Emotionally, even in those brief moments, Nicholas Young stirred her: she was aware of him as she had never before been conscious of any man. And true to her type she in no way shrank from the fact.

At twenty-four, Stephanie was mature far beyond her years. Her tastes were a mixture of intellectuality and romantic illusions. She enjoyed a Bach Fugue no less and no more than a Strauss waltz, or a tuneful, modern composition. Her mind was alert, flexible; her desires normal and healthy even though, deep within her, there was a sense of unfulfilment, as if an integral part of the jigsaw of her life was missing. Thus far, she had regarded men as an amusing and necessary decoration: she had flirted with many, rejected many, but loved none, not because she had any preconceived ideas, or pre-judices, against marriage, but because no one had roused her sufficiently to care, other than mildly, whether or not she saw him again. When she thought in terms of marriage it was as of a complete physical surrender, the impact of affinities, but she refrained from all dogmatic assertion on the subject, maintaining that generalization was a dangerous misconception. In appearance she was arresting and unusual with a mass of dark, chestnut hair, fair skin and tantalizing grey-blue eyes, while her soft red lips curved into the promise of passionate response.

Nicholas was aware of all this in some subconscious fashion as he stood there and, even though he would have denied it, anxious that she should prolong her stay. He handed her the drink, raised his glass, looked at her above its rim and said:

'To your success – and mine.'

Instinctively, Stephanie glanced out at the picture framed by long casement windows. It was a wild, overgrown landscape that met her eyes and she said gently:

'I think I know why you've called this "Wilderness Farm".' A pause, then: 'And yet there's something exciting about it.'

'Wresting success from failure,' he said, responding to her mood, 'is always thrilling. At least to me.'

Stephanie moved and half-knelt on the

wide window seat the better to take in the sweep of countryside – and appraise it.

'At least the orchard looks productive – the blossom is amazing and utterly lovely.'

He spoke abruptly.

'Would you care to wander around?'

She turned impulsively and a trifle breathlessly:

'I would.' It was a deep, sincere exclamation.

It struck her, then, that he was, in truth, a mystery. New to the district, without apparent background. And, obviously, unattached. Had he ever been married? Was he a bachelor, or a widower... No one seemed to know and not even the most curious around him had, thus far, been able to ascertain the facts. Odd, Stephanie thought, for any man to take over such a place as this and to live in its rather dilapidated farm-house, with only a housekeeper to look after him. She supposed it had been the housekeeper who admitted her.

They went out into the silence of the spring evening and her conjecturing turned to unfeigned appreciation of the scene confronting her.

Wilderness Farm was situated within the northern margin of the Cotswolds, rising from the plain of Evesham, and spreading its acres midway between Winchcombe and Broadway. During the last ten years it had passed through several hands and still remained derelict; yet there was about it that promise which Stephanie was quick, intuitive, in sensing.

'This will be paradise one of these days,' she said quietly and with conviction.

'You like farms?'

'Yes; they're real.'

'And you like reality?'

'I like it,' she said, 'when one is able to colour it with illusion, without committing the folly of imagining that illusion *is* reality. Rather involved but—'

'Not to me.' He indicted a wide expanse of upland country. 'I want crops growing there next year,' he said doggedly. 'Cattle grazing in those meadows to your right. I have it all planned.' He looked back at the Cotswold stone house, now glistening in the light of the evening sun. In design, it was typical of the seventeenth-century pattern of the district; virtually medieval, inheriting the Gothic tradition, with its mullions, dripstones and arched doorway. 'I've plans for the interior of the house, too.' He spoke with a whimsical reflectiveness as he added: 'Even as a hermit I take it that I am allowed comfort!'

Their eyes met; silence wrapped around them as though its graciousness offered them sanctuary and the breathless excitement of discovery. Stephanie's heart became oddly still, not able to endure its former throbbing. The enchanted spell of evening, the fragrance, sweet and sharp, of apple blossom and wallflowers, was as perfume sprayed from an invisible bottle. Between them, passion, absolute, demanding, surged – inescapable and inevitable.

Stephanie managed to say tensely:

'I am sure you would hate anything less than perfection.' She averted her gaze. 'I detest compromise, too. Life forces us to indulge it with ourselves, and humans generally, because we are all so utterly im-perfect … let it end there, however. Perhaps that is why I like antiques: they are, in their way, so perfect; specimens of craftsmanship, imagination and artistry.' Her laugh came spontaneously. 'I shall bore you.'

Nicholas knew that he was certainly not bored. He fought against what, he told himself angrily, was the mere treachery of the senses. This girl was a stranger to him and he had done with women, anyway. Not into her hands would he deliver his future peace of mind and happiness; not even by the weakness of desiring her, which would ensnare him mentally once he succumbed to her charms. He said almost curtly:

'On the contrary; your ideas are quite refreshing.' His expression changed. 'That sounded patronizing – didn't it?'

'Very' – frankly. 'You do not intend to yield an inch, Mr Young,' she added, relying on

14

banter to break the spell that seemed to bind them.

'That can be very wise,' he answered.

'And very dull.'

'The voice of inexperience,' he murmured.

'Perhaps; but I hope I shall never run away from life nevertheless.' Her voice was strong, decisive.

He held her gaze.

'And I hope it treats you very kindly,' he added, 'as to make that precaution unnecessary.'

She stared at him, aware of a deepening mystery and finding that she could not entirely curb her curiosity.

'No one has stayed here for very long,' she told him, changing the subject abruptly.

'Then I shall be the exception.' His eyes were drawn back to hers. 'You, obviously, live around here.'

'At Winchcombe.'

'An antique in itself,' he said appreciatively.

'To me, it is always like a village, even though it does happen to be a market town... Do you know Gloucestershire well?'

'I am getting to know it,' he said briefly and, instantly, changed the subject as one who has no intention whatsoever of answering any questions of a personal nature.

'Gloucestershire, Worcestershire, Warwickshire – I love them all. Different, somehow, from the rest of England.'

He looked down at her very intently.

'The heart of it,' he said and his deep voice thrilled her.

'Meon Hill to Winchcombe... Orchard roads; and Broadway Hill with its magnificent view. There's something about it all...' She stopped, aware of the fact that sentiment was welling within her and that the nearness of Nicholas Young created a mood both new and dangerous.

'Something,' he went on almost curtly, 'that makes fools of us all.'

'If you regard emotion as folly,' she challenged.

'And obviously, you do not.' It was a question, sharp and direct.'

'If I did' – her voice was a trifle unsteady– 'I should consider that there was something radically wrong with my outlook.'

'You are young enough to be entitled to all your romantic dreams,' he exclaimed.

Again their eyes met and, with a look, some magnetic force sprang to life. Stephanie knew that should he have drawn her into his arms she could not have resisted him.

'And you are too bitter to allow yours freedom,' she managed to say in a breath.

'Caution is not bitterness,' he corrected her.

'No; just a mist over the face of the sun.'

'A pretty description.'

'A true one.' She flashed him a smile. 'And now I must go.' She took in the sweep of farmland and the garden that surrounded the house and which, even in its neglected state, had an old-world charm, with its rockeries, arbours and masses of lavender hedges. Her tone became business-like: 'Do you intend to sell any of the contents of the house, Mr Young? Or was that merely gossip?'

'Not entirely; some of the stuff I took over when I came here is pure junk' – he hastened with a broad smile – 'certainly not in your line. I shall get rid of that in my own time–'

'I could introduce you to someone who would at least be honest,' she suggested.

'I'd be grateful.'

She stared up at him. They had talked for some considerable time and she realized that she knew no more about him than when she came. Had he gone in for farming that he had taken on such a place? Had he made it a career, or was this a retreat from the past? She pulled herself up critically. Why concern herself … her mission was finished and it was unlikely she would ever see him again; just because he had refrained from broadcasting the details of his life was no reason for wild conjecture or avid curiosity.

'I left my car in the lane,' she explained as he would have guided her back to the house. 'I can reach it through the garden.'

Nicholas resisted the temptation to invite

her to dinner and refused to admit that he was loath for her to go. It struck him that it was a very long while since he had seriously talked to any woman, and found the mere fact of doing so unsettling and his own immunity placed in jeopardy. There was something about Stephanie, he argued, in mitigation of his lapse, that made him review his life from the angle of what might have been. Not a pleasant reflection. He said, despite himself:

'You could come back through the house and have another sherry.'

She flashed him a quizzical look.

'I have intruded enough, Mr Young.'

He made no attempt to persuade her, but a bleak sensation of loneliness stole upon him.

'Do you visit many houses in search of treasures?'

'I'm beginning to do so. I love it; people are so interesting, quite apart from their possessions.'

He smiled.

'I trust I am not the exception!'

'On the contrary. I shall remember the card table I found to be out of reach.'

'I note the distinction.'

She laughed naturally.

'That was open to misconstruction – wasn't it?'

'Definitely.'

'Then allow me to correct myself: I shall remember your courtesy *and* your card table.'

He inclined his head in a mock bow. Then, abruptly:

'Is your business actually in Winchcombe?'

'No – Warwick. I am thinking of moving to Warwick very soon; there is a flat over the premises we have taken.'

'I see.' He wanted to know more, but refrained from questioning her.

They stood facing each other for a brief moment. Stephanie found herself hoping that he would make inquiries that might suggest an interest in her affairs, or promise a further meeting. Faint colour stole into her cheeks; never before had she indulged such adolescent reactions towards any man.

He saw her to her car, helped her in, and remained beside the door while she started the engine.

'Thank you,' she said nervously as she manipulated the gears; 'thank you for being so patient.' Her smile was glowing. 'Good-bye, Mr Young.'

'Good-bye, Miss Reid,' he murmured.

She raced down the lane; a strange emotion tingling in her veins. Nicholas Young! Well, that was that... It had been a waste of her time to go there...

A waste of time...

Curious why she should feel so completely cut off from her surroundings as she covered the short distance to Winchcombe; why the blossom, shimmering with a pearly radiance as it fluttered in a soft, scented breeze, should almost hurt her with its beauty... Strange how it seemed that the face of the man she had just left appeared to be superimposed on every landscape, and as she reached the cottage, which she shared with her brother, a sensation akin to depression engulfed her; a loneliness foreign to her. She glanced at the clock on the dashboard. Twelve forty-five. A restlessness pursued her; there was nothing she desired less than to lunch alone at home, yet it was exceedingly doubtful that Trevor Morly, her partner, would have completed his search for a particular antique – a Regency writing table, ornamented with brass mounts and gilt with an open cabinet for books, above.

A sudden, expansive mood came upon her as she thought of Trevor; he took the edge off her loneliness and loomed upon the horizon like a tower – strong, invulnerable – his friendship ever a sanctuary.

To her delight, as she drew up outside the small, thatched white cottage, Trevor Morly came forward from the garden to greet her.

'Any luck?' he asked with that blithe, carefree manner that typified his approach to life in general.

'None.' Stephanie slid from the car. 'And you?'

'Not with the writing table, but I got hold of a Queen Anne cabinet – you'll be wanting to keep it when you see it.'

Stephanie smiled at him; it was a smile indicative of friendliness and complete understanding.

'Quite probably since I want most of the things I see ... let's go in and have something to eat,' she added naturally. 'I'm starving.'

'Then how about coming along to the Lygon Arms,' he suggested.

'It's an idea. But I must do a spot to my face first,' she added, and went down the flagstone pathway as she spoke, with Trevor following, talking as he did so.

'What was that fellow Young like?'

'Quite pleasant.' Stephanie's heart seemed to quicken its beat.

'But he wouldn't sell.'

'No.'

'The cussed type?'

They had reached the lounge as he spoke, and Stephanie peeled off her hat and threw it unceremoniously into the nearest chair.

'The man has a perfect right to refuse to sell his own furniture,' she exclaimed defensively.

Trevor threw her a sudden, startled look.

'All the same,' he persisted, 'there's something definitely odd about that man ...

21

mind if I help myself to a drink?' He wandered to the cabinet as he spoke. 'Will you have one?'

Stephanie said almost recklessly:

'Yes; I did have a sherry but–'

'Good; glad you got something out of the deal… No, the idea of any man in his right mind, taking over a derelict property like Wilderness Farm and living there alone… Probably a murky past.' He added soda water to his whisky and, handing Stephanie her glass, rambled on: 'Just can't get the mentality of those eccentrics, can you?'

'Aren't you rather jumping to conclusions?' she demanded. 'Just because a man buys a farm that isn't flourishing and doesn't broadcast his private affairs, is no earthly reason why everyone should consider he is either eccentric, or has a murky past.'

Trevor stared at her.

'Rather on the defensive, aren't you?' he exclaimed infuriatingly.

'Nothing of the kind.'

'Don't snap my head off,' he said gaily. 'Evidently the mysterious Mr Young had sex appeal if nothing else.'

'You're positively ridiculous, Trevor.'

'I know; but I am, also, usually right. You liked him – didn't you?'

'I found him charming – yes.' She added rather too carelessly: 'But seeing that I was there less than an hour–'

'Quite a long while in which to receive a negative answer, my pet.'

'You're impossible... I've been to dozens of places recently and you've never cross-examined me like this before.'

'Probably,' he said, changing his tone, 'because I've never sensed that I had a rival before.'

Stephanie had a sudden vision of Nicholas Young as she stood there; she could hear again his deep, attractive voice; feel his penetrating gaze upon her, and be moved by the remembrance of his forceful personality. She avoided Trevor's gaze, saying as she turned towards the doorway:

'Unless you talk sense, I shall refuse to lunch with you.'

'I was talking sense... You could make me filthily jealous.'

'Trevor!' It was a shocked, incredulous cry.

'It's true,' he said in a somewhat subdued tone. 'You know, my dear, that you have always attracted me.'

She stared at him.

'I know that we have always been friends,' she insisted.

He made a somewhat ridiculing gesture.

'That can cover a multitude of emotions, Stephanie, and you know it.'

'I know nothing of the kind.' Her voice was indignant. 'When we went into partner-ship it was perfectly clear that – that–'

'That there was no thought in either of our minds about marriage?'

'Exactly.'

'I wasn't talking about marriage,' he told her quietly.

A sudden feeling of disquiet possessed her. She studied him subjectively for the first time. No one could have denied that he was attractive; good figure, tall mid-brown hair, fresh complexion and the litheness of the athlete. Until that moment she had regarded him very much as she regarded her own brother, with that natural acceptance of their relationship, their friendship of several years. Trevor was... Trevor, someone always there and of whom she was very fond. On rare occasions, perhaps at a dance, or a theatre, her heart had quickened at his touch, but never sufficiently for her to question herself about her regard for him. She would have said that he had no subtlety where sex was concerned, and was far more interested in the latest cricket score than in making love to any woman. She temporized:

'I don't think you know what you *are* talking about!' Her smile was intended to dismiss the topic.

He said doggedly:

'Just like a woman to avoid the issue because she doesn't want to face the facts.'

She stared at him as though seeing a stranger.

'Really, Trevor, this is quite absurd!'

He laughed softly.

'Why? Because I suddenly admit that you attract me, Stephanie. There's no law against it, you know.'

She met his gaze very steadily:

'We've been friends for years,' she said firmly, 'we've started in business together and even though we didn't express the fact in words, there was the tacit understanding that our relationship should continue along the lines familiar to us both. Business and romance – or whatever you care to call it – do not mix.'

'Meaning that had you suspected that my feelings for you were other than platonic you would not have contemplated me as a partner.'

'Since the possibility in no way occurred to me,' she said frankly, 'it isn't easy for me to give you an honest answer; but I can say this: I cannot change my conception of our relationship, Trevor.'

'Meaning that I do not attract you?'

She didn't avoid his challenging gaze.

'We are sufficiently adult, Trevor, to accept the fact that any two people who have affection for each other can, in certain circumstances, be roused physically *by* each other. But that element can be encouraged or otherwise and–'

'You,' he interrupted her, 'wish it to

remain otherwise?'

'Yes.'

'Why?' He was stubborn, defensive.

'Because I hate untidy emotions,' she said swiftly. 'Romantic affairs that straggle through one's life and, in the end, complicate them.' She gave him a direct and challenging gaze: 'You don't want to marry me, and I don't want to marry you, therefore–'

Again he interrupted:

'Do you allow of no compromise, Stephanie?'

'Not with my affections: all or nothing.'

'That is hardly the modern idea.'

'Then I am not modern.'

'And if I did attract you–'

'I cannot answer for what my mood might be in entirely different circumstances.'

'A clever evasion. Do you suggest that, until you seriously fall in love, you are immune from man's attentions?'

The word immune struck against the memory of her talk with Nicholas Young when she had implied that *he* was immune – or thought he was – from the wiles of her sex. Her voice was a little less steady as she replied:

'I should not be so foolish as to suggest any such thing.'

'Merely that *my* attentions are unwelcome?'

Stephanie felt wholly bewildered in that second; the conversation appeared to have become entirely out of hand; words piled upon words without elucidating the problem or bringing them nearer an understanding.

'Isn't all this quite absurd?' she said desperately. 'How did it start? Oh, let's go and have lunch and stop this nonsense before we lose all sense of proportion.'

'The cool, logical business woman – eh?'

'If you like; although that is not how I see myself. I detest that type of business women.'

'How I agree with you, my dear. As much sex appeal as a gnat.'

Stephanie laughed; an attractive, husky laugh that had none of the high-pitched shriek indulged too often by women; there was something very desirable about her as she stood there; a femininity, the charm of gentleness, allied to an overwhelming magnetism that drew both men and women to her in true affection.

'I suggest another drink for you, Trevor,' she said lightly. 'Then you can take me out to lunch before I die of hunger.'

His gaze was stormy, but admiring:

'You'd get away with murder,' he said grudgingly.

'Splendid! So much more comfortable,' she murmured complacently.

'You were determined that I shouldn't tell you what was really in my mind – weren't you?'

'Of course; words, once uttered, can never be retracted.' With that she flashed him a smile and went up to her room to attend to her make-up. But her poise was no indication of her reactions; emotionally she was churned up to a point of frightening tension. First the meeting with Nicholas ... now, Trevor. She knew that he had been going to ask her to become his mistress and he knew, now, that she was not ignorant of the fact. It unsettled her, nevertheless... A matter of hours ago her life had seemed to be as smooth as the sea on a still, calm day; tranquillity, peace silenced her heart and she had joyed in her escape from ecstatic eruptions. She didn't want the complications of love, sex, or their concomitants, at this stage of her life – not because she was cold, or lacking in feeling, but because she knew that, with her passionate, impulsive nature, she could never give less than all and she wanted her freedom several years longer.

Freedom! It was a magic word to her... The thrill of adventure in business ... a different business from that of mere materialism; the search for things from the past, the learning to discriminate between the fake that would seem to be more real than the genuine antique... That was the pulse of her emotional excitement.

She perched herself on her dressing-table stool and proceeded to repair her make-up. Through the mirror she could see the reflection of the bedroom, with its colour scheme of off-white and blue, its quilted, glazed-chintz hangings, headboard and bedspread; the elegance of exquisite Regency pieces, and, finally, the frilled dressing-table at which she now sat. Outside, a small, but unexpected, garden stretched in a riot of blossom. Iris, tall and slender, blended with pale yellow tulips; forget-me-not splashed their colour against grey stone walls and rockeries; wallflowers, prim and old-fashioned, mingled as a reminder of yesterday. It was, she decided, a lovely spot; its quietude, the shady lane in which it was situated; the modern comforts which she and Michael had added after their parents died and left them the property as part of their inheritance.

It struck her, suddenly and irrelevantly, that she had much for which to be thankful. Financial independence of a modest nature which, supplemented by the business which she and Trevor had taken over, could swell to something better; the understanding of Michael who lived there with her in complete harmony... The loyalty and affection of friends...

Her eyes looked back at her with faint ridicule. Was she trying to build up a case for her own happiness ... to balance everything on the credit side, so as to make any change in that same life abortive and unnecessary?

Trevor appeared suddenly in the opening of the doorway.

'I don't doubt but that reflection was most interesting,' he said coolly, 'but do you realize that time is going?'

Stephanie deliberately maintained a calm and natural attitude; the only way to overcome his previous outburst was to ignore it, she told herself complacently.

'I'm quite ready,' she said easily, getting to her feet and picking up her bag and gloves from a nearby table. She glanced up at him and smiled as she passed him, but he reached out swiftly and determinedly, drawing her into his arms. Then, swiftly, bent his lips to hers.

Stephanie made no effort to restrain him; she accepted his kiss without yielding more than its unemotional return. Roughly he released her.

'The ice maiden,' he said remorsefully. 'I suppose I should apologize?'

She shook her head and moved past him to the wide, oak-beamed landing that gave a view of stairs and hall-way below.

'No,' she said gently. 'I'll just apply elementary psychology to all this, Trevor.'

'That's very kind of you,' he said tartly.

Her heart seemed to miss a beat as she countered:

'My visit to Nicholas Young would seem to have produced strange repercussions.'

'That,' he said pointedly, holding her gaze, 'is precisely what I'm afraid of.'

CHAPTER II

During the week that followed Stephanie found herself dwelling upon her meeting with Nicholas Young to a point where, with every ring of the telephone, subconsciously, as she lifted the receiver, she listened for his voice. It didn't matter that she ridiculed the very idea, scorning herself for what she termed her 'adolescent vapouring', the fact remained that, despite herself, she had been shaken out of her complacent unemotionalism. She found that she began to veer the conversation around to the district in which he lived; then casually to mention his farm – but always with a casualness calculated to deceive. When driving back to Winchcombe, after business in the evening, she would imagine herself seeing him walking along the road so that she might stop to offer him a lift... Absurd, annoying things that both shook and infuriated her.

And one evening Michael, her brother, said suddenly, as they sat together at dinner:

'By the way, didn't you go over Nicholas Young's place a week or so ago?'

Stephanie took a deep breath because it seemed that nothing could prevent the

31

blood flaming into her cheeks. She reached for the mustard which she had already used, and answered carelessly:

'Yes – why?'

'No particular reason, only he came into my office today.'

Stephanie's interest more than over-shadowed her intended reserve.

'Your office! But why?'

Michael looked up from his plate.

'My dear girl, I am an architect, you know. Is it so surprising that Mr Young should come to me?'

Stephanie gave a little, nervous laugh.

'Of course not … what did he want?'

'For me to reconstruct the farm-house for him.' He glanced at the clock as he spoke. 'I promised him I'd go over there tonight and have a look at the place.'

'Oh.'

Michael studied her intently.

'You rather like the man, don't you?' he suggested bluntly.

'Can one like, or dislike, a person in a matter of an hour?'

Michael smiled.

'One can fall in love with a person in that time.'

Instantly Stephanie was on the defensive.

'Really, Mike you're utterly absurd.'

His gaze was steady, whimsical.

'Am I? It so happened that I was talking

purely in generalities, but if you have proved my point–' He paused. 'He mentioned you, by the way.'

Stephanie again was off her guard.

'Did he know you were my brother?' It was a breathless, rather urgent sound.

'Naturally ... why else should he mention you?'

'Of course.' She felt confused and hated it; the mood was foreign to her. 'Did you – did you like him?'

Michael poured himself out more wine. His movements were studied and deliberate; the movements of a man with a precise and tidy brain. There was something definitely reliable about Michael, without, too often, the attendant dullness. He was a keen sports-man, a devotee, but not a *poseur*, of art, and his attitude towards life and people was tolerant, kindly. In appearance he resembled Stephanie, in so far as their colouring matched: he had the same dark hair, and grey-blue eyes; the same type of oval face and anyone meeting them, instantly recognized their likeness one to the other.

Michael raised his glass.

'Yes, I did.' His tone was forthright. 'Although I should say there is *something* in the man's life on which he wishes to shut the door.'

Stephanie's heart was beating heavily.

'I really don't see why, because a person

33

doesn't pour out his family history in two minutes, it should be supposed that he has something to hide,' she said defensively.

'I didn't suggest, or imply, that it might be something to hide,' came the imperturbable reply. 'Aren't you rather jumping to conclusions?'

She smiled as a way out. Then:

'It must be a very lonely life at that farm.'

'It is obviously his choice. The absence of human companionship need not always denote loneliness. Some men prefer to be alone.'

'Would you prefer it?'

Michael chuckled.

'You are in a most perverse and provocative mood, my child. I don't know you in it. The impact of Mr Young has certainly affected you.'

'Nonsense!'

'Very well … have it your own way. Perhaps you would care to come to the farm with me?'

Stephanie knew that there was nothing she would like more, but she retorted:

'Of course not. Why should I?'

'You,' he said, getting up from his chair and patting her shoulder, 'are far better qualified to answer that question than I. Shan't be late back, darling. Will you be in bed?'

'No; I've some accounts to grapple with.' She made a wry face. 'How I hate them.'

'Can't Trevor attend to them?'

'Yes; but I must go through them first.'

'How is Trevor these days? He hasn't been over for a week or more.' He looked down at her. 'No complications there, I hope?'

'No – why?'

'You're in a questioning mood, too,' he chipped her. 'But you know my views on men and women in business together. Sooner or later there are emotional complications.'

Stephanie gave a ridiculing snort.

'Don't be archaic.'

'And don't you be coy.'

'You're in a *difficult* mood,' she said firmly. 'I shan't talk to you any more.' Her eyes twinkled. 'Give my regards to Mr Young.'

'I will. And if anyone phones – tell them where I am.'

'Expecting anyone?'

'No.' It was a somewhat vehement sound. Stephanie's voice softened.

'If it should be Felice, I'll suggest that she comes over for a drink later on.'

Michael said a trifle unsteadily:

'It won't be Felice: she's at the Darlington Ball tonight, with Terence Wayne.'

'Why didn't you go, Michael?' It was an anxious sound.

'Because three's a crowd and I'm particularly allergic to Terence,' he said shortly.

Stephanie understood.

'Shall I ask Felice to dinner tomorrow?'

He brightened.

'Would you?'

'Of course... I'd do anything.' She added harshly: 'She's an awful fool.'

'She's young, attractive, wealthy,' he said flatly. 'And has no desire to settle down. Why should she? I've every sympathy with her point of view, odd though it may seem, since I want to marry her.'

Stephanie shook her head.

'You're not very bright, darling, in your tactics?'

'Meaning?' He struck his lighter and held his cigarette to the flame.

'That your very reliability leaves her nothing to worry about.'

'Technique!' It was a disgusted scornful sound.

'You may ridicule it, Michael, but there's an awful lot in a man's approach and, even though it is elementary, it is still a good rule not to overplay your hand and allow a woman to believe that she can wipe the floor with you.'

'Heaven forbid I should create that impression.'

'Not intentionally; but it's either Felice or no one with you; she realizes that you are there, nicely tucked up, loving her and, in effect waiting... I said just now that she's an awful fool, because any woman's a fool who can't appreciate your worth ... but, well, you

36

just *ask* a girl of that type to play you up!'

'Am I supposed to flirt with some dam' woman I don't want?'

'Not necessarily; but show some interest and keep her guessing a little.'

'Is that your idea of romance?'

'No; but you are not wanting to marry *me*,' she said comically. 'Personally, I'd expect to be treated as an adult, and hope to behave like one. But that proves nothing, since I am not Felice's type at all.'

Michael sighed.

'Love's completely cock-eyed, if you ask me.'

'Perhaps; I wouldn't know, except through the medium of what I've seen and read. I've had infatuations, but I know I have never been seriously in love.' She added almost fiercely; 'and I have no desire to be.'

'A look, an inflection of a voice, my child, can soon alter all that. Even so, you're lucky to have escaped thus far: it's worse than the measles – believe me. Hell, I must be going ... sure you won't change your mind and come with me?'

'Quite sure.'

'Technique?' He spoke teasingly.

'No; just the overwhelming desire to wallow in my bath, slip into a house-coat and read a new book on furniture I've just bought.'

Michael looked at her with obvious affection.

'You're a pretty nice person, Stephanie.'

'If I am, then it is probably because life has been very kind to me. No emotional upsets, entanglements; comfort …. those things tell.'

'True; but very often they make people smug, self-satisfied and unsympathetic. As a general rule, give me the man, or woman, who has suffered.' He stopped. 'Good lord, what a way for me to talk. Must be getting mawkish!'

Stephanie bathed, donned a blue satin house-coat, and stretched herself like a well-fed, slinky cat on the divan in the lounge. A fire had been lit in the miniature chimney corner and its blaze sent out a comforting heat to take the edge off the chill of the spring evening. Hilda, her faithful and expert housekeeper, who had been in the family for twenty years, appeared with coffee, setting the tray down on a table at Stephanie's side.

'I knew you'd be wanting some more of this,' she said with that degree of familiarity and respect which made her the old-fashioned 'treasure'.

'You always know what I want, Hilda – like a magician!' Stephanie's eyes twinkled. 'This is luxury, your excellent dinner, a fire awaiting me; now more coffee … what more could I ask?' A sigh. 'I'm very lucky – aren't I?'

'Yes, Miss; but you deserve it.' Hilda nodded her grey head as if to agree with her own utterance. 'I've switched the electric blanket on in your bed; you'll be needing it this cold night.' She gave a little snort. 'And they said over the radio that it would be warm again tomorrow! *Warm!* With a north-east wind to cut you in two!'

Stephanie laughed. The weather was Hilda's pet topic.

'It was warm in the sun today,' she teased.

'When there was any sun,' came the retort.

'I shall have to pack up and take you to some warm climate.'

'Oh no!' It was an emphatic sound. 'No leaving England for me.' She turned her bright brown eyes upon Stephanie: 'Not even for you, Miss. I can talk about the weather as much as I like; but that doesn't mean I think there's another country in the world as can touch England. Oh no,' she added again.

Stephanie chuckled softly.

'Then we shall have to remain here.'

'Yes, Miss; and you find yourself a nice, sensible husband. That's what you'll be needing before long... Good night, Miss.'

'Good night, Hilda.'

Stephanie sighed, relaxed and day-dreamed. Against the windows laburnum, lilac and pink May were etched in a magnificent blending of colour; beyond the bright green of newly cut lawns glowed in the mellow light of the evening sun; a sun dipping down into the west like a giant golden circle, its rays striking into soft, cloud patches, turning them to crimson, amber and mauve. The rose arbours, miniature rockeries, shimmered in the reflection, and in the very stillness there was an enchantment. Home, thought Stephanie, with a sense of satisfaction.

Home... The word caught at her imagination and she wondered just what it would embrace were she married and living within those same walls. The breaking down of all her habits; the realization that upon her actions evolved the happiness of another human being; the surrender of individual freedom; a complete revolution of her daily life.

Emotion stirred within her, vital, physical. The touch of soft satin against her warm skin sent a faint shudder, a thrill over her body as though, in imagination, it were a man's hand caressing her. Colour flamed into her cheeks; never before had she been beset by such thoughts and she fought to dismiss them as she tried to read the book in which, she had told herself, she would find so much interest. The print, however, danced before her eyes; the sentences telescoped, and did not make sense... What was Michael doing now? And Nicholas Young... She stirred impatiently. Since it was no concern of hers why bother. The phone rang just then and she reached out, lifted the receiver, and felt a certain breathless suspense as she did so.

'Felice?' A sense of disappointment over-whelmed her, although she could not have said why. 'I thought you were at the Darlington Ball.'

And the voice came back. 'I was, but it bored me... Michael in?'

'Afraid not ... but, obviously, I am; and Michael will be home in an hour or so. How about coming over... As you are? We'd love to see you resplendent in your ball gown... Or your *négligé*. No formality here... Very well – just as you please. I'm wallowing in the comfort of a fire, bathed, in my house-coat, and enjoying every moment of it... Sybarite? I know I am. Why not? *You* should talk!'

Stephanie replaced the receiver. She was glad, for Michael's sake, that Felice had phoned, but sorry for her own. Reflections in solitude could be very intriguing, she decided, even if dangerous.

Felice Morgan arrived some forty minutes later, having changed and driven from Chipping Camden.

'In a way,' she announced decisively, 'I'm glad you're alone.' She wandered unceremoniously into the lounge as she spoke, moving instinctively to the fire.

'Lovely to see that glow,' she said approvingly.

Stephanie studied her with a certain curiosity as she stood there, tall, slim in her pale, lime moss crepe gown and short, mink jacket which she discarded and threw over a nearby chair, revealing a figure of almost sculptured perfection. Difficult to sum Felice up, she decided, without doing her an injustice, for she was by no means the spoilt, wealthy girl, vain and selfish.

'I was unutterably bored at the ball,' she announced firmly. 'Oh, Stephanie, how fatuous some men can be!'

'Then why,' said Stephanie practically, 'go out with them?'

Felice shrugged her slim shoulders, threw herself into a deep arm-chair, took the cigarette that was offered to her and, when it was lit, blew a tiny cloud of smoke into the air.

'Possibly *because* I was bored,' she said, 'to begin with. I don't think I really know what I want – to be honest.' She turned a lazy gaze upon Stephanie: 'Do you?'

Stephanie went back to the divan.

'I think so – as far as we can possibly know.'

'Marriage?' It was a sigh.

'Eventually – yes.'

'But not now?'

'No,' replied Stephanie almost too emphatically, 'not now.'

'I feel like that; but I get so restless. Oh, I know I'm a fool and want a damn good thrashing if you like. I've far too much of everything, doting parents, no problems except those I create myself.' She looked at Stephanie very steadily: 'Do you mind if I'm very frank?'

'I'd appreciate it.'

'Then, I'd marry your brother tomorrow if I trusted myself more and could be sure that I'd make him happy. Obviously I realize his worth – any woman who didn't would be an unutterable fool but–' She paused, the expression in her eyes gentle and appealing: 'You most probably regard me as a fool, anyway.'

Stephanie didn't hedge as she answered:

'I have certainly thought along those lines! But, naturally, I am prejudiced in Michael's favour.'

Felice nodded so that her platinum-gold hair shimmered in the now fading light.

'If Michael were just the ordinary man it would be different, but he isn't: marriage, to him, is a serious, profound business, and unless I can see it that way, too– Oh, Stephanie it's such a muddle.'

'I always understood that love made everything very simple.'

'Possibly; that's the danger. It would be so easy to marry Michael, but not so easy to make that marriage a success. I'm used to my own way, my freedom: one half of me says that I could never compromise over either, and the other insists that Michael would more than make up for the loss of them. Do you believe that love is the magic potion that ensures eternal bliss?'

'Heavens – no! Love's the foundation and structure of the house, as it were, but it requires a tremendous amount of furnishing and decorating to make it habitable.'

'There you are! That's what worries me.' She looked at Stephanie very searchingly: 'Would you marry a man just because you were in love with him without weighing up the debit side?'

Stephanie stared out at the dark tapestry that was now the garden.

'Would I be able *to* weigh up the debit side if I were in love?' she asked reflectively. 'Wouldn't it rather appear to me that there was no debit?'

'Meaning that love is blind? But you said just now that you knew it wasn't any magic potion and that–'

Stephanie smiled wryly.

'I may *know* that,' she insisted; 'know it to be true, but love isn't reasonable and even the things a person may *know* they refuse to *see*. That's the tragedy – and the ecstasy, I suppose.'

'Imbecile.'

'Perhaps; but it still remains. What I believe as I sit here in cold blood is theory based on observation and substantiated by fact … but were I to be in love–' Her voice dropped, 'I should be deprived of my reason

44

and think along the lines that most suited me. Women know that it is crazy to marry drunkards, thieves, liars, but does that fact deter them? Of course not.'

'Sounds grim – absolutely grim.'

'Not necessarily.'

'Do you believe in marrying just for love?'

Stephanie didn't hesitate.

'I should have to be in love before I could marry,' she confessed. 'As I see it, one requires a great deal of affection in order to live with another person for the rest of one's life!' She paused, then: 'Not only that; I'm a romantic at heart and nothing would shake my faith, or make me believe that anything else was worth while as a substitute.'

Felice grunted.

'I just don't know,' she murmured. 'I don't think I shall ever marry – too great a gamble.'

Stephanie smiled.

'Suppose we let the matter take care of itself.'

'Just so long as you do not imagine I am being unfair to Michael.'

'I think I understand your feelings.'

'Perhaps I care too much.'

Again Stephanie smiled. Then:

'That's his car,' she said swiftly.

Felice jumped to her feet, raised herself on top-toe and peered into a wall mirror, feverishly grabbing for her compact and vigorously powdering her face.

Michael's key went into the front door; his voice was heard from the hall; the next second he appeared on the threshold and, as his gaze leapt delightedly to Felice in silent greeting, he said:

'I've brought Mr Young back with me for a drink, Stephanie.'

Stephanie's heart missed a beat as, across the intervening space, her eyes met those of Nicholas.

'I'm afraid,' she said in greeting, 'that I am hardly dressed to play hostess, Mr Young. Please excuse me.'

Nicholas took in every detail of her attractive, beautifully cut house-coat, aware of her perfect figure and the emotional appeal of the picture she presented.

'You could not,' he said quietly, 'look more charming.' He turned towards Felice who had already stepped forward to Michael's side.

Michael said:

'Felice, may I–'

She interrupted him with a warm smile as she held out her hand to Nicholas.

'Nicholas and I have met before; almost old friends, in fact.'

'Really!' He looked surprised.

'Quite three times,' she said gaily. She added swiftly: 'I came over about an hour ago: the Darlington Ball was just about the end... Stephanie and I have been enjoying a

46

natter together.'

Michael flashed Stephanie a grateful glance.

Nicholas, sitting down beside Stephanie on the settee, exclaimed:

'This is a most attractive cottage you and your brother have here, Miss Reid. The name intrigues me, too: Willow Corner. Original!'

'Simple! There just happens to be a corner in the garden that boasts of three rather lovely willow trees!'

Felice said instantly:

'I never noticed them.'

Michael held her gaze.

'Then, if Mr Young will excuse me, I'll take you to see them.'

Nicholas grinned.

'By all means,' he said smoothly.

They went out, shutting the door behind them. To Stephanie there appeared something almost fateful about the action. A soft, golden light from a standard lamp mingled with the radiance of the afterglow that was diffused through the lattice windows, falling gently upon polished surfaces and striking through the shadowy corners of the room, like limes upon a darkened stage. The fire had burned low and spread a fan of orange upon the wide hearth that was decorated with copper and brass. The cream of an Indian carpet formed a background for delphinium blues and soft pinks in chintz and curtains. A grandfather's clock ticked away into the silence.

'Peace,' said Nicholas suddenly, hoarsely.

'The hush of evening,' Stephanie mused, responding to his mood. She got up as she spoke and offered him a cigarette from a jade green box. Then: 'Whisky?' she asked.

'If I may... I hope I haven't intruded, Miss Reid, but your brother assured me you were not the conventional type who would object to an unexpected caller.'

Stephanie spoke to him from a far corner of the room where she was pouring out their respective drinks. Returning, glasses in hand, she answered him:

'No, I am not the conventional type – in anything,' she said with a smile. 'The fact that I didn't rush upstairs and dress myself properly rather proves that!'

He held her gaze.

'I like naturalness in a woman,' he insisted. 'You have that quality, if I may say so.'

'You may...' She rested back against the cushions and relaxed, but her heart was beating heavily and her awareness of the man beside her was greater than her interest in any words uttered. She noticed, anew, that his eyes were steady, but disturbing; that his features were finely etched and that there was an artistic magnetism about him which appealed to her. Not for her the materialistic, business type whose world was bounded by 'deals' and decimal points. She noticed the looseness of his limbs, the sureness of his movements, the delicate strength of his hands as they held his cigarette; even the manner in which his tie set in perfect grooming, without any suggestion of untidiness, and that the white collar gave a certain intensity to his faintly tanned complexion. 'How,' she asked, somewhat breathlessly, 'is the farm going?'

'Improving slowly. Your brother knew instantly what I wanted done with the place. I liked him.'

'Michael's a wonderful person,' she said warmly.

'And you live here together.'

'Yes; it works amazingly well. Freedom; no questions asked, and yet complete confidence one in the other.'

'The perfect formula.'

'I think so. I don't like cages – either mental or physical, and I'd hate to swallow my victims whole!'

'Most women imagine that to be an achievement,' he said with faint cynicism.

'They should regard it as a confession of failure.'

'How true.' He looked at her.

'That which one keeps by force, one has never really possessed – nor ever will,' she added.

He studied her with an intensity she found

unnerving. Emotion, sharp, inescapable surged between them; his gaze upon her lips was as a passionate caress.

'An exceptional philosophy for a woman.'

'You have,' Stephanie said, fighting to control herself, to pretend that every nerve in her body was not tingling or that the temperature of her blood was not degrees higher than normal, 'a poor opinion of women – haven't you, Mr Young?'

He didn't avoid her inquiring glance.

'Don't you think that most men have – when it comes to speaking in terms of women in general?'

'I think,' she said firmly, 'that they are apt to speak purely from their own experience. It needs only one disastrous love affair to reduce some men – and women – to cynical bitterness.'

'I cannot contradict you without wholly agreeing with you.'

Stephanie sipped her sherry.

'It is always so easy to excuse one's follies by generalizing about the defects of others!' She spoke lightly.

A shadow crossed Nicholas's face; a certain grimness tightened the line of his jaw.

'Are you suggesting that I come into that category?'

'I hadn't,' she answered him honestly, 'though of it. But I should imagine that you could be rather bitter – since you ask me.'

'Probably... And you?'

She met his gaze and allowed herself the pleasure of surrendering to the emotions he awakened, the excitement, the delight of passionate contemplation as she replied:

'I have never had anything in my life to be bitter about. If I say that I've known many men without loving any of them, I do so to illustrate my point. Who can say what one's reactions would be in the face of disillusionment or unhappiness? One can but surmise and base that supposition on the experiences and behaviour of others.'

Nicholas felt his pulses quicken as he said hoarsely:

'But many men have loved *you?*'

She didn't retreat coyly into false denial; she said casually and truthfully:

'Many is rather an overstatement; several would be more correct.' She smiled broadly. 'But would they still be in love with me had it been possible for me to marry them each in turn!' She sighed. 'Perhaps the greatest loves, after all, are those that never reach fulfilment.'

He looked at her very steadily:

'Do you,' he demanded, 'believe that?'

She stared reflectively into the fire. Then:

'I'm not quite sure,' she said frankly. 'All I know is that I could not endure the marriages of many whom I see around me. The bickering, nerve-wracked couples, clinging together because of the habit of years; drawn together, even, by their own incompatibility! Neither could I endure the life of those who build up an elaborate edifice labelled: "The happily married couple," while behind locked doors they nurse frustrations, grievances as they squabble, cajole, nag and indulge a mawkish reconciliation!' She gave a shiver of distaste. 'That makes marriage merely a masquerade, the trappings of which might be likened to the cap and bells of the jester!'

Nicholas nodded understandingly:

'With the man cajoling, pandering to, and appearing to dote on his wife because he is, in truth, scared of doing the wrong thing and knowing that his only salvation lies in keeping peace and subjugating his own inclinations and desires! A pitiful, nauseating spectacle.'

'Then we are agreed.'

He looked at her with a penetrating, compelling glance:

'Just what do you want from marriage?'

'Reality,' she said stoutly. 'And an adult appreciation of each other's needs. A companionship born of genuine unity of ideas and respect for individual freedom.'

He looked down at his glass, sipped his whisky and then raised his gaze to hers.

'And – love?'

The blood seemed to be rushing, warm

and turbulent, over her body in a fierce wave as she answered him:

'That above all.' Her voice was uneven. 'While appreciating that it is not enough in itself.' A sigh. 'Perhaps I seek the impossible but I know, at least, what I could not *bear!*' She laughed a trifle nervously. 'You must be unutterably bored by all this.'

'You know perfectly well that I am not,' he retorted calmly.

She stared at him with great directness.

'That being so ... what are your views on the burning question?'

He appeared to withdraw from her as he said stiffly:

'I am not qualified to pass an opinion.'

'I cannot agree with that ... my inexperience doesn't preclude me from having my own ideas. It is the same with you.'

'Then perhaps it is my experience,' he said subtly, 'that precludes me.'

Stephanie started; her heart feeling suddenly painful. What did he mean by 'my experience'? Could he be married and... She resisted the suggestion, aware of the disconcerting fact that it hurt her.

The silence deepened; the shadowy darkness of night crept stealthily upon them as the afterglow faded from the sky, leaving only the faintest spear of silver against billowy cloud. The ticking of the clock beat like imaginary wings about them; the warmth from the fire brought a luxurious sense of relaxation, sensuous in its appeal and effect. Passion, urgent, insidious stole between them like an invisible pulse throbbing in the heart of each.

Nicholas got restlessly to his feet. He was tense, aware of his own desires, conscious of Stephanie's presence to the exclusion of all else. It was a very long while since he had wanted to make love to a woman but he knew, beyond all doubting, that he craved to make love to her. His thoughts raced: would she rebuff him, imagine that he held her cheaply after such a brief acquaintance, or would she expect him to follow it up with a proposal of marriage he had no wish to make. He said, as one escaping from himself and feeling the words to be both defensive and protective:

'I'm afraid I have little time for marriage... I hate counterfeit or compromise and, in it, I've seen so much of both.'

'Surely in marriage compromise,' she said breathlessly, 'can be a good thing?'

He stood facing her from his position on the hearth rug; his eyes met hers almost stormily:

'And the fact that it is necessary stands as the hall-mark of failure between two people.'

'Isn't that rather a violent statement?'

'No.' He held her gaze. 'I think you know what I mean.'

'Yes,' she whispered. 'The sharp edge of ecstasy blunted and sacrificed to the commonplace.'

'Exactly.'

'I think,' she murmured as one whose views were crystallizing as she spoke, 'that it is because I yearn for so much in marriage that I cannot see myself ever being married ... yet, perversely, I cannot picture myself as a spinster for all time!'

'Quite neutral at the moment – is that it?'

Nicholas found that his pulses were racing as he awaited her answer. And, in turn, Stephanie struggled to be honest... Neutral ... when the very presence of this man roused her to a feverish longing; when the sound of his voice, the expression in his eyes obliterated all normal thought. Flippantly, however, she managed to say:

'Naturally! Free, white and ... twenty-four!' She peered out of the french windows – stretching herself over the edge of the settee. 'Michael and Felice are certainly studying those willow trees,' she said with a swift smile.

Nicholas made a low sound that was half sympathy and half ridicule.

'Let's hope they never quite find them,' he said, 'wasn't that your original theory?'

'Hardly a theory; more a question, or a statement made to be contradicted.' She got to her feet as she spoke and poked the fire.

The fragrance from her stole upon him and he moved slightly away.

'Who would be strong enough to resist the temptation of fulfilment in order to prove your statement true,' he said tensely.

Stephanie straightened herself.

'Life sometimes parts people, irrespective of their desires,' she suggested.

'Not two people both equally in love,' he replied firmly.

She arched her brows.

'So you do *believe* in love?'

'Have I given you to understand anything to the contrary?'

Stephanie plunged.

'It could hardly be said that you have given me anything to understand by way of any definite assertion.'

He walked slowly to the window; outside the garden was bathed in the opalescent glow of a half-moon; the trees a dark frieze against the sapphire of the sky. He said jerkily, ignoring her utterance:

'They are just coming in.' Swiftly, then, he turned and looked at her. 'I must be going.'

'Why?' It was a breathless sound.

The tension mounted as he moved back to her side. They were as two people mesmerized, held by some magnetic control, speechless in the face of inexplicable emotion.

'I thrust myself upon you tonight,' he said, as one at war with himself.

'Then I assume Michael didn't even suggest your coming back with him,' she said, trying to sound bantering, but without much success.

'You know how I meant that,' he murmured.

'Yes.' Stephanie's senses were swirling in some curious, unfamiliar world of excitement and ecstasy; a thrill went over her body as from a caress. And although she told herself fiercely that this was only the second time she had met Nicholas, her heart accepted the fact that he was more real to her than any other man she had ever known.

The front door opened, the sound of Michael's voice and Felice's intermingling, came to them. For a second the atmosphere vibrated with a certain breathless urgency as though time had become an invisible enemy they were both fighting. Swiftly, tensely, Nicholas said:

'Will you have dinner with me tomorrow?' He drew her gaze masterfully to his as one who will not take 'no' for an answer.

Stephanie's heart lurched and seemed to lift itself within her breast.

'Yes,' she murmured.

'Shall I come over to Warwick for you?'

'If you could or–'

'I'll be there – about six?'

'Yes.'

He looked down at her; no further words

were uttered, but they were as two people who had found a new world.

Michael and Felice came into the room. Felice's cheeks were flushed, her hair slightly ruffled; Michael had a certain self-conscious air about him. He didn't speak for a brief moment, then gazing down at Felice said jerkily:

'Congratulate me, both of you; a miracle's happened. Felice has just promised to marry me.' He gave a little, nervous laugh and looked at Stephanie.

Stephanie gasped:

'Michael! Felice... Oh, I'm so happy for you both.' She went forward and kissed them in turn. 'For a girl who didn't think she'd ever marry,' she said in an affectionate, teasing voice, as she smiled at Felice, 'you are doing awfully well!'

Felice shook her head.

'You were so right, Stephanie, in all you said. There just didn't seem any debit side!'

Nicholas added his good wishes. Then:

'I must be going,' he said as one who hates the idea of outstaying a welcome.

'Nonsense,' said Michael stoutly. 'Can't leave until you've drunk our health!' He grinned boyishly and grasped Felice's hand. 'I'm going to get a bottle of champagne, darling. No, better stay here or we'll forget what we're going for!' With that he swung on his heel and, a few moments later, returned. 'Here we are!' He proceeded to uncork the bottle and poured out the wine.

They drank, both Stephanie and Nicholas contributing a brief toast.

'And how about letting the next bottle be opened in your honour, Stephanie,' said Felice laughingly. 'I know how you feel about that "freedom" stuff and waiting, but–'

'Having taken the plunge yourself you don't intend to give me any peace,' Stephanie chuckled.

'Exactly!' Felice turned to Nicholas. 'And what about you, Nicholas?'

Nicholas looked faintly grim as he said swiftly:

'Marriage is rather like a garment – it suits some people but not others.'

Felice gave Michael a meaning glance.

'We'll remind him of that somewhat caustic remark when we're dancing at his wedding – eh?'

Nicholas edged towards the door. His nerves were taut, the present conversation irritated him. His entire mood was at variance with his preconceived ideas; he criticized himself for having been weak enough to accept Michael's invitation in the first place, and thus risk the fascination of Stephanie's presence.

'And now I *must* go,' he said firmly.

'I'll run you back... Or had you forgotten you came in my car,' Michael exclaimed as

Nicholas had been about to protest.

'Frankly, I had, but I could walk–'

'Three miles!' Felice gasped in horror. 'We'll drive you. Or if you care to take my car, Michael will see me home,' she said softly.

Nicholas declined that.

'Of course,' Michael said absurdly, 'if my sister were decently dressed we could all see you home!'

Stephanie gave him a loving glance.

'And wouldn't you just hate that,' she said gaily, without being conscious of the words she uttered. Her mind was completely absorbed with Nicholas and the fact that she was to dine with him the following evening; it was as though a radiance flooded her world, leaving her breathlessly expectant, awed by the impact of emotion.

They went out into the hall, standing there talking as though loath to break up the little party. Stephanie opened the front door and Nicholas said instantly:

'Don't catch cold.'

She looked at him swiftly:

'I shan't; this is really quite warm.' She tightened the satin girdle about her waist as she spoke.

Felice kissed her affectionately.

'It's going to be worth marrying Michael in order to have you for a sister-in-law,' she said sincerely.

'So that's why your marrying me,' com- mented Michael absurdly.

Nicholas faced Stephanie as he said:

'Good night … and until tomorrow.'

'Until tomorrow,' she echoed unevenly.

She stood and watched them get into the car; watched until the pin-point of light from the rear lamp vanished into the dark- ness. Around her the world was still and in its stillness was the pulse of a passionate anticipation. For her, earth and sky were one and she a miraculous part of both; the beauty around her – moonlight spilling upon the fresh green of trees, hedges, lawns; blossom gleaming as with the lustre of newly fallen snow, and in the soft breeze the fragrance of gardens and countryside.

Stephanie felt a swelling, a surging emotion flooding her heart, as though it must burst with the force of its own happiness; exult- ation lifted her to heights hitherto unknown in the contemplation of the scene around her; music, as from throbbing, muted strings, filled her soul. It was a moment of enchant- ment, when she was bewitched by the ecstasy of her own dreaming. She knew, then, swiftly and surely, that she was in love with Nicho- las; that from the very second of meeting him that fierce attraction had burned within her, and that in her passionate desire there was a sublime spiritual quality, an affinity trans- cending all else.

She went slowly up the stairs to her room. Strange that in the space of a few hours a life could be so transformed. Her eyes, wide, starry, looked back at her from her dressing-table mirror; she was almost shy of them, for they spoke for her.

Nicholas Young... Could she deny that his attitude had betrayed a definite interest...? Faint colour mounted her cheeks. Tomorrow ... dinner... Her sigh was heavy with her own unspoken longings. For that brief moment, the stars were hers; the universe trembling on the brink of her awakening, and her sudden absolute belonging.

CHAPTER III

Nicholas set out for Warwick the following evening in the mood of one accepting the fact that he was being exceedingly foolish. For three years, he argued to himself, he had refused all contacts with women and, thus, manoeuvred his life into those quiet and peaceful by-ways where conflict and tumult were unknown. And he had enjoyed his own immunity, vowing that nothing should jeopardize it. Why suggest this dinner? Why plunge, now, into a friendship the repercussions of which might well be dangerous.

Stephanie attracted him... That was no excuse, he told himself contemptuously, despising the weakness that prompted the need of explanation.

By the time he had reached the town, driving along Mill Street, with its fringe of ancient houses, he had decided to make this evening his swan song so far as she was concerned. Useless pleading that Stephanie was 'different': all other women were different in the initial stages of a man's infatuation. The cynical observation brought him a measure of satisfaction, and he clung to the reflection as he drew up outside the address which bore the name: 'Stephanie' in old English lettering. The premises were near Castle Street and early fifteenth century. In a low – almost pavement level – latticed window a Bacon settle stood sharing the honours with a William and Mary chest of drawers while, as a background, rich, purple velvet was draped in artistic carelessness, to throw into relief the wood of the furniture for sale.

Nicholas had, without knowing why, expected something after the old 'Curiosity Shop' type, with Dresden, Minton and Worcester set in contrasting array against a collection of chairs, crystal and old jewellery. This was entirely different and, as he went inside, the feeling was borne upon him that he had stepped back into the period to which the building belonged. The faint, and not

63

unpleasant, smell of damp soot came to mingle with the almost imperceptible perfume which Stephanie left in her wake. The low ceilings, heavy oak beams, timbered walls and swaying lantern lights, appealed to his love of yesterday. He found himself reluctantly thinking that, despite her modernity, Stephanie belonged there.

Trevor Morly came forward in that second, regarding him as a prospective customer.

'Can I help you?'

Nicholas looked at him very levelly.

'My name,' he said smoothly, 'is Nicholas Young. Would you be good enough to tell Miss Reid that I am here?'

Trevor was not in a patient mood; the day had been difficult and tiring, and if there was a name he had come to loathe it was the one which Nicholas bore, since he was aware of the fact that Stephanie appeared to be unduly sensitive to it. With bare politeness he said:

'If you will wait here.' He indicated a chair.

'Thank you.' Nicholas watched Trevor's tall figure, in its impeccable grey suit, disappear. Evidently that was the partner. Not the type he would have imagined, he decided. But, then, there was no accounting for the relationships between men and women. The fellow was good-looking and probably charming... He lit a cigarette rather impatiently: what did his opinion matter and why waste time.

Stephanie appeared some few seconds later, Trevor following.

'Sorry to keep you waiting,' she said rather unsteadily, 'but I've been dealing with a rather irate customer; she was furious when I told her that her settle was a fake and that a power-driven saw had given the fretted design, instead of a fretsaw. She insisted that power-driven saws, in any case, were perfectly well known in the seventeenth century!' Stephanie laughed nervously, trying by plunging into business-like conversation to keep a firm control over her emotions, and finding her poise deserting her the moment she met Nicholas's eyes. She remembered Trevor and said hastily, 'Let me introduce my partner, Mr Morly.'

'We have spoken,' said Nicholas formally. Then: 'This is a gem of a place,' he went on with enthusiasm, as he looked around at the artistically furnished room – the obvious sanctuary for customers – the rich, ruby velvets, the Queen Anne furniture with its purity and marked simplicity of line.

'I love every inch of it,' Stephanie agreed. 'Would you like to see the cubby hole I'm having done upstairs?'

'It's really a flat,' Trevor insisted.

Stephanie made a wry face.

'It sounds sacrilege for us to use that word in a fifteenth-century house!'

Trevor frowned, glanced at the clock and said:

'I shall have to be going.' His tone suggested that she and Nicholas should leave with him.

Stephanie knew that there was nothing she desired more than his departure. She wanted to show Nicholas this love of hers – this house she had tended and developed – without the intrusion of a third person. She said calmly:

'Yes, I know; you'll be late and then Lady Molby will be furious ... you have the designs? Would you tell her that I shall be over there tomorrow?'

Trevor said in clipped, uncompromising tone:

'Very well. You'll lock up?'

'Of course ... good night, Trevor.'

He left them rather after the manner of a volcano, seething and on the point of eruption. Nicholas said swiftly:

'I'm afraid I'm hardly popular.'

'Trevor,' she said frankly, 'can be wonderful and very difficult.'

'And – jealous?' Nicholas wanted to retract the words the moment they were uttered; it was foreign to him to make such observations.

Stephanie smiled.

'Perhaps,' she said lightly and led the way up the narrow, winding stairs to a small

66

landing from which four rooms radiated.

'This,' she said, stepping down two steps into a large unfurnished apartment, 'will be the lounge. Chimney corner, oak beams, half-panelled walls. Gate-legged tables, chintz, and clever reproductions will make this homely for me.'

'For *you?*'

'Yes.' Their eyes met deliberately for the first time. 'I shall let Michael and Felice have Willow Corner and move here. Be quite fun.'

'To live here – alone?' His voice was hoarse.

'Yes.' She averted her gaze. 'I don't mind being alone and there should be at least one ghost to keep me company.'

He stared at her.

'Will Michael agree to that?'

Her laugh held a note of nervousness.

'Agree! He knows he could never stop me once I've made up my mind. Obstinate is my second name!' She moved to a corner of the room, indicating a window at floor level. 'I adore that; so lovely to have to kneel down in order to look out! They were nothing if not original in those days!' She opened a small door, went down a short, narrow passage, Nicholas following, then: 'I shall make this my bedroom,' she announced. 'I can then look out and see the castle; dream of days of feudal grandeur – in nine hundred and fourteen.' She laughed. 'Before William the Conqueror's reign.' Her sigh was eloquent of her appreciation of the scene. 'All this speaks to one, somehow: Shakespeare's England ... the very breath of history.' Her voice trailed away. 'Take no notice of me – I'm quite mad.'

'Then I am mad, also. I love it all,' he said gently. 'The riverside walks, the yew hedges and lawns fringing the water's edge ... the romantic beauty of the unseen yesterday.'

'The reality of a past more real than today.'

'How true; today is never quite real.'

'The impermanence of fleeting hours and the falsity of retrospect.'

'Falsity?' He drew her gaze to his.

'Yes ... in retrospect, yesterday acquires glamour; misery even the semblance of happiness; happiness the wild ecstasy of perfection... Looking back is such folly,' she finished uncertainly.

'Are you speaking from – experience?'

Stephanie looked out of the window, taking in the majestic sweep of Caesar's Tower rising to its great height and soaring into the mist of the evening sky. Then:

'No; not really, except in trivial remembrances.'

'There must surely have been some outstanding ones,' he said hoarsely.

She shook her head.

'The flirtations of adolescence – nothing more. I am not an experienced woman, Mr Young, as I have already told you; but it is not my belief that one must always live through things in order to understand them.'

'And there,' he said gently, 'speaks the voice of inexperience, if I may say so.'

She nerved herself to meet his gaze; her heart was thudding wildly and a certain sickness born of fear possessed her. Again there came to her the instinctive feeling that there was something in Nicholas's life that was a closed book ... a chapter of which still had the power to hurt him, make him cynical and on the defensive. It struck her, as she stood there, just how inexplicable love was... She loved him without knowing him, or anything about him – beyond the merest details. She would have been prepared, at that moment, to take him on trust, asking no questions, and content so long as she could count on his love in return. She said quietly:

'Perhaps you are right; only I have always felt that I could sit in the other person's chair, think with their mind, feel with their heart and not my own.' She forced a laugh. 'Possibly we have very odd notions about ourselves.'

'Which is a kindness; could we really see ourselves as we are, it might not make for our peace of mind!'

They stood for a second looking somewhat uncertainly at each other. Then, abruptly, Nicholas said:

'How many rooms have you here?' His voice was matter of fact and Stephanie was quick to appreciate the fact; to be aware, also, of a subtle change in his general attitude towards her; a change that brought a bleak sensation to her heart as of being shut off from him.

'Five,' she said, maintaining her poise. 'Four without the kitchen. I've had to attend to the plumbing, as you may imagine, and turn one other room into a bathroom. It was originally a dressing-room.' She added swiftly. 'Being alone, I shall not need it.'

'A state which I hardly imagine you will retain for long,' he suggested, congratulating himself on the powers of his resistance, as the subtle fascination of her nearness surged upon him, quickening his pulses and awakening within him the overwhelming desire to take her in his arms.

Stephanie remained very still in that second. A sudden dramatic silence fell; a silence charged with drama and bringing a tension unbearable.

'I cannot speak for the future,' she said, as one fighting for control. 'It depends.' She added hastily: 'We'd better go.'

'I suppose so ... thank you for showing me all this. It has a charm quite indescribable, almost as though we were, in fact, dressed in the period. Rather a disembodied feeling.'

'We may,' he said fancifully, 'have stood here before, you and I... Hundreds of years ago. I know you so well–'

'And I you.' It was a whisper.

'Some people could never be strangers.'

'And others never be anything else even if they lived together for years.'

'How right,' she said quietly.

They left the room, looking back at it through the heavy, latched oaken door. Rays from the evening sun rifted from the windows, catching the particles of dust and holding them in mid air; the stillness was uncanny; the atmosphere heavy with a certain expectancy.

'I wonder just what this old house has seen,' Stephanie murmured as they went slowly down the stairs, their footsteps echoing hollowly through the silence. 'Sometimes I think I can hear voices.' She managed to laugh. 'My trouble is an incurable romanticism – as you have already guessed.' She glanced back at him over her shoulder. 'I was born in the wrong age.'

'Perhaps; but I cannot be expected to agree with you.'

They reached the hall, standing together, held as by some spell.

'Why?' It was a breathless sound.

'Could I have guaranteed meeting you – in that other age,' he said tensely.

Their eyes met in a look, deep, penetrating, as though each would draw the other irrevocably into that world wholly their own. As Stephanie, her heart thudding madly, moved away, their hands touched and, at that touch, a spark was ignited that flamed between them violently, inescapably. Nicholas's gaze lowered to her mouth then back to her eyes seeking, silently, the permission which, involuntarily she gave him.

Swiftly, almost desperately, his arms closed around her and his lips found hers in a kiss, passionate, demanding, as he held her with a suffocating nearness, his heart seeming to beat within her body, as hers within his, so fierce was that heavy thudding; so complete their surrender and the ecstasy it awakened. Stephanie floated into a world far removed from any she had ever known; a world of sweet, soft darkness pierced with dazzling light, as she swirled dizzily to a rapture indescribable; a rapture where resistance was forgotten and only the wonder, the fulfilment of the moment remained.

And suddenly, almost abruptly his arms fell from her; the warmth of his mouth against her parted lips was no more; the exquisite surging of desire vanished, killed as he murmured:

'I'm sorry ... forgive me.'

She stared up at him, seeking, but not finding, an explanation, aware that even without conscious thought, she had believed he cared as she ... believed that they were two people who had met and loved on the breath of a first sigh. With a superhuman effort she said, her voice low and yet strangely harsh even in its quietness:

'Of course ... I will put it down to the spell of an old house and–' She paused, adding swiftly: 'And perhaps for you the nostalgia of memory.'

Nicholas was wrestling with emotions with which he was totally unfamiliar, warring with his own weakness and aware of a tearing, smarting sensation of loss as he heard Stephanie's words. He was not, he told himself, fiercely the type to make love to women on the slightest pretext; he despised the very idea as adolescent or flagrantly sensual – neither of which provided any explanation for his conduct. It angered him to think he had made such a fool of himself and, in all probability, jeopardized her good opinion of him. Yet, since he had decided that this evening was to be his swan song why allow the matter to concern him. He could not stay the words:

'The spell was of your casting.'

She looked up at him, baffled by his attitude which was not that of a flirtatious man. She was the last woman to imagine that because a man kissed her, he was in love with her; nevertheless, Nicholas in no way conformed to her idea of the average man to whom making love was part of life's normal routine – irrespective of whether his affections were involved or not.

She managed to say casually:

'Those other centuries catching up with us, perhaps.' A light laugh to prevent his suspecting the fact that she was trembling with emotion and the force of the desire he had awakened.

Nicholas deliberately brought the conversation back to the commonplace.

'Shall we dine at the Lord Leycester?'

Stephanie tried to overcome the blanket of depression that almost stifled her.

'If you wish.'

Nicholas glanced around him.

'Everything locked up... Your partner was very particular about that, I seem to remember.'

Stephanie turned the key on a nearby show-room.

'Men are always fussy about barricading everything up.' She managed to keep her voice steady. 'Half the time I forget that doors *have* locks.'

Nicholas said unexpectedly:

'It could be that, footing the bills, men are forced into a position of safeguarding their possessions.'

Stephanie felt again that strange, tugging sensation of curiosity.

'That sounds rather like a cynical husband.' She waited tensed, breathless for his comment.

It came, in a clipped staccato tone:

'Cynical, perhaps. Husband – no.'

Stephanie felt the blood rising to her cheeks; a certain relief flooded over her. That, at least, told her he wasn't married. And as if reading her thoughts, he added hoarsely:

'Does that tell you anything you want to know about me. Or do I flatter myself?'

Their eyes met; they stood poised, tensed with emotion; both caught again in that spell; both aware of the other's need, even though Stephanie fought to suppress her yearning and Nicholas to overcome his. She said fearlessly and honestly:

'I am not impressed by the misunderstood married man – if that is what you mean.'

'I see.'

Something in his voice arrested her attention and she hastened:

'Oh, not because I'm a moralist, or, I hope, smug; but because I can never tolerate the person who whines, yet has not the courage to do anything definite about it.'

'Did you wonder if I came into that category?'

Stephanie caught at her breath.

'No.'

'You don't sound very sure.'

'I was trying to be absolutely frank.'

'A great virtue,' he said slowly. 'Well?'

'I merely wondered–' She stopped. 'No; I detest the person who asks questions by making statements that require an answer.'

'And if I were married you would not be dining with me – is that it?'

'Yes – exactly.'

'You are nothing if not frank.'

'Sincerely I hope so,' she said quietly. 'I have seen too much heartbreak through the feeble declarations of spineless married men, ever to plunge to my own doom by accepting their attentions.'

Nicholas held her gaze.

'And suppose I happened to be married and you happened to fall in love with me?'

She managed to keep an iron control upon herself.

'I should have run as fast as I could the very moment I realized that you so much as attracted me. Self-preservation.'

'Life isn't as simple as that, you know.'

'I don't agree,' she countered.

He shook his head.

'When one *can* run one is not in love.' A sigh. 'That's the tragedy.'

'But one can run before one reaches that stage.'

He laughed softly.

'Love, its realization, can be a matter of split seconds.'

'Perhaps…' Her voice faltered.

'Your principle is excellent,' he said softly. 'But in practice it doesn't really work.' He added: 'The divorce courts should convince you of that.'

She flung up her head.

'That is very different; the divorce courts *solve* the problem; the people in question have the courage to break away and begin again... But what of those who haven't that courage and seek solace without discomfort...? I could never be a shadow, a ghost, in a man's life.'

'And no man who was sincere would wish you to be.'

Without knowing why, she felt a certain relief at his words. Strange how, in those few seconds, she had been on the defensive; rabid on a subject which, hitherto, she had regarded quite casually, her views merely impersonal.

'I'm glad,' she said with a smile, 'we are agreed on that point.'

They went out into the street; the light from the sun dazzling them after the subdued and mellow glow within the house. It was a matter of seconds in the car to the Lord Leycester, which stood at the top of the High Street.

'I love every inch of this district,' Nicholas said abruptly, as he led Stephanie into the smoking-room of the hotel, ordered cocktails and settled himself in a deep arm-chair beside her.

'So do I; I want to travel and am determined to do so, but I know that when I'm away I shall crave to be here. That is the trouble; one's mind is so contradictory: away from England I shall remember only its beauties, never its restrictions and its climate. Retrospect again!'

Nicholas said ruefully:

'That is the trouble with people – away from a person and you recall his or her virtues – seldom his or her vices.'

Stephanie looked at him searchingly. Long afterwards she recalled those words.

'That could be the kindness of indifference,' she suggested, feeling again that surge of emotion, that provocative mood stealing upon her.

'It could; but seldom is. Kindness usually follows in the wake of a great love that is dead. Memory, too often, clings to the mediocre.'

'You seem,' she exclaimed, 'to know.'

He held her gaze.

'*I* have not claimed to be inexperienced,' he murmured with a half-smile.

Stephanie's thoughts were swirling dangerously; the realization of love unsettling and disarming her. She said, trying to meet his mood banteringly:

'I have placed myself at a disadvantage by admitting that I was inexperienced.' She took a cigarette from the case he held out to her, and leaned forward so that he might light it. 'Don't,' she added subtly, 'confuse that word with ignorance – will you?'

He looked at her above the flare of the match.

'No,' he said briefly.

'I sometimes wonder,' she went on, 'if the capacity for great feeling is not the enemy of experience. Is it better, perhaps, to have several light-hearted affairs, rather than to wait for the real thing.'

Nicholas shook his head.

'One cannot generalize,' he said reflectively. 'Every case is so individual, and each of us can behave only according to our instincts and desires. We cannot follow any preconceived plan; determine any set course of action. Something, or somebody, always confounds us in the end.'

'Yes,' she echoed quietly, 'someone always confounds us in the end.' A tiny flame of anger burned within her in that moment. She had not wanted to fall in love with this man beside her; she had intended to continue in a pleasant backwater that allowed of her basking in the serenity and peace of a life devoid of complications or tumult. Now, in the space of days, she was no longer mistress of her emotions, but completely, irrevocably, at the mercy of someone named Nicholas Young for her future happiness. A word, a look from him could transport her to heaven; a frown, the suggestion of indifference and she would be plunged into the abyss of gloom. And, worst of all, it was quite useless her pretending there was anything she could do about it – beyond bear it in secret.

Nicholas refused to allow his thoughts to dwell upon Stephanie subjectively as he sat there. It would be fatal for him to give rein to his feelings for her and, thus, build them up out of all proportion. Far better, he argued, to accept the truth that she attracted him and to avoid her, for that very reason, in future. Almost defiantly, defensively, he insisted that his reaction to her was violently physical and that for him to be ensnared by the appeal of the senses, would violate every instinct and destroy his every plan. He said conversationally:

'You don't look like a woman who understands antiques!'

'So long as I don't look antique.'

He held her gaze.

'You look very beautiful and very disturbing,' he said hoarsely.

A thrill went over her body. But she said flippantly:

'I cannot imagine any woman disturbing you for longer than a minute or so.'

He glanced down at his glass then raised his eyes.

'Is that the impression I give you?'

'Yes.' She managed to laugh. 'But I am quite ready to admit that, beyond that, you are entirely inscrutable.'

'That could be defensive.'

'It could be.'

'But it isn't – is that what you mean?'

Stephanie sipped her cocktail.

'I think I do. I should say that you deliberately cut yourself off from people; retreat the moment you feel they might be making headway or coming to understand you.'

'You are very discerning.' He breathed sharply. 'But not quite right in your deductions... How about dinner?'

She felt again that sharp withdrawal mentally; as though he had pulled down an invisible blind between them. She got up from her chair and stood beside him, conscious of his nearness, alive and quivering in the floodlight of her own love for him, craving in turn his response and despising herself for the weakness.

'When,' he asked, as some minutes later they sat over their meal, 'does your brother propose to get married?'

'In a month,' Stephanie replied.

'So soon?'

'Michael is not a patient man,' she said, forcing a smile.

'I hope that he will never have cause to regret his impatience,' came the sombre and somewhat bitter reply.

Stephanie's heart beats quickened.

'They are very much in love,' she hastened. 'I cannot imagine Michael failing at

81

anything he undertakes.'

'The responsibility for failure, or success, hardly rests entirely with him.'

She looked at him very levelly:

'You wouldn't be a pessimist by any chance – would you?'

'Sorry.' He smiled.

She said quickly:

'Marriage doesn't appeal to you – does it?' A faint laugh. 'Or do you object to my questions?'

'On the contrary. No; marriage does not appeal to me,' he said almost roughly. 'The idea of it – perhaps when I'm feeling senti-mental, romantic ... the reality, no!' It was a harsh sound.

Stephanie felt unutterably wretched; a sick-ness overwhelmed her... The very thought of indulging unrequited love offended her sen-sitivity...

'I can well appreciate any man desiring to keep his freedom.' She added defiantly. 'As I told you I wished to keep mine; but recalling what you said a very short while ago, what do you propose to do should you ever fall in love– Oh, yes, let us ignore that immunity of yours for a moment?'

There was a sudden, dramatic silence between them. Nicholas twisted the stem of his wineglass as though it held the answer. Then, raising his eyes very directly to hers, gazing at her with an unnerving intensity he said softly:

'Quite frankly, I don't know what I should do... No one does, really. In this life we know only that which we imagine we should do.'

'How true ... Nicholas?' She stopped, colour rising to her cheeks as his name slipped out unawares. 'I'm sorry,' she said, 'but–'

'Isn't the Mr rather absurd, Stephanie,' he whispered, and there was something in his attitude that made the memory of his kiss flame between them as though he had, again, taken her in his arms.

'I hate formality,' she agreed shakily.

Nicholas struggled to draw the conversation back to generalities; his mood was dangerously susceptive, his senses inflamed; passion crept upon him with shattering insistence; he could not ignore Stephanie's attractiveness, or his desire for her.

'You will,' he said irrelevantly, 'come here to Warwick to live, after your brother is married?'

'Yes.'

Nicholas could not resist he question:

'And your partner – does he, also, live here?'

She didn't avert her gaze.

'Yes; within a stone's throw of the shop – if you can call it that.'

Nicholas found that a sense of frustration possessed him. He said jerkily:

'Human relationships are very unpredictable, aren't they? All this because you had a customer wanting a Chippendale card table!' He smiled. 'Oh, I know that remark is thoroughly irrelevant, but it struck me that our conversation has been of an unusual character from the very beginning!'

'I like unusual things,' she insisted. 'And detest the kind of relationships where only the commonplace thrives.'

Suddenly, almost harshly he asked:

'Are you eventually going to marry Morly?'

She stared at him in surprise; excitement surged through her as she became aware of the intensity of his gaze. 'Not to my knowledge,' she answered, rather unsteadily.

'But he is in love with you?'

Stephanie's voice shook as she said:

'No word in the English language is used quite so lightly as that word "love".'

He drew her gaze to his.

'That is evasion.'

'And is this intended to be a cross-examination?'

Nicholas lit a cigarette, his movements were somewhat agitated; his composure oddly threatened.

'At the risk of being accused of asking a question in order to avoid answering one, are you telling me politely to mind my own business?'

She forced a smile. The tension was mounting between them and she was at a loss to know how to maintain that casual acceptance and interest in the conversation.

'On the contrary; perhaps I was wondering,' she flashed back, 'whether or not I might take over, and do a little probing as a reward for telling you my affairs!'

His eyes appeared to darken.

'You haven't yet attempted to satisfy my curiosity,' he suggested. He was endeavouring to curb the quite unreasonable anger that was beginning to possess him.

Her smile was slow and faintly tantalizing.

'Then if I say that Trevor imagines he has a proprietary right where I am concerned, and that we are very good friends and business partners, that is, frankly, as far as I can go. I cannot speak for him beyond that.'

Nicholas's heart was beating heavily and his fury on account of his own vulnerability in no way lessened it.

'Proprietary is a word that could mean many things.'

She turned a disarming gaze upon him.

'It could – but it doesn't.' There was a quiet strength in her voice. 'Trevor is not my lover, if that is what you really mean.'

He looked annoyed.

'It was not what I mean.' There was a sternness about him. 'And you know it.'

'I'm sorry if I shocked you.' Spirit came to her rescue; excitement flamed to life at his attitude.

He made an impatient sound.

'You know perfectly well that I should not be shocked,' he rapped out. 'But it so happens that some things *count* to me.' He stopped abruptly. This was absurd; why delve into her life, allow it to concern him.

She sipped her wine while still looking intently at him.

'You are a very strange man,' she said solemnly.

'Not nearly so strange as you are tantalizing,' he retorted.

They were silent for the next few minutes while they lingered over their coffee and liqueurs; but the tension remained and increased; they dared not lower their guard lest they betray the weakness of their armour.

'Shall we,' he said suddenly, 'go for a run after dinner? Anywhere you wish?'

Stephanie's heart-beats quickened at the idea of prolonging their time together.

'It would be lovely; the country around here is so wonderful just now.' She added swiftly: 'I've wanted to ask–' she paused and there was a significant and rather unnerving stillness as he said tersely:

'What?' And, again, there was that instinctive resistance in his attitude.

'Why you took Wilderness Farm ... I mean,' she hastened, 'farming is not your vocation – is it?'

He stared at her in frank astonishment.

'How did you know that?'

'I didn't – except by instinct. And, perhaps, helped by the fact that you do not look the part.'

'Really?' It was a question. 'And where do I fall short?'

Stephanie didn't smile, but her eyes became expressive of her interest.

'You haven't that ruggedness that deep tan; and your hands–' She shook her head. 'Just that indefinable *something*.'

He allowed his gaze to rest in hers; allowed the attraction he felt for her, to betray itself in the look he gave her.

'Since you are such a wonderful detective – what was I, before?'

She was thoughtful for a moment, then:

'It could,' she suggested almost sharply, 'have been the army.'

'It was.' There was a grimness in his tone.

Her reaction to that brought a certain fear. Was it possible that, after all, there had been some chapter in the past of which he was ashamed. She dismissed the very idea with scorn, the loyalty of love refusing even to consider it.

'You didn't like it?' she prompted tentatively.

'I was negative,' he said gravely. 'And one should never be that about anything. I resigned my commission. It might have worked in different circumstances.' There he stopped as one drawing sharply back from the edge of a confession. 'Shall we go?' he asked, subtly conveying that he had no intention whatsoever of continuing the conversation along those lines.

They went out together and, when seated in the car, he suggested:

'How about taking the Tamworth road to Coleshill?'

'Ideal.' She waited until they were out of Warwick, then:

'I'm giving a little dinner party next Saturday for Michael and Felice – just to celebrate their engagement among our special friends. Will you come?'

He glanced at her.

'Do I qualify, even in this short while, as a "special friend"?' His voice was low and exciting.

Stephanie fought against the emotion that engulfed her like some wild, surging tide leaving her helpless in its power.

'I think so,' she answered him guardedly. 'If you wish it.'

Nicholas warred with himself. This was to be his swan song; the end of a brief interlude, before his affections became inextricably and irrevocably involved. Caution battled against desire; discretion against recklessness. Finally, in a breath, he said:

'I'd like to come.'

'Are you quite sure of that, Nicholas?'

The words throbbed dangerously between them like soft, sensuous music holding them spellbound. Neither spoke. He drove on...

Later, as they reached Coleshill, lying snugly between Shustoke and Maxstoke, Stephanie murmured:

'Sanctuary.' It was a loving sound. 'I cherish every inch of this little place – sleepy, agricultural; I love its pool, the Georgian houses, and specially its bridge – medieval almost – whispering of the past.'

'Not forgetting,' he managed to chip in lightly, 'its stocks, pillory and whipping-post!'

'That,' she admonished feeling suddenly gay, 'is your bloodthirsty army training coming out!'

'Possibly. I must say that such relics hold a particular interest for me.'

'Could you,' she asked breathlessly, 'bear to wander through the church with me?' She looked into the near distance where its spire – one of the finest in England – rose to the soft, evening sky, seeming, finally to lose itself in a haze of opal cloud.

'Yes, I think so.' He forced the note of banter to enable him to stifle the desires that surged upon him. 'I have a special affection for empty churches.'

They stopped the car and walked up the hill to the peace and quietude of those sacred precincts. After the brightness of the sun, its ancient walls appeared in shadow;

shadow speared with dazzling light that pierced the stained-glass windows, and fell in shafts of crimson, amber, sapphire – like reflected jewels – upon the altar and perfect Norman font.

Stephanie was aware of an exultation as she moved slowly down the aisle with Nicholas; she felt the sting of tears behind her eyes, moved by an emotion spiritual and all sufficing. She could not stay the thought that seeped into her mind... She and Nicholas there together; if it could but be prophetic...

No word was spoken; only the echo of their footsteps broke the impressive silence. The air was cool, heavy with the fragrance of incense, musty books, ancient wood.

And it was when they, eventually, walked again outside into the light of evening, that Nicholas said hoarsely:

'Stephanie ... there's so much I must tell you.'

She lifted her gaze to his, her heart feeling that it would burst with the force of its own emotion.

'Never unless you really feel you must, Nicholas,' she said gently. 'I am always ready to take my – my friends on trust,' she added softly.

'Do you think that, between us, friendship would suffice?' he asked hoarsely. 'Will you come over to the farm tomorrow evening?'

Stephanie felt the bleakness of disappointment as she murmured:

'Oh, Nicholas, I'm so sorry. I can't.'

'Morly?' It was a bitter sound.

'No!' She shook her head. 'I'm going down to Oxford to bring a friend of mine back to stay for a few weeks.' Even as she spoke there came the sharp awareness that no longer did she want the intrusion even of Hester, her friend of school-days, and that, since meeting Nicholas, she had almost completely forgotten the arrangements made for her visit.

'I see.'

Stephanie hastened:

'She's recently lost her husband. I haven't seen her for almost six years: they lived abroad. Quite tragic, for they'd been married less than a year.'

'Of course... Then it will have to be Saturday – the party.'

'Yes – Saturday.' A little chill wind blew across her heart; a tremor went over her body. Just what had he meant by friendship not sufficing... Was the alternative marriage, or had he some other conception of their relationship in his mind. She glanced up at him. Impossible to gauge his mood; to fathom the inner workings of his mind. Was it, she asked herself, presentiment that made it seem that the light had gone from the sky of their future relationship; or was it that her need of him, her desperate love for him, was inspiring a fear for which there was

91

no possible justification? In her impulsive, warm-heartedness was born the yearning to learn the truth of his feelings; vague innuendo could but create an agony of suspense.

He looked at her.

'What is it?' he asked in a breath.

'Nothing.' She smiled up at him. 'Just that "someone walking over my grave".' There was a pause in which time she waited, hopefully, for him to speak, to set her mind at rest. Suppose, after all, he was married... Yet he had said that he was not. She tried to recall his words: 'Cynical perhaps; husband – no!' That hardly made it definite that he was a bachelor. She pulled herself up sharply; what folly was this ... might that something – that 'so much' he had to tell her be a declaration of love. Faint colour stole into her cheeks. How often had she heard, and read about, the emotions of women in love; how intolerant she had been of its turbulent effect and the torments it awakened.

Nicholas maintained an iron control. He was aware of the fact that the evening had got quite out of hand; that he was fast precipitating himself into a situation he had sworn to avoid.

They returned to the car and drove back to Willow Corner. There, seeing her to the door, he said quietly:

'Good night, Stephanie ... until Saturday, then.'

'Until Saturday,' she breathed.

For a second his eyes met hers in a passionate, lingering gaze.

'Good night, my darling,' he whispered hoarsely and the next second was gone.

CHAPTER IV

The lounge of Willow Corner bulged with people. It was a gay crowd assembled there and Hester Wincott was the only stranger in the midst. She held court rather after the manner of a queen receiving her subjects. Much travelled, wealthy, exquisitely gowned, Hester at thirty had the playful appeal of a kitten allied to the scratch of a tigress; used in conjunction with each other, these characteristics had served her well. Few, however, had any suspicion of the scratch beneath the purr.

She was blonde, blue-eyed and there was the suggestion that, at middle-age, she would be plump. Her voice was inclined to be high-pitched, but she could lower it to a rather babyish whine on occasion, which she fondly believed to be highly effective. Her regard for Stephanie was deep and sincere, but for humans on the whole, she had very little time, neither liking nor disliking any of them, and bored by their problems and tragedies. Friendships were not essential to her, provided there was a man in her life, and her outlook, in consequence, was entirely subjective and unashamedly selfish.

'Is everyone here?' she asked Stephanie suddenly.

Stephanie was tensed as she awaited the arrival of Nicholas.

'No; not everyone. Why?'

Hester looked smugly complacent.

'You'll soon know, my pet.' A little giggle. 'Trust Hester ... never can tell what she is up to!'

Stephanie smiled.

'I see ... a stray admirer in the offing?'

Hester showed a row of very even, white teeth as she flashed Stephanie a smile.

'How did you guess!'

Stephanie said suddenly.

'You've changed, Hester.'

'Six years is a long time and–' There was a significant pause, 'a great deal happened to me during that interval. You don't know the half of it... Darling, I like Felice, but she would never *mean* anything to me.'

Stephanie's tone was bantering:

'Would anyone? You're far too self-contained to–'

'Like my own sex?'

'Rather an extreme view but–'

'Perfectly true,' came the self-satisfied

reply. 'You're the only woman I've ever known who counts.'

'I'm flattered!'

Hester said:

'My dear, you're hardly hearing a word I'm saying ... don't worry, he'll come, who-ever he is!'

Colour mounted Stephanie's cheeks and, in that moment as she turned away, Nicholas was admitted.

The murmur of voices died down as Michael stepped forward and made a general introduction; the near-silence gathered to itself a certain dramatic expectancy. Few, if any, of the guests had considered the possibility of Nicholas Young being invited and they had all, at some time or another, regarded his hermit-like existence with conjecture and suspicion.

Nicholas bowed his greeting, aware of the tension. Then, suddenly, Hester's voice came with a deadly, shattering significance as, walking towards him she said in a soft, purring voice:

'Nicholas, how *nice* to see you!'

Stephanie's heart seemed weighted.

'You – you know each other?' She was too startled to consider the obviousness of the remark.

Hester's laugh was light, provocative.

'We should do, since Nicholas happens to be my husband!'

The words fell upon the silence like the clashing of cymbals and suddenly, sharply, Nicholas rapped out:

'Your *ex*-husband, Hester.'

Stephanie had never before done other than ridicule the cliché of 'being turned to stone' but in that agonizing second she felt the full force of that apt description, for she appeared to be clamped to the floor, her body cold and rigid and, in that body, her heart thudded like some maimed, imprisoned thing, suffocating her.

Michael gasped.

'Good heavens!'

Felice laughed.

'My book of rules didn't teach me the correct thing to say on an occasion such as this.'

Stephanie mastered her emotions sufficiently to remark in a tone of flippant cynicism:

'I'm sure that Nicholas would agree that silence is golden.' She nerved herself to meet his gaze, her own hard, faintly derisive. 'The mystery is now solved.' Before he had time to comment, she added, smiling at Hester: 'We'll leave you two to wallow in your reminiscences.'

And with that she moved deliberately towards Trevor, saying audibly:

'Trevor, I can see some empty glasses – of which mine is one.'

Trevor was quick to sense her mood.

'Then why not come and help me replenish them?'

She nodded.

'I will.'

In the adjoining room where a buffet supper awaited them and the cocktail cabinet groaned under its weight of bottles, Trevor said quietly:

'So *that* explains away our friend...'

Stephanie sat down on the edge of a chair; she felt weak, conscious of a sickening disillusionment.

'Yes.'

Trevor gloated inwardly. A hated rival had been miraculously removed.

'Of course I have heard rumours about him,' he went on as he poured out the drinks. 'Undoubtedly, he was the guilty party. Someone told me the other day that his name was linked with a Valerie Brown – some actress or other.'

'Rumour,' said Stephanie disgustedly.

Trevor raised his gaze and said warningly.

'If he is the guilty party then, obviously, he has ratted on the woman in the case. Charming fellow.'

Stephanie was torn between a desperate loyalty and an equally desperate unhappiness; her thoughts were in turmoil; her emotions tumultuous. Nicholas, whom she had fondly imagined was coming to her that night to tell her he loved her... How easy it was to understand his general attitude now... And she had cherished the foolish notion that he had marriage in mind... Colour crept up over her cheeks. When, obviously, he was in search of another mistress. She stopped abruptly, horrified with the progress of her jealous conjecturing, yet feeling that a burning gimlet was boring mercilessly into her brain, stabbing her to bitterness and retaliation... Hester's husband... Her ex-husband... How well had he loved her ... well enough to marry her ... to live with her. She got up as if the very inactivity were unbearable.

Trevor strode to her side and handed her a glass.

'Drink that,' he said authoritatively. 'You look as though you need it.'

She obeyed him gratefully. Then:

'I wonder if Hester knew he lived here in the district?'

'Bet your life she did.' He added: 'She's pretty cute, Stephanie, make no mistake.'

Stephanie echoed:

'"Cute"?'

'Yes.' There was a grimness about him. 'Oh, I know you think she's wonderful – the cloying little girl type one moment, and the sophisticate the next – you have yet to see the *virago*,' he finished.

Stephanie laughed; the very idea was absurd.

'I think I know Hester better than you,' she said, thankful for any conversation that forced her mind a fraction from Nicholas.

'The best in her – yes.' He shook his head. 'You're so disgustingly trustful, Stephanie – it's almost tragic.'

'That makes me sound unsophisticated and naïve.'

'Which in many ways is precisely what you are!'

'Nonsense!' Her voice was indignant.

'Very well ... whatever you are, my sweet, you're quite adorable,' he whispered. 'And utterly desirable.' He moved to her side. 'How about going back to the rabble?'

'Is that polite – this is my party and Michael's.'

'I know ... but it is still a rabble! Singly, everyone is charming; collectively they are quite unattractive.'

Stephanie said swiftly:

'You take the drinks in, Trevor, I'm going outside for a little air; the smoke in there' – she inclined her head in the direction of the lounge – 'is stifling.'

Trevor wasn't deceived, but he was far too wise to challenge her.

'Very well ... I'll get rid of these glasses and join you.' He spoke reassuringly.

But even as he left the room, Hester entered it.

'There you are,' she said brightly, as she

glimpsed Stephanie. 'I've been looking for you.' Her expression became faintly coy. 'I told you to wait and see – didn't I?' she went on confidentially.

'You knew that Nicholas–'

'Lived in the district?' Hester settled herself beside Stephanie. 'Of course. I made it my business to find that out the moment I landed in England from Rio.' She added knowingly: 'He's an absolute devil and quite unreliable but–' She lifted her gaze and raised her eyebrows: 'No one can compare with him as a lover.'

Stephanie felt sick, desolate. She was trembling violently and nothing offered her escape from the torment. She fought to keep her voice casual as she asked:

'Did you divorce *him?*'

Hester looked surprised.

'Naturally!' A sigh. 'Perhaps I was foolish.'

Stephanie was torn between the desire to know more and the anxiety to spare herself hurt.

'And – and the other woman?'

Hester kept a very tight rein upon her emotions. Plans were formulating in her mind and, even as she sat there, she was making swift calculations.

'An actress – Valerie Brown.' She added triumphantly: 'But Nicholas didn't marry her afterwards. I knew he wouldn't.' Her voice became an effective purr: 'Poor Nicky, he was always in love with me, really; begged me to forgive him.' She shook her head. 'One can be so very stubborn when one has been hurt.' A sigh. 'And I suppose I trusted him too much; put him on a pedestal. Doesn't do! My dear, it just doesn't do,' she went on solemnly. 'One is just asking for disillusionment.'

'It is,' Stephanie managed to say, 'natural for a woman to imagine the man – the man she loves is above reproach.'

Hester darted a sudden, inquiring glance in Stephanie's direction. The germ of a thought fertilized in her mind. Was it possible that Stephanie was in love with Nicholas? And he with her? Frustration gripped her. It couldn't be that she, herself, had returned too late... She said quietly and significantly:

'Perfectly natural and utterly foolish. No, my pet ... the best a woman can hope for is to be that one woman whom a man cares for, *above all others.*'

'I should loathe to be one of many,' insisted Stephanie violently.

Hester smiled pityingly, but affectionately.

'Ninety per cent of women are that,' she said knowingly. Adding with studied intent: 'I knew that Nicholas was a philanderer when I married him, but, like so many women, I imagined I could change him.' A tinkling little laugh. 'How naïve I was.' She paused, then: 'Have you know him long, darling?'

Stephanie held her breath as she tried to control her emotions, to maintain a calm that should prove deceptive.

'Not very.'

Hester wanted to know more.

'How did you meet him?' Her voice was encouraging without being curious. 'He said something about your wanting to buy some furniture!' A laugh.

Stephanie explained; and Hester registered the thought that there was no discrepancy in her story and that already told by Nicholas.

'And you liked him?'

'Michael and I both liked him.'

'I think it is too sweet how he's lived the life of a hermit all this time. It really touched me, Stephanie. Just shows what a man can do when he loses the woman he really cares for.' Hester hurried on: 'Don't think I'm flattering myself, darling, but–' A little pouting smile.

Stephanie felt slightly sick and sickened.

'Do you want to re-marry him?' she asked bluntly.

Hester resorted to her childish act of somewhat flippant vagueness.

'Never know what little Hester may do... I'm just going to let things take their course. He's been terribly sweet to me tonight, and

I may relent. Just depends!' Her expression changed to a certain impressiveness, tinged with a suggestion of secrecy: 'We might even go abroad – who knows!'

Hester was talking deliberately for Stephanie's benefit. Couldn't be too careful, and if Stephanie had any ideas in her mind of a romantic nature regarding Nicholas now was the time to kill them. Hester never deceived herself about the things in life that she wanted, and the things she wanted she was quite determined to have. Nicholas was the next item on her very long list! And, equally, while she was genuinely fond of Stephanie, she most certainly wouldn't study her happiness or temper her own desires to Stephanie's needs. She could not quite rid herself, also, of the suspicion that Nicholas's attitude over Stephanie had been somewhat strange and quite inscrutable.

Stephanie's heart ached as from a wound. How easy to see that Nicholas had merely been interested in her as a new adventure to relieve the monotony of his life.

Hester babbled on:

'It's wonderful to have you to talk to, Stephanie. Some people are so stuffy: they never really come within a thousand miles of what one is trying to say.' She glanced around her. 'I love this old place... How can you bear to leave it when Michael marries?'

Stephanie said quietly:

'It is always easy to do anything when one has a purpose in mind. Michael and Felice will be very happy here.'

'But I really don't see why *you* should have to uproot yourself, darling. Felice's people, apparently, are rolling in money – let them provide the house.'

Stephanie shook her head.

'You don't really think like that, Hester. Can you imagine a man of Michael's character being beholden to his in-laws? Besides, I'm free: a flat in Warwick will suit me equally well.'

'And even if it didn't, you'd still move.' Hester smiled: 'You certainly haven't changed...' Her expression hardened. 'All I ask is that you don't allow Felice too much rope.'

Stephanie's voice was affectionate.

'Felice and I understand each other. She is an utterly frank person to whom one can talk and trust.'

Hester laughed, not unkindly.

'My dear child, you trust everyone.'

'Thus far, I've never really regretted it,' Stephanie said, adding almost harshly: 'Obviously one misplaces confidence on occasion, but that doesn't prove anything.'

Hester asked unexpectedly:

'Were you surprised about Nicholas?'

'In a way – yes. Although I sensed there was some mystery in his life.'

Hester sighed.

'So like Nicky; close as an oyster unless he happens to be infatuated,' she said meaningly. 'Be rather funny if we were to marry again, wouldn't it? Heaps of people do. Half the time they're thoroughly miserable apart – even if they are not happy together.'

Stephanie could not resist asking:

'Were you happy together?'

Hester put on her child-like act.

'I thought we were, Stephanie. That was what was so *awful.*' Her voice dropped to a pathetic whisper. 'I thought the shock would kill me when I first *had* to believe that Nicky was unfaithful. I just wanted to die.'

'I'm sorry.' It was a low, sincere sound of regret and sympathy. Stephanie's nerves were taut as she endeavoured to avoid betraying her own reactions.

'For all that,' came the steady comment, 'Nicky was always in my thoughts; he isn't the type a woman forgets easily.' She pouted prettily. 'I suppose the real truth is that I love the man.'

Stephanie shivered.

Hester watched her carefully; not a gesture, nor an expression, escaped her notice; she was by no means satisfied that there was nothing between her, Stephanie, and Nicholas. And she congratulated herself that, were her suspicions correct, she had prepared her own defence in advance and deterred Stephanie from regarding Nicholas as a possible husband.

'Coming back to the others?' she asked lightly. 'It's a good party, my dear. Michael's really charming. You know, it has just struck me that the Brown woman knew Felice's people.' A shrug of the shoulders. 'Although, of course, I could be mistaken.'

'Did – did you know Valerie Brown personally?'

Hester looked rather pathetic.

'Yes.' The word broke on a note of misery. 'My *dear*, he brought her to the house. Oh, yes, I knew dear Valerie – unfortunately.'

'Was she very attractive?' Stephanie hated herself for being concerned.

'I suppose so. Rather the obvious type that men always profess to detest and then sneak around corners to sleep with. Theatrical, naturally. I thought she bored him.' A smirk. 'Never does to believe anything men say about women and always beware of them when they decry any particular type – that type is precisely what they make for.'

Stephanie looked at her intently. Somehow the sentiments were not in keeping with her conception of Hester. It struck her that she had become hardened in the past six years. Hardened ... the word caught at her imagination. Wasn't that natural in the circumstances and after all she had been through. What could be more agonizing than to discover that the husband in whom you believed, and with whom you were happy, was, in truth, unfaithful and that the whole edifice of marriage was a hideous sham.

Hester was anxious to get back to Nicholas and paused in the doorway on her way out of the room.

'I'll join you in a few moments,' Stephanie murmured.

'Don't be too long.' A light laugh. 'I'll go and see where that ex-husband of mine is!'

Stephanie opened the french windows and stepped out into the coolness of the night air. Around her the scene had all the beauty and serenity of a painting by a master. The sky, still flushed with the afterglow, formed a background for towering trees, and in the far distance, the spire of the village church rose delicately, like an etching. The garden was in shadow, yet against that sombreness, light was shot with a curious iridescence, every flower, seemingly every blade of grass, stood out stereoscopically, and the orchard became a dark, mysterious tunnel where the blossom-laden trees, like pearly tinted snow, gleamed wanly in the half-light.

She stood very still, as one endeavouring to gain strength from the beauty around her and finding in it only the tearing, smarting anguish of memory. This, she thought, is the hurt of love; the deep and desperate pain which makes of yearning a dagger twisting in the heart.

A voice beside her said hoarsely:

'Stephanie...'

She turned to meet Nicholas's intense gaze.

'Oh! Hallo,' she said, carelessly hating the need for breaking the spell which the inflection of his voice cast upon her. Fiercely, however, she told herself that it was up to her to retreat from further danger and to make it quite plain to him that their association – other than mere acquaintanceship – was at an end.

'I've been looking for you.'

She flashed him a faintly cynical glance.

'Really.'

He said roughly:

'There was so much I had to tell you.'

She raised her eyes and nerved herself to meet his gaze without flinching.

'Suppose we don't go into that,' she said firmly. 'I think I understand the situation very well and Hester has filled in quite a few of the gaps... In any case, Nicholas, you don't have to explain anything to me.' She spoke in the tone of one dismissing the subject as she turned away from him with an air of finality.

Fiercely, masterfully, he gripped her shoulders, forcing her to look at him.

'And do you imagine those few words are

108

adequate between us,' he demanded. 'Listen, Stephanie—'

'Please, Nicholas,' she said almost irritably because her resistance was fast ebbing.

His voice dropped to a passionate whisper.

'Do you imagine I am going to allow you to dismiss me like that?'

She remained maddeningly calm.

'There is no question of my "dismissing you" as you call it. You are certainly not answerable to me for your actions in any case. Our acquaintance could hardly have been more brief. And even if it were not, it so happens that I *am* a friend of Hester's,' she finished staunchly.

'How little you understand.' It was a low sound of regret.

'There is absolutely no reason why I should do so.'

'There is to me,' he insisted hoarsely, his eyes meeting hers in fiery challenge.

With a superhuman effort she managed to smile up at him as she forced herself to say, with an air of casualness:

'I warned you that I had no time for married men.'

Roughly, he countered:

'I am not a married man.'

She said, jealousy and pain goading her:

'Neither have I any time, Nicholas, for the divorced husband of my friend. I cannot imagine anything worse than a relationship haunted, not only by the ghost of a former wife, but of a mistress as well,' she ended harshly.

For a second there was a deadly silence. She saw him wince; saw a shadow cross his face. Then, very softly, but with a compelling forcefulness he asked:

'Just suppose Hester had not come into the picture at this stage and I had told you, as I intended, the whole truth about my marriage ... what then?'

Stephanie beat down the sudden, overwhelming love that engulfed her; fighting it as she would fight a turbulent sea, the waves of which threatened to submerge her. Briefly, she retorted:

'It so happens that Hester did come into the picture...'

'That is pure evasion.'

'If it is,' she challenged, 'then I'm sorry; but it remains my answer.'

'Very well.' His eyes darkened in the light of passion that blazed within them as looking at her, making it impossible for her to avoid his gaze, he demanded: 'And suppose I had told you that I was in love with you and had asked you to marry me ... would you, then, have held the past against me?'

She was trembling so violently that speech appeared to be almost impossible.

'It would never,' she said, seeking by trying to avoid the issue, to escape from the danger of her own desires, 'have been a question of holding the past against you.'

'Isn't that precisely what you are doing now?'

'No.' Her voice shook with determination.

'You still haven't given me an answer to my question, Stephanie.' He spoke sternly.

With equal firmness, she replied.

'It is a question based on supposition. A question,' she continued scornfully, 'that I doubt very much would ever have been asked.'

He didn't avert his gaze from hers as he said:

'Your lips say that, but your heart rejects every word. Stephanie, can't you *see–*'

'So very clearly,' she rapped out, knowing that only by fighting him could she hope to prevent complete capitulation.

'That's where you are so wrong.'

'I know what Hester has told me,' she insisted. 'I take it that you do not deny *she* divorced *you?*'

Nicholas spoke very quietly:

'No; I do not deny that.'

Stephanie hesitated.

'And if you are thinking that I am the type of woman who expects to be the first in a man's life, or sets for him impossible standards of conduct, let me abuse your mind.'

'I do not,' he said generously, 'jump to any such conclusions. But I dare say that, at this moment, the only ghost that separates us is jealousy.'

'I'm afraid you flatter yourself,' she retorted lightly.

'Anything but that... But I know you, my darling,' he said hoarsely, 'as any man who loves a woman deeply knows her.'

For a second she stared up at him, her heart thudding wildly, every nerve responding to the caress of his voice, the intensity with which he uttered those words she had so craved to hear.

'Yes,' he repeated, 'I love you ... and I know in my heart that you love me,' he added almost triumphantly. 'You can deny me, scorn me, condemn me, but the fact remains that, even as you stand there, you can hardly trust yourself to look at me because your emotions respond to my need of you.'

Stephanie clenched her hands as contempt blazed into her eyes:

'How professionally you utter that word "love",' she said challengingly. 'Practice makes perfect, Nicholas...' Her whole body was trembling as she spoke. 'Don't make me despise you.' She added swiftly: 'I could love a man who had lived his life, shall we say, as the splendid sinner? Never one who had betrayed both his wife and the woman who, doubtless, trusted him sufficiently to be identified with him in the divorce court.'

She expected some violent denial, prayed for some word that might defy her accusation. But in that second it was as though he drew a blind down between them as he said slowly, with great deliberation:

'And you believe me capable of that?'

Standing there, Stephanie was fortified by Hester's words to justify her attitude. Hester was not the type to distort, or accuse falsely, and she had admitted that she was still in love with him... No venom there; no bitterness; only the almost pathetic desire to blame the other woman and defend him! She was – and Stephanie had not the slightest doubt on this point – ready to forgive him and re-marry him. That Nicholas was obviously unworthy of such generosity in no way affected the issue. And for her, Stephanie, foolishly to be weakened by his insincere protestations of affection would be not only endangering Hester's future, but jeopardizing her own. She said and her voice was low:

'I have to believe *facts*, Nicholas. You have said nothing that could possibly prove them to be a distortion of the truth.'

'I see.'

'I hope sincerely that you will atone to Hester for all the misery you once caused her.'

'That is very kind of you,' he said icily.

'I am thinking of Hester.'

'I'm sure you are.' He looked at her intently: 'One day, Stephanie, you will be forced to believe me; to remember this conversation. I cannot plead, justify myself at this stage; and without your faith I would not accept your love – the two must be indivisible. One day you will understand... At the moment, love, hatred, bitterness and contempt are surging within you. You believe me to be the philanderer making love to every woman, even seducing every woman or seeking her as a mistress ... so be it. And that is your hurt, your–'

'My instinctive distrust,' she managed to say sharply. 'I am not a trusting girl of eighteen, Nicholas.'

It was strange, Stephanie thought, how even as she stood there, she had added years to her experience. She felt curiously older, as though the anxious, impulsive and trusting adolescent in her had tip-toed away, leaving in its place a woman mature and disillusioned. It seemed incredible that only a matter of hours previously she had been keyed up with excitement at the thought of seeing Nicholas again, clinging to the hope, the belief, that he would tell her he loved her, even ask her to marry him. Colour tinged her cheeks. Useless to deny that yearning; to deny, also, how she had refused to dwell upon any other possibility, or to remember his secrecy and guardedness after those moments when their lips met... And now – now... She drew in her breath sharply. He *had* told her he loved her and she could not believe him. Love to him was a game; quite possibly he even found sadistic pleasure in making women his slaves and then discarding them.

He looked down at her steadily, passionately.

'Very well, Stephanie; I accept your verdict.' He added tensely: 'For the time being. Even friendship without trust would be quite intolerable to me.'

'I agree.' She spoke stiffly. 'And so long as we understand each other–'

His laugh was half-smothered, cynical.

'Just so long as you *think* you understand, we can but be strangers.'

'But–'

'Ah,' he said more gently, 'woman-like, you fear that; your emotions are far too involved to make that thought pleasant.'

She scoffed:

'That is absolutely ridiculous.'

'No, my darling... It is just – human nature. And it heartens me. At this stage, however, I realize how futile it would be for me to argue with you, attempt to change your somewhat jaundiced outlook.'

That whipped her to anger and she was grateful for the fact; anything rather than that she should have to listen to his insidious appeals which weakened her more than she would ever admit – even to herself.

'My outlook,' she said icily, 'is consistent with the normal reactions of any woman in such circumstances. But I shouldn't expect you to appreciate that.'

Around them the shadows deepened; the trees were no more than a frieze against a shimmering sheet of opal; the hush was unearthly as though the world were waiting, tensed, listening to their heart-beats. Stephanie was shaking and, unable to bear any more, turned to go into the house.

Nicholas moved swiftly; his eyes met hers penetratingly, unnervingly, as he said in a hoarse whisper:

'You belong to me, my darling. Never forget that. Never imagine I shall forget it either.' And with that his arms closed around her, his lips met hers, possessively, masterfully, in a kiss there was no escaping. For a second Stephanie's will power failed her as desire, passion, love surged turbulently to life at his touch and her body relaxed against his in response. Then, as one disgusted with herself and the treachery of the senses, she tore herself away.

But not before the caress had been seen by Hester who noiselessly detached herself from the shadows of a nearby rose arbour and, moving forward, said as though completely unaware of the situation:

'Sensible people to come out here in the cool... Isn't this an attractive garden, Nicky? Reminds me of the one we had at Tonbridge when we were first married... Stephanie dear, they are asking for you and Trevor just cannot escape from that Reynolds woman.'

Stephanie was grateful for the kindly darkness that hid her embarrassment and the colour that had flamed into her cheeks. She said lightly:

'Then I must go and rescue him.' And with that she turned and disappeared into the house.

Hester said deliberately:

'I think that she and Trevor will be very happy – don't you? Well suited.' Her voice was smooth and conversational.

'I don't quite follow,' Nicholas said tensely.

'Are you so blind, my dear?'

'No; but equally I do not jump to conclusions.'

Hester maintained perfect poise, although inwardly she was seething and a little afraid. Suppose there was some understanding between Nicholas and Stephanie, how best could she combat it... And she was determined to do so, she told herself defiantly, no matter to what lengths she was forced to go.

'Neither do I; but it is quite obvious–'

'That,' interrupted Nicholas, 'Trevor is in love with Stephanie.' He drew in his breath

117

sharply: 'But not that she returns his affections.'

Hester knew that she must not be provoked into a display of jealousy or ill-temper and she said lightly:

'Do I sense a little wishful thinking?'

Nicholas found it wholly impossible to understand her; there was something faintly absurd, even fantastic about meeting her again in such circumstances and he was at a loss to fathom her attitude. It had never, he reflected sombrely, been easy to follow the trend of her thoughts, or co-ordinate those thoughts with her actions; her mind appeared to him as a labyrinth, mysterious, inaccessible, and during the years of their married life he had become increasingly aware of her unpredictable and incomprehensible behaviour. At no time could he have gauged, with any degree of certainty, just what her conduct would be.

'I hardly think it necessary to answer that question, Hester.'

'Meaning you refuse?'

'Meaning that you have no right to ask it.'

Hester bit her lip in mortification.

'Won't you even meet me half-way, Nicholas?' It was a pleading, cajoling sound. 'After all, since I was the injured party, surely–'

Nicholas interrupted her.

'Let's not hold any post-mortems, Hester.

They cannot possibly serve any good purpose. We happen to have met again–' His pause was significant, 'whether by design on your part, or accident, remains to be seen and isn't, in any case, important, but for heaven's sake don't expect me to introduce any sentimental note into the proceedings. So far as I am concerned, yesterday is dead – quite dead,' he added adamantly.

She peered at him through the gloom.

'Is that any reason why we shouldn't be friends?' she said gently.

'None; but I certainly cannot see any purpose being served by it.'

'I can.' It was a low, purring sound. 'I'd love to see your farm, Nicky, if you'd show it to me; love to know just a little bit about you ... surely that isn't too much to ask. I take it I am not exactly repulsive to you.'

'Don't talk nonsense,' he exclaimed with some impatience.

She continued to look up into his face.

'You've changed,' she whispered. 'You're harder.'

'Is that surprising?' he demanded.

'You sound as though the fault lay with me,' came her swift response.

'Suppose we agree that our marriage was not exactly a success,' he suggested somewhat cynically, 'and leave it at that. Trying to apportion the blame in any human relationship is pretty fatuous.'

'I wasn't in any way endeavouring to do so,' she insisted hotly, and gave a little light laugh. 'How absurd it is for us to argue,' she purred. 'May I come up to see you tomorrow? I want your advice – if you'd be good enough to give it to me.'

'What about?' He was suspicious.

'Money; oh, several things.'

'Surely your solicitor is better fitted to give it than I?'

'Don't you want to help me?' It was a wheedling cry.

'Yes, but–' Nicholas had no desire to be drawn back into any relationship with Hester; he was aware of Stephanie's attitude and what her reactions to such a situation would be. 'Look here, Hester, I think it would be far better if we didn't take this meeting further than tonight. I–'

'Oh, Nicky, how can you be so cruel?' Her eyes gushed tears that gleamed wanly in the light of the moon. 'Didn't you hurt me enough in the past without adding to it now?' She added tactfully: 'I shall not be down here very long and surely–'

Nicholas recoiled from the possibility of a scene and, manlike, capitulated.

'Very well,' he said resignedly.

Hester felt triumphant. Once she could establish herself again in his life, even in friendship, the rest would be easy and Stephanie soon made to realize that there was no future for her in clinging to any romantic hopes of becoming the second Mrs Nicholas Young. It would require great tact, restraint and patience, but Hester flattered herself that she was possessed of all three in abundance. There was no question about it, she argued, Nicholas had that charm and fascination which made all other men appear tame and boring, while his obvious interest in Stephanie had sharpened the razor edge of her desire for him, as to make the issue both vital and urgent.

She slipped a hand through his arm.

'Let's go in,' she said softly. Then: 'Oh, Nicky, this is such fun and I feel so much happier. I've hated our estrangement so much.'

Nicholas was too distracted to comment, subconsciously realizing that to do so would, inevitably, provoke further argument. His thoughts were entirely obsessed by Stephanie and a certain bitterness tinged his reflections as he dwelt upon the fact that, but for Hester's reappearance, the whole pattern of his life might, even at that moment, have been irrevocably changed and Stephanie's future linked with his in a sweet, sharp ecstasy and affinity. But, now, what?

His voice was a trifle harsh as he exclaimed:

'Aren't you rather dramatizing and sentimentalizing a quite commonplace situation... Ah, Michael,' as they stepped into the house through the french windows, 'Yes, a drink would be most welcome.'

Michael took one look at Hester, then back at Nicholas.

'A good stiff whisky?'

'A good stiff whisky,' said Nicholas grimly.

Across the intervening space, between the double doors of dining-room and lounge, Nicholas met Stephanie's eyes, holding her gaze with a passionate, penetrating determination that defied her efforts of escape. He had forgotten Hester's presence until, arrested by Stephanie's swift expression of faintly cynical challenge he realized that Hester's arm was still through his own...

Stephanie was aware of what represented to her the intimacy of rediscovery and, slowly, deliberately she moved forward until she stood facing them both. Then, raising her glass she said flippantly:

'To both of you; the scene looks quite domestic.'

Hester experienced a sharp thrill of conquest. And took advantage of it as she said with a little, contented sigh:

'Divorce is by no means always the swan song.' Then, anxious not to provoke Nicholas, she adroitly moved away a few paces and, smiling at Felice said: 'And remember, my dear, if Michael should ever get out of hand ... they always come back!' A laugh. 'These misunderstood married men are just not to be trusted but are ... *so* charming.'

'And very transparent,' said Stephanie blithely. She turned upon Trevor a little, confident smile that disguised the misery tearing at her heart, 'but so long as one does not take them seriously, they can provide a certain diversion and amusement.'

She felt the intensity of Nicholas's gaze upon her, almost as though it were burning her eyes; she could feel the force of his anger, his disapproval and found a certain pleasure in it; for nothing could ever approximate the sickness of disillusionment she had experienced as she realized the truth about his life and his behaviour to Hester.

Nicholas sipped his drink and continued to hold her gaze in defiance of her attitude.

'It would be comparatively easy to apply that philosophy to women,' he said sardonically.

Stephanie took in her breath rather sharply.

'Haven't you already done so and put the philosophy into practice, Nicholas,' she retorted smoothly. Then: 'Trevor, do you think anyone would notice if we slipped out for half an hour. I feel like driving at seventy miles an hour through the moonlight.'

'Say the word,' Trevor promised.

'Let's go,' she exclaimed firmly, and flashing a glance at Nicholas, added: 'Good night ... if I don't see you again.'

'Good night, Stephanie,' he said solemnly.

Again their eyes met and again it was as though he were challenging her, even condemning her.

He commented with a deadly calm:

'The implication of any event cannot rightly be assessed until one can study the facts in retrospect. Tonight will not prove the exception, Stephanie.'

Something in his voice silenced her; the muscles of her throat contracted making sound impossible. It was as though he exercised some uncanny power, the forcefulness of which destroyed her defences, rendering her helpless in the face of his magnetism. Swiftly, almost blindly, she turned. Hester watched, vigilantly, critically and as one weighing up every phase of the present situation. The conversation had not been intended for her ears, but, nevertheless, she had strained every sense in order to hear it above the din of the room.

When Stephanie returned, having been upstairs to fetch a light woollen coat, she found Nicholas standing alone in the hall.

'Your friend has gone out to the car,' he said deliberately.

'Thank you.' She glanced into the now overcrowded rooms through the open doorways. 'We shall certainly not be missed for a little while.'

'No?' It was a statement made with the inflection of one querying the issue. Through the entrance porch the soft, opalescent darkness of the spring night beckoned mysteriously, romantically; the sudden rays from the headlights of Trevor's car, swept over flowers, arbours and lawns, giving them sudden life, like limelight spilling upon a stage previously blacked out. The perfume of blossom, lilacs and moist earth was heady, intoxicating. Stephanie's heart ached as she stood there, aware of the fact that she had but to put out a hand to touch Nicholas, so close was he and yet, a world, a universe, separated them. No escape was possible; she was in love with him wholly and irrevocably. Why pretend otherwise? Yet ... would she forget, lose herself in other loves ... look back on all this with an indulgent smile, thankful for a kindly fate that had thus delivered her. She knew it would not be so. Love was rather like the negative of a photograph ... it remained, even though no further prints would ever be taken of it and those already in existence destroyed. She would, because she despised weakness, sentimental clinging to what might have been, go on to other experiences, but, never again, would she be able to retrieve that part of her heart which Nicholas had made his own.

She managed with a superhuman effort to meet his gaze and say flippantly, even though the words hurt her:

'Your technique is quite perfect, Nicholas … in fact just a little too perfect.'

Hester caught up with them, having been impeded by a couple from whom she could not escape.

But Stephanie merely smiled and before further comment could be made, was gone.

CHAPTER V

Trevor drove some few miles in silence, aware of the fact that Stephanie was in no mood to talk and had suggested the drive with him merely to escape from Nicholas Young. The idea neither flattered nor appealed to him, but he accepted it as a progressive step in the right direction. Hester would soon absorb Nicholas and, thus, Stephanie's romantic dreams would receive further setback. He began slowly:

'Quite an original evening – eh?'

'Quite.'

Trevor glanced at her and then back at the road ahead.

'You're in love with him – aren't you?' It was said quietly and conversationally and as though the statement were a perfectly normal one.

Stephanie was not conscious of annoyance. Inertia followed in the wake of tumultuous emotion, jealousy, anguish. She was so tired in those moments that keeping awake became an agony yet, paradoxically she knew that could she be spirited into bed, no sleep would offer oblivion.

'I rather think I reserve the right not to answer you,' she said flatly.

'Very well; I don't need your answer, my dear. I told you that first day when you'd met the man that you were more than interested. I'm seldom wrong,' he added complacently. 'Hester's quite a complication. That is the trouble with wives – they litter a man up so!'

Stephanie forced a smile.

'You're quite incorrigible.'

'I don't want to see you hurt – at least not more than you have been tonight, my sweet.' It was said quietly and sincerely.

Stephanie fought against the sudden violence of her emotions that seemed to burst into her heart like water through a dam.

'Experience,' she said laconically.

He gave a snort.

'The price is hardly worth it in this case.'

'That's prejudice.'

'Is it? Do you remember a conversation we had one day – the day, in fact, you first met Young?'

Stephanie's voice was uncertain.

'Quite well.'

'Do you still feel the same as you did then about life and things in general?' He bent his cigarette to the flame of his lighter, catching her eyes above the flare.

'I see no reason why I should have altered in so short a time.'

'That is not an answer.'

'I know.' She sighed wearily.

Trevor slowed down, stopped and drew on the brake with a vicious movement.

'The finest antidote for one man is – another,' he said firmly.

'Please–'

'Listen to me.' He spoke almost harshly. 'I'm an opportunist, Stephanie, and, unlike you, while I believe in romance and all the rest of it, I certainly don't subscribe to the view that there is only one person out of millions who can give one happiness; I don't even believe – if what I see around me is any criterion – that love, as such, is the alpha and omega and that without it there's neither ecstasy nor happiness. Far too often it damned well means misery and torment.'

Stephanie protested.

'I don't quite follow what you are trying to say.'

'I am doing my damnedest to prevent you nursing the misery you feel at this moment,' he said roughly. 'I know what is going

128

through your mind as you sit there... I'm a fool rushing in at the wrong moment, when you've hardly got your breath from the shock of Hester... Well, if I am a fool then I'm choosing the role deliberately, for it is my belief that the very best time to readjust things is when they are at seething point. Never stand on the brink of icy water – plunge only to discover how warm it *becomes*. Do you see what I'm driving at?'

Stephanie felt the pressure of his arm along the back of her shoulders; felt the tenseness of his body, the emotion of his desires.

'I think so,' she said steadily.

'I don't profess to be madly, insanely in love with you,' he went on frankly, 'and I've very little time for this swearing away of one's future in marriage. Human emotions can't be tied down and no human being, if absolutely honest, can say with truth what he, or she, is going to feel in ten years' time. But, I'll guarantee one thing: I'd not make you miserable.'

Stephanie shook her head.

'That being so, how could you possibly make me happy, Trevor? One must have the positive and the negative to produce that spark.'

'Then I'll settle for a little less than that spark,' he replied. 'We're friends, good comrades, you attract me physically – far more, in all probability, than any overwhelming love could inspire... And I respect you,' he added firmly.

'I told you once that, for me, it must be all or nothing, Trevor.'

'I haven't forgotten; but you don't mean to tell me that, from now on, it is going to be nothing,' he insisted, 'merely because Nicholas Young happens to be your friend's ex-husband and, quite obviously, there will be a reconciliation.'

'I've not even begun to think of the future,' she said wearily. 'This whole evening has seemed fantastic.'

'Exactly.' He looked at her very levelly. 'If I asked you to marry me—'

'I'd refuse,' she said instantly.

His pulses quickened.

'Meaning that you would look upon me with more favour as a lover?'

Stephanie did not hesitate; a certain hardness crept into her voice; a hardness born of pain, and the anguish of hope defeated as she answered him:

'Yes.' She looked at him. 'Yes, Trevor, at least there would be no pretence about *that* and I should know where I was. Just as I know, now, that I am not the type of woman to marry one man while—'

'Loving another,' he finished for her quietly.

She made no attempt to lower her gaze; concealment seemed to her to be childish and feeble in that moment.

'Yes,' she murmured. 'Bitter though that truth is.'

Trevor's hand moved from her shoulder and came to support her chin. Then, deliberately he leaned forward and kissed her lips; it was a swift, persuasive and yet passionate gesture and while she remained passive, unmoved, she in no way recoiled.

'We understand each other,' he said firmly a second later as he turned the ignition key and started the car again. 'One day you will belong to me, Stephanie, and ... I have infinite patience I assure you.'

Stephanie shivered. The echo of Nicholas's words came back to haunt her... 'You belong to me, my darling. Never forget that. Never imagine that I shall forget it, either.'

The name of Valerie Brown obtruded, suddenly, sharply, and Stephanie felt the tearing pain of jealousy which, oddly enough, flamed to destructive life far beyond the intensity of that which could be applied to Hester. Nicholas had married Hester and that marriage had, evidently, failed in some way. But he had sought Valerie Brown out ... been her lover .. made love to her. Stephanie clenched her hands because the torment of reflection became an agony; she could have groaned from its pain, its shattering, searing emotion. Never would she have believed it possible to suffer so intensely through the mere contemplation of a relationship; never would she have credited the fact that mind, body, soul and spirit could so rise in revolt against any act of infidelity ... of sexual satisfaction. The thought of Nicholas in Valerie's arms – even though Valerie was but a name – made her writhe... And the agony of her own longing for him so sharp as to become a gaping wound.

Defiantly, as one clutching at gaiety as the only hope of salvation, she cried:

'Let's not be so serious, Trevor; and we must get back or everyone will think us most frightfully rude. I suppose it was quite unpardonable that I should sneak away like this.'

Trevor said easily:

'By this time they will be far too merry to notice our absence.'

'Sincerely, I hope so.'

Trevor said in a tense, clipped voice:

'Come to Coventry with me when that Kilnorth Grange sale comes on, Stephanie.' He added: 'On your own terms, my sweet...' A pause. 'You look unutterably lovely as you sit there in that pool of moonlight ... your frock, your eyes – everything about you drives me mad. Yes,' he finished hotly, 'if that is an extravagant word I'll still use it. I hate to admit it, but I must be more than a little in love with you for all this to be so important to me.'

'Don't be,' Stephanie cried.

'Why?' It was a hoarse whisper.

'Because I distrust love and those who profess it...' A little sigh. 'Let's not be serious any more, Trevor – please.'

'Very well... Let's go, then!' And with that, he jammed the accelerator down and the car shot forward into its tunnel of amber thrown ahead by the brilliance of the lamps. 'Close your eyes,' he insisted, 'and you shall be home almost before you have time to open them!'

Music floated through the open windows of Willow Corner as they reached it; lights poured upon the garden, catching now and then the outline of lovers who blended with the shadowy trees and arbours. And Stephanie thought dismally, desolately: 'Nicholas will have gone!'

She looked for him as she entered the hall and then moved swiftly into the lounge; her heart seemed suspended; her breath jerky, her lungs solid, as fear possessed her.

And suddenly above the din, yet softly, resonantly, his voice came to her:

'I hope the run came up to your expectations, Stephanie.'

She turned, jumped violently as one startled, while Nicholas detached himself from his position in a far corner, but nothing could conceal the light that sprang to her eyes in welcome, even relief at his presence; nothing could conceal the desire that curved her lips as they parted in anticipation. Only the inflection of her reply broke the spell as she said coolly:

'It certainly did … you still here.' A brief laugh. 'Obvious remark.' She was nervous now, and unnerved by his steady scrutiny; a condition which made her talk too much and, inevitably, say the wrong things. 'Like asking if it is raining when a person comes in drenched to the skin… We've not been missed, I see … I think a nice, cool Pimms is what I need.' A swift glance: 'Can I get you anything?'

'Thanks – no! I merely waited to say good night to you.'

'We said good night ages ago.'

'Then I substitute "good-bye", Stephanie,' he said gravely.

'"Good-bye"–' Her voice broke. 'But–' She pulled herself together. Obviously they had no reason for any further meetings unless by accident and equally obviously, he wished to make this perfectly clear, she told herself rebelliously, and with all a woman's illogical reasoning.

'That was charming of you… Good-bye, Nicholas,' she murmured. 'So dramatic – eh? And where's Hester?'

'Here,' came Hester's somewhat challenging voice. 'You leaving, Nicky?' Hester said sweetly. 'I'll walk to the car with you and, then, I'm going to be very rude, Stephanie, and go to bed. I find,' she added, addressing

Nicholas, 'that the English climate makes me so *tired*. Lack of sun and the kind of warmth to which I've been accustomed.'

'I wonder,' he said vaguely, 'you returned here.'

Her smile was slow, confident.

'England is always a magnet, especially when one is away from it.'

'As are people – when one is away from them,' said Stephanie jerkily. She tried desperately hard to regard Nicholas impersonally, instead of viewing him subjectively in his association with Hester, but the sickness of contemplation overwhelmed her, making it impossible for her to escape from the torments of longing and the sharp, poignant awareness of her own love.

Nicholas despised himself because of his reluctance to leave, but it was as though he were fighting some invisible enemy whose ghostly presence had obtruded the moment Hester stepped into the picture. Yet, could he say, with certainty, just what would have happened had she not reappeared at that crucial period... Would Stephanie, his story told, have accepted him as her future husband, or was it a case of building up possibility to the proportions of actuality and drawing upon his own desires, rather than correctly assessing hers. Nevertheless, there was something about her which gave him, he told himself fiercely, the right to believe that she was by no means indifferent to him... And he had no intention of resigning himself to the fate she had decreed for him, or of accepting her attitude as eloquent of her true feelings.

Hester followed him out to the car, standing by it as he slid into the driving seat.

'I'll come up to the farm tomorrow, Nicky,' she said with smooth complacency. 'Stephanie will lend me her car.'

'Very well.' His voice was flat, disinterested. 'Good night.' And with that he drove swiftly away.

Hester appeared at breakfast the following morning looking radiant and self-satisfied. Her pale daffodil crepe frock, severely tailored and piped with blue, enhanced the fairness of her skin and brought out the colour in her eyes. She looked cool, confident and exceedingly smart.

Stephanie, studying her, said warmly:

'The years have added to your attractiveness, Hester. There's something about you now–'

'Experience,' said Hester swiftly, smiling so that her even, white teeth flashed dazzlingly. Then, aware of the role she must play for Stephanie's benefit, she toned down her enthusiasm and went on: 'Even unhappy experiences are better than none. I've learned so much from Nicholas, really. If one can rise above hurt, without becoming bitter, it is a triumph over self, after all.'

Stephanie said impulsively:

'I really do think you've been wonderful, Hester... Was your – your second marriage happy?'

Hester lifted her cup, sipped her coffee as one weighing up the facts before giving her answer.

'I suppose I could claim that it was. I know that I made Hector happy, at least. But–' She drew in her breath on a sigh– 'For me there was always the ghost of Nicholas – wondering if I had been harsh, unforgiving. It's funny,' she went on reflectively, 'how violent the shock is when one realizes that one's husband isn't the man one thought him. Nicky was always so convincing, so plausible.' She watched Stephanie very carefully as she spoke, calculating the effect of her words and aware of the shadow that crossed Stephanie's face.

'I can well believe that,' Stephanie said somewhat cynically.

'The trouble is,' Hester went on, 'that we cannot love to order. And I suppose I should have understood and forgiven him his affair with Valerie... I was so shattered and wounded at the time, that I just couldn't think straight. It was as though my whole life disintegrated.'

Stephanie could not stay the words:

'Do you know why he and Valerie Brown parted?'

'Not really; of course he insisted that he would never marry her, but I was far too jealous of her to listen to reason, I suppose. She enticed him – no question about that – and Nicky never could resist a pretty woman.' A slow smile. 'I must admit that she *was* a very pretty woman.'

Stephanie felt that the toast in her mouth had suddenly turned to ashes and that someone had opened a vein and drained all the strength from her. Emotion, sharp, inescapable assailed her; she could not dismiss it. A terrible sickness of jealousy was upon her; jealousy embracing hurt, the pain of conjecture, the vividness of imagination that painted tormenting pictures.

'Do you know where she is, now?'

'Back in London,' said Hester shortly. 'Damn her.'

Stephanie said abruptly:

'Of course; she's been touring South Africa – hasn't she? Now, I remember.' She added fearfully: 'She's only been back a matter of days.'

Hester buttered her toast with the viciousness of one mentally scraping a knife over an enemy.

'She'll probably be down here,' she said fiercely. 'If I know her.' She added: '"The woman scorned" stops at nothing, you know.'

'But since Nicholas doesn't want her ... there must have been something very drastic that prevented his marrying her after she had been involved in the divorce.'

Hester smiled at Stephanie rather pityingly:

'You have far more illusions left than I, my dear, Nicholas isn't the type of man who thinks of anything beyond that which he wants at the moment. He'll always be the same.'

'And yet you talk as though you would consider re-marrying him,' said Stephanie hotly. 'That doesn't make sense.'

'Of course it doesn't ... love never does.'

'No, murmured Stephanie, shakenly. 'I suppose not.'

'Of course,' Hester went on, determined to preserve Stephanie's good opinion and behave 'in character', 'if I didn't know, beyond all doubting, that I was terribly important to Nicky I'd never have returned. I want *his* happiness because only that way could I ever be happy myself.'

'You are very magnanimous,' said Stephanie slowly. 'I don't think I could ever compromise with life like that.'

Hester sighed and looked effectively sentimental.

'I've learned that I cannot go on without Nicky,' she insisted. 'I can say that to you, darling, where I could not possibly confide to anyone else.' Her expression changed to a rather pathetic solemnity. 'I must face the facts as they are and accept him as he is. Useless deceiving oneself, after all. You like him – don't you?'

Stephanie managed to keep her emotions under control.

'You asked me that last night, Hester.'

Hester said swiftly:

'Of course; how silly of me… All the same, I didn't feel that there was any enthusiasm in your answer.'

Stephanie, in an effort at understatement, overplayed her hand.

'Since I hardly know him, I am not really qualified to give one,' she replied.

Hester made a doubting sound.

'Darling, your judgments of people are usually of the "snap" variety. You like, or dislike, on sight. Be honest.'

Stephanie was aware of Hester's gaze intently upon her and unnerved by it. It would be agony should she suspect the truth. She said swiftly:

'Very well, then: I liked Nicholas the first time I met him – which was precisely what I told you,' she finished coolly.

'Would you – trust him?'

Stephanie's reply came somewhat disarmingly:

'I might have done had it not been for you. As it is, I can but accept him at your value, Hester. Most certainly I am disillusioned as to his character.'

Hester leaned forward, saying agitatedly:

'But I didn't want to lower him in your eyes, darling. I just wanted to be frank with you about the whole situation. Nicky has some wonderful qualities and so many men are philanderers at heart and–'

'You,' suggested Stephanie cynically, 'are suggesting that he is a philanderer who, if given the chance, would always come home?' A pause. 'Is that it?'

'Exactly. I couldn't bear to do him an injustice, Stephanie. His weakness over women...' A sigh. 'There it is.'

'I'm afraid,' Stephanie could not resist saying, 'that I should use stronger language in describing a man who, having involved a woman in a divorce action, doesn't ultimately marry her.'

Hester's suspicions were more than confirmed in that second. Stephanie was obviously in love with Nicholas. Why the vehemence, otherwise. Fear turned like a knife in her heart. She had not been prepared for such a complication and was the more vulnerable, she argued, because she was unaware of the true significance of the relationship existing between them. Keeping an iron control on her emotions, she said smoothly:

'Perhaps ... but, again, my dear, Nicky and I have been married; the ties that bind us are, in reality, irrevocable and therefore I can look at it all so very differently. Naturally, to me, the fact that he *didn't* marry her proves so much about the nature of his true feelings. It may be horrid of me, callous; but I cannot be expected to consider *her* point of view.'

Stephanie agreed. Depression submerged her in its deadly, stifling grip. How deeply Hester was in love... She recoiled from the thought that such devotion created yet another barrier between herself and Nicholas.

'You are,' she asked, 'going up to the farm this morning – aren't you?'

'Yes.' Hester lit a cigarette and relaxed in her chair. 'What kind of a place is it? Nice?'

'A heavenly setting and when the structural alterations are complete it should be very attractive.'

'Michael is doing those?'

'Yes.'

'Amusing if I were to settle down on a farm, Stephanie! Can't somehow picture myself, and yet–' A dewy tenderness came to her eyes. 'Be rather fun to help Nicky.' She responded to a thought that struck her sharply: 'Didn't you associate him with me in any way when he first came to live here?'

Stephanie answered promptly.

'Why should I? To me, the man you first married was Major Barrington Young. Your letters, my dear, were, if I may say so, anything but coherent! You were always going to tell me "the whole story" of your parting, but never did!'

Hester laughed.

'I'm a ghastly correspondent,' she admitted. 'But our friendship never depended on letters, thank heaven... No, I suppose plain Nicholas Young could hardly mean anything to you.'

Stephanie started.

'Strange,' she murmured. 'Nicholas did tell me that he'd been in the army but even then–' She stopped abruptly. Hadn't she been too excited, too wrapped up in her own emotional reactions seriously to reflect upon half that was said that night ... hadn't she been just a woman in love, a woman bewitched by the promise of tomorrow... Hester ... the entire world ceasing to exist for her in those hours.

Hester was satisfied.

'When one hasn't actually met a person, or seen a photograph of them, they don't really register. But, afterwards, it seems quite absurd that they shouldn't have done!'

'Life seems to be made up of being wise after the event,' Stephanie mused.

'Just like Nicky to drop the "Barrington",' Hester said and decided that she would insist on his using it when they were re-married. 'What are you doing this morning?'

'Working.'

'Do you like being tied like that?'

'Naturally! It's exciting rummaging around for antiques.'

'Clever person ... of course' – slyly – 'I don't doubt but that Trevor Morly adds zest to the proceedings.'

'Not in the way you mean,' Stephanie said flatly.

Hester smirked.

'Darling, of course he does ... women always pretend about men. What is life without a man? I mean, it's all so dull and–' She sighed. 'Couldn't stand it myself. Women bore me to tears.'

Stephanie said stoutly:

'I disagree; I'd far rather be alone than with just a *man*. And one's own sex can often be infinitely more entertaining then some Romeo who bores one to death.'

'Does Trevor bore you?'

'No; we have far too much in common.'

'Exactly ... would you have been as eager to have a woman for a partner?'

Stephanie didn't hesitate.

'Yes,' she insisted with absolute truth. 'Provided she could pull her weight. It so happened that Trevor was a man. The fact of his sex just didn't come into it.'

'Then you don't agree with the theory that women cannot agree in business?'

'No. It isn't a question of sex, but of

individuals. Some men can be as petty and jealous as the most half-witted women on earth. And just as vain – if not more so. I like men, but I most certainly do not subscribe to the fallacy that they have the monopoly of all the attractions.'

Hester smiled and put on her child-like face. She traced a pattern on the table-cloth as she said in a thin little voice:

'I suppose I have been spoiled ... I like being spoiled and feminine and helpless.' Her blue eyes became seemingly very much rounder than usual. 'That was the very thing that both Nicky and Hector liked about me.' She hastened: 'The fact of Nicky being unfaithful didn't alter that. One can be so weak emotionally, alas, and that's the trouble.' An imperceptible pause. 'On the whole, men just do not like business women, I've found.' A smile. 'Unless they happen to be called Stephanie!'

Stephanie shook her head.

'My dear Hester, you have no need to add that. I agree with you, but I would add this: half the time they fear the woman in business because she has become the formidable rival. A man has far greater intellectual powers than a woman; but a woman has far greater *intelligence* and is far more quick-thinking and intuitive, flexible, than a man. She will grasp a thing and make a decision before he has had time to get the gist of it at all. If there is one thing I cannot endure it is a slow-thinking man!'

'Would you call Nicky slow thinking?'

'Heavens no! Why?'

'I just wondered.'

Stephanie spoke half to herself:

'I'm afraid I expect too much of a man,' she said ruefully. 'But, somehow, he must be interesting and a good conversationalist; someone who I know is far superior mentally, and whose views and opinion are backed by experience, travel, a knowledge of life and of art. I'm quite ready to sit at his feet and learn. But anything less–' A sigh. 'It wouldn't work out even if I were in love; so much of me would be left barren and unfulfilled.'

Hester shook her head. Then, cunningly, she asked:

'Would you put Nicholas in the category of what constitutes an "interesting man" in your opinion?'

Stephanie dared not draw back. She said as easily and frankly as was possible:

'Yes, I should.'

'He would be flattered.'

Stephanie's gaze darted to Hester's face. Was that jealousy she caught in the inflection of her voice. She said quietly:

'Unfortunately character and the attributes I've mentioned, are not always found together.'

'You condemn him – don't you, Stephanie?'

How to answer that without being a hypocrite? How to answer it even with a modicum of truth? Slowly, she began:

'Not as one sitting in judgment – heaven forbid! But I do appreciate certain codes and I'm terribly sorry you've been hurt so badly.'

'Bless you, darling.' A telling appeal crept into Hester's eyes. 'And you won't despise me for being so weak – will you? You're different, Stephanie – strong and full of character. I'm not... Oh, I know my own shortcomings,' she insisted cleverly. 'I suppose I'm all heart and no head and may be terribly foolish in wanting Nicky back ... asking, even, for more unhappiness – but I just cannot help myself and there it is.' A thought registered swiftly in her brain and she finished breathlessly: 'I'm like a parrot – aren't I? All on one note!' She changed the subject abruptly: 'I'm longing to see your place in Warwick. May I run over there, later on?'

'You could fetch me home,' Stephanie suggested.

'Since I shall have your car this morning that's fair enough. What time?'

'Sixish.'

Hester showed consternation:

'How are you going to get in this morning?'

'Trevor is calling for me at ten.'

'Oh!' A little smirk. 'You know, Stevie,' she lapsed into her old pet name, 'you don't fool me one little bit... I thought Trevor most fascinating. If I hadn't been such a nit-wit over Nicky, I might have constituted myself your rival.'

Stephanie could not help recalling Trevor's words. 'She's pretty cute ... you have yet to see the virago'. Certainly Hester had not made any conquest with him. Never for a second did it occur to Stephanie seriously to consider the possibility of Trevor's opinion being in any way correct. She *knew* Hester and believed in her. Trevor was merely prejudiced because she happened not to be his type, she argued.

He arrived in that second, coming into the cottage as one completely at home.

'Good morning, Mrs Wincott,' he said formerly as he caught sight of Hester. He paused, somewhat possessively, behind Stephanie's chair and smiled his greeting. 'Any coffee left in the pot?' he asked naturally.

'Enough,' she exclaimed.

He sat down at the table.

'What about some bacon and eggs,' suggested Hester.

'No; just coffee,' he said with absurd seriousness.

She had returned to the table and taken

up her place at it the moment he entered the room, studying him thoughtfully; indulging all manner of wishful thinking. If she could establish some kind of relationship between him and Stephanie... Find even the minutest clue to work on, it might prove invaluable in her fight for Nicholas.

'Do you live near here?' Hester asked him.

'In Warwick – near our business premises.' He drank the coffee which Stephanie had poured out for him.

'Oh, so you will be a neighbour of Stephanie's when she moves to the flat.'

He arched his brows. What was the woman driving at. He decided that he liked her even less in the somewhat harsh and critical light of morning and that his distrust was as strong as his animosity. She irritated him, with her alternating moods of coyness and bold, sophisticated challenge; the latter might ring true, but the former was a sickly and sickening pose. It wasn't possible that Stephanie couldn't see through her. That reflection inspired another: the vulnerability of human beings the moment their emotions were involved. It mattered not whether it be the love of man for woman, or love between the same sexes, there was always that blind spot in the matter of calculation; that margin for deception. That a friend should meet the faults of a friend with understanding and generosity of spirit was

149

reasonable enough and laudable but why, *why* he demanded of himself, was it that in the process of that same friendship, people were so often incapable of seeing beneath the surface.

To him, the outsider, Hester shrieked of insincerity. To Stephanie, fond of her, she was merely 'complex and lovable'. People, he decided, were like paintings: each individual read into them precisely what they wanted to see. Stephanie, while fiercely critical in the general sense, was singularly blind to the faults of those around her. He wondered if it was a case of *knowing* but refusing to *see...* Or was it that, not having seen Hester for six years – in which time she might have changed – Stephanie was still mesmerized into believing that the Hester she knew of old had returned. Nothing is more difficult to destroy than the ideal created from illusion and preconceived notions.

Trevor took his cigarette-case from his pocket and handed it first to Stephanie, then to Hester.

'Yes, I shall be a neighbour,' he replied briefly.

'How nice for you, Stevie,' Hester said sweetly. 'Someone to look after you. Trevor – may I call you that – don't you think she needs looking after? I know how clever she is – she always was clever at school – but no woman should be on her own and–' She stopped and smiled – a smile full of solicitude.

'I can't agree,' he said tersely. 'Provided a woman is on her own from choice and not because she cannot find a companion, then, obviously, she is happier doing as she pleases. Admittedly when a woman wants a husband and cannot get one, or has to *scheme* to do so, the whole thing is vastly different.' He added pointedly: 'Stephanie will never come into that category.' A pause. 'Thank heaven.'

Colour stole into Hester's cheeks. There was something in the look that Trevor gave her which made it perfectly plain that he saw through her and placed her among the scheming women whom, obviously, he despised. She got up from her chair. On no account must this argument, or discussion, develop so that Stephanie began to see with his eyes.

'I couldn't agree more... Stephanie, dear, I'll be off now... Fetch you around six. Don't work too hard.' She kissed the top of Stephanie's head. 'Bless you for being such a dear to me.' She threw a somewhat challenging and triumphant glance in Trevor's direction. 'Nothing in the world like picking up the threads of an old friendship. And finding each other unchanged ... 'bye ... 'bye, Trevor,' she added deliberately.

Trevor remained silent until her footsteps died away on the stairs. Then:

'I certainly congratulate Hector Wincott. How long did you say they were married?'

'A year.' Stephanie looked puzzled. 'Why?'

'After a year with her I should think dying was a pleasure.'

'Trevor!' Her voice was sharp. 'Hester is my friend and if you expect me to sit here—'

'I don't.' He sighed. 'All I ask you to do is to – oh, never mind; you wouldn't listen to me.'

'In that you are perfectly right.' She added fiercely. 'I went to school with Hester; I've kept in touch with her all these years—'

'And you treasure the idea of a life-long friendship – build it up, in fact, out of all proportion.'

'I do nothing of the kind,' indignantly.

'How often have you seen her during those years? What do you know of her life—'

'Precisely that which she tells me.'

'And you believe.'

'Implicitly.'

He groaned.

'Women like you should be certified!'

She laughed. Then:

'I hate the idea, Trevor, that no one is right for you. First it was Nicholas; now Hester; you're not even keen on Felice, and so it goes on. If you're not careful it will become a habit. Everyone,' she finished sombrely, 'cannot be wrong and you right.'

He lowered his gaze.

'I think,' he admitted rankly, 'that I must have a complex about you. I seem to dislike everyone – with the exception of Michael – whom you like.' He pondered the idea as he spoke, aware that it was mainly true even though it had never, before, occurred to him. 'Can't always be coincidence, because, mostly, I get on pretty well with people.'

'Exactly.' Stephanie was conscious of a certain relief.

'All the same,' Trevor went on darkly, 'I wasn't wrong about friend Nicholas. My suspicions about him were right enough – you can't deny that.' A pause. 'Can you?'

Stephanie drew rather sharply on her cigarette and puffed a tiny cloud of smoke into the air.

'No,' she said painfully, 'I can't deny that.'

He looked at her.

'Don't tell me that you want to plead extenuating circumstances even for *him!*' It was a gruff sound.

She flashed back:

'I don't want to plead anything and I have no wish to judge anyone.'

'Least of all Young?'

'If you like.'

He got to his feet.

'Let's get to work,' he cried, 'before I throttle you.'

They laughed together.

'If you want me to be serious, or indulge any long psychological discourse, then I am going to be a very great disappointment to you, Trevor. I'm not in the mood and I doubt if I ever shall be again. From now on, I'm out to enjoy myself – *live*,' she added almost fiercely.

He turned her around so that she faced him.

'Am I allowed to help in that cause?' he demanded.

'Why not,' she answered flippantly.

The phone rang in that second and Felice's voice came over the wires.

'It was a simply wonderful party, Stephanie. I could never have enjoyed anything else half so much.' A laugh. 'Head's a bit heavy this morning, but otherwise I'm walking on air. How about lunch? I'll be in Warwick; we could go to the Leycester.'

Stephanie had a vision of the hotel and of Nicholas... For a split second she recaptured the ecstasy and excitement, the thraldom of that evening, and said as one about to go into battle:

'Very well... One o'clock?'

'Perfect... Oh, I say! I've just heard that Valerie Brown is coming down to stay with us next week. Mother's giving a party for her...' A chuckle. 'How about inviting Nicholas and Hester? Mother hasn't a clue that *he* was the

154

man in the case... No? Perhaps you're right. Just my love of the dramatic. I was dumbfounded when I learned the truth last night. Certainly lent drama to the proceedings... One o'clock, then. 'Bye.'

Stephanie replaced the receiver and stood looking down at the inanimate instrument as though expecting it to become alive. Every nerve in her body was taut, painful; her strength ebbed, her head ached.

Trevor said sharply:

'What is it? Stephanie, you look–'

She pulled herself together sufficiently to interrupt him:

'Just making a few calculations. I ought not to have said I'd meet her–'

'Felice!'

'Yes... I've that Hardby tapestry to examine this morning. Oh, but perhaps I can manage.' She edged to the door. 'Won't be a minute; just get my hat.'

He stood looking after her with puzzled contemplation. Impossible to gauge her moods. Probably that was what made her so tantalizing and desirable. His thoughts raced on like film clicking through a projector. If he could persuade her to accompany him to Coventry...

155

CHAPTER VI

Hester was aware of a certain elation as she began the drive to Wilderness Farm. It wasn't she told herself, that she expected her task to be easy. Nicholas was a stubborn man and not easily influenced. She went back, in imagination, over the years asking herself just why she had taken the trouble to come back to England in order to seek him out. The answer was simple, she decided.

Firstly, the idea that she had been forced to divorce him rankled in the light of retrospect. Whatever her feelings might have been at the time (and it suited her purpose to gloss over that phase) now, widowed, Nicholas came into focus as the most satisfactory proposition she was likely to encounter. Marriage wasn't an easy state and the ill of which one was aware was, in all probability, far better than the promise of an ecstasy that faded after the honeymoon. Love? She doubted it; physically he attracted her and that was enough; for the rest, she had very little patience with those who believed in spiritual and mental affinity and all the romantic nonsense instilled by poets and novelists alike.

Obviously, she argued to herself, she must be *very fond* of Nicholas to bother with him now. A little smile touched her lips. Of course the picture had changed considerably since her advent at Willow Corner. Originally, it had been her intention to seek Nicholas out in the hope that he might still be nursing a secret passion for her. She had always discounted the idea of his *loving* Valerie. And, such was her temperament, that had he been enthralled by the possibility of a reunion she, on the other hand, would have been thoroughly disinterested. Curiosity had prompted and inspired her thus far and, now, frustration was to take her the rest of the way.

In danger of being out of reach, Nicholas became the only man on earth she wanted, or had ever truly loved! He became the husband who had wronged her, but whom she had forgiven and, as the sweet martyr, was prepared to offer that second chance. The moment she had heard Stephanie's remarks about him, caught that inflection in her voice, seen the expression in her eyes, she had decided to fight... And became the woman with a purpose instead of one merely exploring possibilities for the future.

Hester had a very convenient philosophy. She accepted love as a fact when it was directed towards her. Nicholas had 'adored' her; Hector had 'adored' her and so had – in her imagination – every other man of her acquaintance. Nevertheless, in relation to the rest of women generally, she ridiculed love and regarded it with cynical contempt. Hers was the prerogative of being loved, yet never, herself, truly loving. She had that fortunately rare, but absolute, ability to cut herself off from all rules applicable to the rest of mankind. What *she* believed was right; what was right for her was sheer folly for others... For her to want to re-marry Nicholas was normal and sane. For him, on the other hand, to want to marry Stephanie, or Stephanie to marry him, was absurd and ridiculous. Her inability to adjust herself to the views of others had, during her years of marriage, reduced both husbands to despair. And when she was in the wrong she became 'little Hester' coy and child-like, but with the stubborn resistance of a mule.

Her ever-changing moods, her theatrical playing of many parts, made it impossible for anyone wholly to appreciate the depths of her cunning or the ego-mania that urged her on. She never *seemed* to be the woman she actually, was. And therein lay her strength. Hers was the nature to abhor the success or happiness of the other person – be it friend or foe. This was not a conscious reaction, but rather that deep-seated inhibition that allowed of neither generosity nor inherent kindliness. All outward display was false and she found an intense and malicious delight in the misfortunes and miseries of her fellow creatures. Had this been suggested to her she would have shrieked in derision and considered it so fantastic as not to be worth consideration. Thus far in her life, few had seen through her ... but Trevor could be counted among that same few.

She planned her campaign after the manner of a general planning an attack. Nicholas would appreciate her readiness to concede that, apart from his own shortcomings and infidelity, she, herself, was not entirely blameless: he was that kind of man, she argued. A man ever receptive and, she had to admit, tolerant. Useless indulging in any form of attack, or playing the role of the coy, wronged wife. It wouldn't be easy, but she had never been beaten yet in any undertaking. Her heart quickened. Of course if Stephanie proved the stumbling block... Then, she decided calmly, Stephanie must be disposed of in whatever way was propitious. Fortunately, Stephanie was riddled with codes and principles and would be easy to deal with.

She caught a glimpse of the farm before actually reaching it, but no emotion stirred within her as she gazed on its far-flung lands; the smell of damp earth and newly turned soil meant nothing to her; the quietude and peace, of which the song of the birds was a part and not a discord, offered her neither sanctuary nor delight. In truth the wailing of a saxophone in a night club appealed to her far more.

By the time she had reached the old Cotswold stone house she had quite made up her mind that when she and Nicholas were re-married, they would certainly not remain *there!* The very thought of it made her shudder. Isolation, deadness and the dull routine of country life. Not for her.

Nicholas, in riding kit, greeted her and took her into his study and, as she gazed out upon the still wild and overgrown landscape, she could not stay the exclamation:

'This is a terribly neglected place, Nicholas.'

He settled himself in a chair opposite her.

'It is,' he said uncompromisingly. Then, changing his tone: 'Perhaps that is precisely why I like it.'

She puckered her brows.

'I don't quite follow.'

'The desire,' he said firmly, 'to build something; to take this land and wrest crops from its barren acres. Sounds dramatic perhaps. Thus far in my life everything has been destructive and a failure. I want to prove, this time, that I can achieve success.'

Hester said flatteringly:

'But my dear you've never been anything but a success. You certainly didn't leave the army through any lack of it ... and you have money–' She stopped, aware of the fact that the reference to the material side of things might irritate him.

'I didn't mean that *kind* of success,' he said.

She leapt at the advantage offered her.

'No ... you meant that need of success springing from within. If it doesn't sound too sentimental – the desire to fulfil one's own destiny.'

She congratulated herself on taking that line. It would appeal to him. And it did.

His gaze rested upon her with an in-creasing curiosity:

'You've changed, Hester,' he said solemnly.

She looked down at her hands and then back at him – a direct, penetrating gaze.

'There was room for it, Nicky.'

He sighed.

'We could all say that.'

'You were ever generous.' She sat back more composedly in her chair. 'Life's strange ... here we are again, you and I ... with many rivers between; many worlds traversed ... and nothing can alter the fact that once we were husband and wife. I think I'm glad of that above everything else.'

Nicholas endeavoured to sum her up as he listened; tried, accurately, to gauge his own feelings and found them to be entirely negative. He had no wish to be harsh, but, equally, no intention of allowing her to intrude in his life. He was, however, faintly intrigued by the subtle change in her and prepared to give her credit for it. But he most certainly would not encourage any sentimental note. He said deliberately:

'You wanted my advice, Hester; about money, I think you said.'

She had allowed for that and replied.

'It is about income tax, actually. Everything seems in such a mess, Nicky, and you know how hopeless I am over those things. I just cannot begin to understand them.'

She put on her wheedling, helpless expression and no one could have denied that, as she sat there, she looked exceedingly appealing. The sun glinted upon her soft, golden hair and cast little shadows upon her expertly made-up cheeks; there was something faintly voluptuous about her and she was well aware of the fact.

Nicholas said practically:

'Then the answer is, obviously, a good accountant. I will give you an introduction to mine.'

'Will you?' She made it sound infinitely important.

'Of course.'

'Perhaps you would be kind enough to go through the papers with me first and then explain things to him.'

'I can seldom manage my *own* affairs,' he

said and forced a smile.

'Then would you have any objection to coming with me when I see him? Just the first time? I don't want to make myself a nuisance, Nicky, but–'

Manlike, Nicholas found it exceedingly difficult bluntly to refuse her. The effort of doing so would involve greater strain than accompanying her, he argued to himself.

'I could arrange that,' he said hastily.

'You're awfully kind.'

'Not at all.' He felt ill at ease, anxious for her to go; unnerved by her expression and her attitude. It struck him suddenly that he had not mentioned Wincott's death and he said:

'I'm sorry about your bereavement, Hester. It was very hard for you.'

She looked correctly sad. Then:

'Yes; life wasn't very kind. On the other hand...' There was a dramatic pause: 'It wasn't all I would have liked it to be, Nicky.' Her voice was hushed.

'I'm sorry,' he said again, a trifle awkwardly.

Hester recognized the fact that she was making very little headway; his resistance was as a wall dividing them. Anger began like a tiny flame within her, mounting as she reflected that he was obviously impervious to her physical charms. She tried another approach as she leaned forward slightly as one impelled by some overwhelming force within her.

'You know, Nicky, I've learned a very great deal since the old days. I realise that so much of all that happened was my fault.'

He stared at her. Hester blaming herself! Incredible! His voice became slightly more natural.

'As I said last night, Hester, trying to apportion the blame in human relationships is pretty fatuous.'

She sighed.

'I ought never to have divorced you. But I was hurt and bitter and jealous–' Her eyes met his very levelly: 'And, now, since you didn't even marry Valerie–'

Instantly, he retreated.

'Suppose we do not go over old ground,' he said almost curtly. 'Raking up the past never serves any good purpose. You did divorce me and–' He added with a brutal frankness, 'I certainly bear you no grudge on that account. I wanted my freedom.'

Hester bit her lip. How dare he!

She said, holding her emotions in check:

'You could hardly bear me a grudge, Nicky; after all, you *were* unfaithful and I had every justification.'

Nicholas got up from his chair; his expression was tense, even grim; he had the appearance of a man wrestling with a problem and endeavouring to come to a decision. For a second he stood framed against the windows, gazing out upon the landscape. Then, almost harshly he said as he swung around to face her:

'That's where you were so wrong.'

Hester's voice came sharp and fearful:

'What do you mean – "wrong".'

'Precisely what I say.' His tone was clipped, incisive. 'It so happens that I was never unfaithful to you; I told you so at the time, but you refused to listen.' He shrugged his shoulders. 'But the fact remains that it is so.' A cynical smile touched his lips: 'And you can hardly accuse me of having an axe to grind *now*,' he added calmly.

Hester paled. For a second she floundered; the very thought of the past unnerved her: she had no wish to discuss its intimate details, merely to play upon its advantages – from her own point of view. But her act was perfect as she cried brokenly:

'Oh, Nicky … I can hardly bear to think of it.'

He lit a cigarette.

'My dear,' he said coolly, 'don't let it worry you: it has all worked out for the best. In all fairness you cannot be condemned for believing the circumstantial evidence against me. I certainly harbour no grudge. Our marriage was hardly a state of bliss and it was the best possible way out for us both. At first, when you flatly refused to believe my story I was, I'll admit, bitter but, later on, I realized that to attempt any further defence would merely prolong the state of our incompatibility. After all, you seemed quite eager to be rid of me.'

Her eyes opened wide; she was startled into crying:

'I ... eager to be rid of you? How can you suggest such a thing! I was so absolutely disillusioned and hurt that I hardly knew what I was doing... Oh, Nicky, and to think I suffered all that hell for nothing,' she cried desperately.

'I'm glad at least,' he said somewhat irrelevantly, 'that you will accept my word, today.'

She made a sound almost like a groan:

'If only I had accepted it, then.'

He shrugged his shoulders.

'Just one of those things. I suppose it was asking a great deal of any woman to expect that she would.'

'Then you weren't in love with Valerie?'

A smile touched his lips.

'No; we are, and always were, merely the best of friends.'

Hester fought the warring elements gathered within her. This is no way pleased her. Now she could no longer play the part of the wronged wife – even by implication. A weapon had been taken from her and the knowledge of Nicholas's fidelity was a very doubtful substitute and no consolation. It, of course, appeased her vanity, but that was all. The thought flashed through her mind that he had not told Stephanie the truth. For that, at least, she had to be thankful.

'But,' she insisted, 'I just don't understand Valerie's attitude. She was divorced by her husband because of – of our case–'

'She, also, was disbelieved … and no happier in her marriage than we were.'

Hester fumed because now she was aware of the fact that there was nothing between him and Valerie, she could not fall back on the hackneyed: 'We were happy until *she* came into the picture!' She said protestingly:

'But we were ideally suited, really, Nicky; and much of our life together was happy – you know it was.' She looked dejected – with intent to do so. 'If only I'd realized the truth and not been such a fool… I was so blind.' She knew that no other line would provide a basis for discussion.

Nicholas was calm, impersonal as he said:

'It was for the best, Hester; don't dwell upon it. It was just that seeing you again… Well, I wanted you to know the truth.' He added tensely: 'It was always rather strange to me that you should think for a moment that I was the type of man who could live with one woman as her husband and then crawl around corners with another. And lie to them both.' His jaw hardened; his expression became grim. 'I'd feel cleaner as a murderer.'

Faint colour stole into Hester's cheeks and, swiftly, she changed that particular trend of the conversation as she hastened:

'And what of your feelings for me, since you were not in love with Valerie. Does that mean that—'

He shook his head.

'No, Hester; I was not in love with you any more than you were in love with me.'

She looked pathetic and feminine.

'I was always in love with you,' she said quietly and with great impressiveness. 'Oh, Nicky,' it was a broken cry, 'I still am.'

It was not what she had intended to say, but summing up the situation as she now found it, she could think of no other subterfuge. Before he had time to answer her, she went on:

'But apart from that… There's life ahead; years in which we might find happiness together and blot out the past. You spoke just now about reclaiming this land… Couldn't we reclaim our marriage? We're both wiser and I'm so ready to admit my failings if you will meet me half-way… The ghastly mistake I made in divorcing you, misjudging you—' She shook her head. 'Don't you *see?*'

Nicholas didn't hesitate and his voice was slow and very calm.

168

'Yes, my dear,' he said solemnly. 'Very, very clearly. And it wouldn't work; going back is not progress and it rarely, if ever, pays... One brings to the present the emotions of the present, but one cannot project those emotions into a relationship that is dead... Only greater misery could result – for us both.'

'But heaps of people – heaps of people remarry,' she cried. 'And are happier than ever.'

'Possibly.' He was adamant. 'But they are the people who were once deeply in love; people who, perhaps, parted in a fit of anger over some trivial discord. Not two people who had never found fulfilment together – either mental or physical.'

'But we–'

He shook his head.

'No, my dear; face the facts as they are. We've had this talk together and there are no hard feelings...'

Hester was far too wise to pursue the subject; she had, for her own guidance, discovered precisely what Nicholas's feelings were for her. With supreme confidence, she decided that she must now inspire within him a new love for her, fresh admiration, respect. He must be made to see her as woman outside the circle of the past, not merely as his ex-wife. She must appear interested in his welfare, eager for his happiness and, above all, create the impression that she fully realized and appreciated the fact that he regarded her merely as a friend.

She said quietly, and with what appeared to be great understanding and sincerity:

'Perhaps you are right, Nicky; you are so much wiser than I and less impulsive.'

He stared at her, trying to accustom himself to the new Hester. In the old days, the attribute of sweet reasonableness had been entirely missing from her make-up and those things she wanted, and wanted to do, loomed on her horizon to the exclusion of everyone else's point of view. He wondered, as he studied her, just how deep her regard had gone for him – or went now – or whether it was something built up in her mind through opposing circumstances.

'I hope,' he said genuinely, 'that the future will more than atone for the past, Hester.'

She smiled, a gentle, appealing smile.

'I hope so... I shall not, of course, be here very long and my plans are quite unformed.' She paused effectively. 'But, while I *am* here, it will be nice to feel that when we meet, Nicky it will be as friends.'

'I agree,' he said heartily.

She stared at him.

'Ours is quite an incredible story – isn't it?' She picked up her bag and gloves. 'Have you time to show me your farm?'

'Yes, of course.' He was smoothly confident. Thank heaven he'd made her understand that there was no question of any romantic repercussions from yesterday. As a casual friend Hester could be charming and good company. Beyond that, he shuddered.

'You are having a great many alterations done here,' she said carefully.

'Yes; Michael has some brilliant ideas for converting this place from a barn to something habitable.' He didn't offer to show her over the house and she, tactfully, refrained from making any request that he should do so.

They went out into the brilliant sunshine that filtered through the tall, ancient trees and cast deep, impenetrable shadows.

'The sweep of the Cotswolds,' he said, embracing a view of panoramic grandeur. 'It has become very much home to me.'

Hester had absolutely no love for the country and remained unmoved, even though she said:

'It is beautiful, Nicky... I wouldn't mind a small cottage somewhere in the district.' A sigh. 'But it is always very difficult to know where to live when one can live anywhere.' She glanced up at him. 'Last night I thought you'd become hard and bitter; today, you are different, somehow – far more generous and understanding. I think we've both changed, you know!'

'Quite possibly.' He smiled down at her

with a friendly, inconsequential air. 'One's experiences must add to the sum total of our development. The trouble is not to allow those experiences to set us back in the general evolution.'

Hester had already formulated a new plan of attack and said deliberately:

'I think, in your case if I may say so, love has changed you, Nicholas.'

He jerked his head back in her direction.

'Meaning?' It was a challenge, even a warning.

'May I speak, shall we say, as a friend wholly detached from your life?'

'If you wish.' He sounded dubious.

'Then I realize that you are in love with Stephanie,' she said suddenly, a trifle amazed at her own daring, but aware of the fact that to be ignorant of his true feelings, or to deceive herself about them might well be responsible for ultimate failure.

Nicholas retreated. He was a man who detested any kind of intrusion into his private world and shrank from discussing his personal feelings in relationship to any sentimental matters. On the other hand the very idea of denying his love for Stephanie would appear as an insult to her. He said with a quiet and yet firm emphasis:

'I have no wish to deny the truth of that fact, Hester.'

Hester recoiled from those words; they

made her own suspicions so much more real and inescapable and she could not ignore them. She said carefully:

'I'm sorry, Nicky.'

'Sorry!' He jerked his head up almost challengingly.

'Because she does not return your affection,' she said with what appeared to be genuine regret.

Nicholas fought to ignore the pain that encircled his heart. His voice was harsh as he exclaimed:

'That remains to be seen, Hester.'

Hester made a little, appealing gesture.

'That is true and one can never be absolutely certain about anyone's feelings, but ... I should be doing you a disservice if I wasn't honest. Stephanie's interests and affections, from all I can gather, are very definitely linked with Trevor.' She added quickly: 'She is always far too ready to insist that there is "nothing" for the denial to be strictly true. But, alas, a woman cannot protect her pride in any other way until her love affair is made public.'

'And what is to prevent that being done – in their case?'

Hester retreated.

'I shouldn't have said so much, Nicky; it was indiscreet, perhaps. But I do know Stephanie rather well and am, naturally, in her confidence.' Her smile was warm, encouraging. 'Don't forget that I'm on your side and if I can help the cause you know I will.' She added easily: 'Stephanie has some very rigid ideas and some equally unconventional ones... She's a perfect darling and I love her and I certainly do not blame her for being flirtatious. Heaven knows men don't deserve to have things all their own way.' A beaming smile. As she spoke, Hester recalled the incident in the garden when she had seen Stephanie in Nicholas's arms; she must be careful not to make any statement that he could flatly disprove.

'Suppose,' Nicholas said coldly, 'that we don't discuss the matter further.'

Hester looked pathetic.

'I didn't mean to annoy you, Nicky... Since things are as they are between us, there is no one I'd love to see you with more than Stephanie and, with all my heart, I hope things work out for you.'

Nicholas said swiftly:

'I appreciate that; I'm sorry if I sounded boorish.'

'I understand... What a complex business life is. If only we could love to order how simple it would be.'

'And how dull.'

Nicholas saw her to her car. Silence fell between them which she broke as she slid into the driving seat.

'Will you phone me about the appointment with your accountants?' she asked quietly. 'Any day will suit me. I know how busy you are, Nicky, and do appreciate your help.' She put her hand through the open window and rested it on his cuff for a fraction of a second, then: 'And bless you for being so sweet over everything. I feel so much happier now that we are friends again and understand each other.' She paused, adding hastily: 'Any message for Stephanie?'

'No,' he said in a clipped, decisive manner. 'I shall probably look in one evening.'

'You've an ally in me, anyway!' She gave a little laugh. 'But Stephanie has a very great aversion to married men – even the "ex" variety!'

Nicholas drew in his breath; his teeth were clenched. How well aware he was of that fact!

Hester swung the car away, racing it down the drive. Nicholas stood and watched... It struck him very forcefully that Hester might well have been a complete stranger and that the past embracing her was completely dead. One thought, however, did register: that she had improved and become tolerant, even reasonable. No need for friction and, since she was to be in the district for a while, far, far better that they should be on friendly terms.

With that reflection he returned to his work, forgetting her as completely as though she had ceased to exist.

CHAPTER VII

Stephanie found that work was exceedingly irksome as she faced it that day. The only hour likely to have significance was that when Hester fetched her from business and she found herself tensing when six o'clock approached as one who waits for her fate to be sealed.

Trevor said knowingly:

'Worrying won't help, my sweet.'

She stared at him.

'"Worrying?"' Her gaze was innocent.

'Precisely.' He looked at her indulgently. 'It isn't worth it, you know, Stephanie. No man is.' He added swiftly: 'And no woman. You've hardly heard a word said to you today and your expression has certainly not been flattering to me. I hate being part of the furniture we hope to sell,' he finished comically.

Stephanie laughed. She knew it was foolish to argue against his truths, or her own preoccupation.

'Wait until I can make fun of you,' she warned him. 'When that one woman comes into your life–' She stopped.

Trevor burst forth roughly:

'If Young qualifies, as he does, for the role of that one man in yours, my dear, then heaven help you.'

Stephanie was thinking of Valerie Brown at that moment. What would Nicholas's attitude be towards her in the event of their meeting again; what fresh complications, what repercussions would follow in the wake of such an impact and how would Hester behave? A shiver went over her. In all probability, by now Hester and Nicholas would already have become reconciled. Cynicism mingled with the hurt she deliberately inspired.

At that moment the phone rang and she answered it, hearing Nicholas's voice with a sense of shock and greeting him with business-like politeness.

'I'm in Warwick,' he said urgently. 'May I come along to see you?'

Stephanie mastered the sudden, sharp yearning that possessed her and said adamantly:

'I don't think we have anything to say to each other, Nicholas. The situation between us was made perfectly clear last evening. And in any case I have another engagement.'

'Then,' came his voice firmly, 'I shall come to the cottage tomorrow evening. This whole thing is absurd and–'

'Quite absurd,' Stephanie said curtly. 'And

I do not talk for the sake of talking, Nicholas. I'm sorry.'

'Neither do I,' he insisted quietly. Then: 'Very well... I shall, nevertheless, come over to Willow Corner tomorrow night.' And with that he replaced the receiver, leaving her wretched, uncertain and trembling with emotion.

It was after dinner that night when Hester struck her first blow, realizing that to win the battle she must first attack. She studied Stephanie objectively in that moment, taking her in relation to her entire background, aware of her assets, virtues and defects. In the soft light of the lounge, with its artistic atmosphere and old world appeal she looked, Hester acknowledged, infinitely desirable and it was not difficult to understand why Nicholas had, apparently, been infatuated with her. Not even to herself, would Hester use the word 'love'.

In turn, Stephanie waited, tensed, agonized for the confidence she knew would be forthcoming and, finally, Hester began solemnly:

'I want your help, Stephanie. Want it desperately.'

Stephanie's heart seemed to be beating at twice its normal speed.

'My help,' she echoed. 'In what way.'

Hester leaned forward.

'With Nicholas,' she said honestly. And it

came to her, then, precisely what attitude to adopt. Useless relying completely on lies; far better to stake all on Stephanie's loyalty. Nicholas, she knew, was in the mood to plunge into marriage with Stephanie, should she give him any encouragement. Nevertheless, Hester appreciated that Stephanie – believing him to be the unfaithful husband and lover of another woman – would resist even her own love for him provided she, Hester, was involved.

Stephanie remained very still in her chair, her hands resting somewhat limply on its arms. A certain depression stole upon her, making body and mind weary; touching her with a sadness unbearable. The thought of Nicholas tore at her, like knives into flesh; she could not begin to pretend that it didn't matter, or that his character and defects were not of import. They were; she could hardly bear to recognize him as the philanderer who had so grievously wronged the woman now sitting beside her. She said slowly:

'I hardly see how I can help you.'

Hester sighed.

'It isn't easy to explain and I can only hope to do so by taking you completely into my confidence. We're sufficiently close for me to be able to let you see into my heart. I've talked to you already about my feelings for Nicholas; but I was not entirely sure of myself until now. It is always fatally easy, when one is away from a man, to imagine that he means far, far more than he actually does, and I'd been prepared for a violent reaction on seeing him again ... possibly even to a point of dislike, as I recalled my earlier sufferings on his account. But ... it hasn't worked that way, as you know. I realized when I was with him at the farm today that he is my whole life and that I want to marry him again more than anything else in the world. It isn't any use pretending. You knew, didn't you, how I felt?'

Stephanie said honestly, fighting to keep her emotions in check:

'Up to a point; your bantering attitude was apt to cut across your more serious remarks. But–' She felt her body tensing: 'Now you are sure?'

'Surer than I have been about anything in all my life,' came the solemn reply.

Stephanie prompted:

'And Nicholas?'

Hester said remorsefully:

'Nicholas hasn't changed, alas, Stevie. Oh, to blind myself to that fact would be quite fatal. I know him too well ... he just cannot help wanting every attractive woman he sees – or, perhaps it would be fairer to say: every woman who appeals to him. But, fundamentally that bond remains between us and he is quite ready to admit it.' She paused significantly. 'Unfortunately, however, it so happens that at the moment, you happen to be in the ascendant. That's what I want to talk to you about.'

Stephanie's heart felt that it was bursting with the force of its own emotion.

'You could hardly expect me to take that very seriously, Hester,' she said unevenly. 'In view of all you have told me, I may be forgiven if I regard Nicholas with the greatest possible scepticism and, since, also, he has treated you as he has, disgust.'

'Nevertheless,' Hester persisted, wanting to know precisely where she stood with Stephanie, 'I felt that he has shown you some attention?'

Stephanie's voice was low and, at the same time, bitter as she answered:

'That is true; but I've no illusions that it was anything more than flirtatiousness. At first, I must admit, I was inclined to take him seriously but—'

'I can imagine how you felt when you realized he had not even told you about me, or even that he had *been* married.'

Stephanie struggled against the overwhelming desire to defend him, aware of the absurdity and perversity of the emotion.

'He said that he had intended telling me last night.'

Hester sighed.

'So like him. How well I know it. I found

it the most difficult thing in the world to disbelieve him…'

'I could never tolerate lies,' Stephanie said harshly.

Hester went on:

'I can't blame him for being attracted by you, my dear, and if I thought there was anything really serious in it then I'd behave very differently. As it is … I must be quite sure that there is no rivalry between us, Stevie… I want the chance to win him back! Yes, I know I'm a fool, as I've told you before, but there it is. Time is passing and, in the end, he will settle down. Years of marriage cannot lightly be dismissed. I've suffered so much that–' She broke off pathetically, hastening: 'And he is ready to atone for all that.' There was a second of heavy silence, then: 'Will you help me? Without any encouragement from you he will allow his true feelings to dictate his actions… It is so difficult to explain, Stevie but–'

Stephanie felt that she was sitting back listening to herself uttering the words that followed; they had all the unreality as of muted sounds coming from a darkened stage.

'I don't think it is difficult, Hester. You are my friend and, therefore, your happiness is important to me – without being smug. I can certainly give you my word that I shall have

182

nothing further to do with Nicholas and, quite honestly, I am hardly flattered by his attentions, in any case.' She added swiftly: 'With you it is different, because your background is different. It is perfectly feasible to me that what affection he is capable of feeling for a woman, he feels for you. His rather hermit-like existence since he has been here would seem to prove that point, particularly, since before your divorce, he was so unreliable. I was merely a temporary diversion,' she finished somewhat cynically.

'I don't want,' insisted Hester with appealing pathos, 'to blacken him too much in your eyes. It is so difficult to explain my reactions.'

'Again, I disagree,' Stephanie said boldly. 'Women in love are crazy enough to cling to the worst type of man and particularly if he has hurt them deeply. We're queer, paradoxical creatures. I can sit in your chair and understand... The very fact of his not marrying Valerie Brown is enough to influence *you*... And I know you well enough to realize that, unless you were quite convinced of his affection for you, there could be no question of your seeking, or wishing, to re-marry.'

Hester looked impressively frank.

'I can honestly say that, Stevie. I'm really in the position of a woman fighting to preserve the remnants of the past and to create a new life for the future out of the

183

experiences of that past. I can see everything so much more clearly now, and while nothing alters the fact of Nicholas being hopelessly weak where women are concerned, I was not entirely blameless. We discussed it all this morning and agreed that we had both learned a very great deal since the divorce. Also, we realized that our common interests, and friendship, at this stage might lead to complete reunion. Rushing things could be fatal and I must not be possessive – I simply must *not*,' she added, knowing that her readiness to criticize herself would appeal to Stephanie and further her own cause.

'There is certainly nothing that men hate more,' Stephanie agreed.

'Then we understand each other?'

Stephanie got up from her chair and moved to the window as one impelled by an unforeseen force. The memory of Nicholas's phone call earlier that evening came back and smote her. Her need and longing merged with the breathless hush of the spring night that hung like a picture from the frame of the room in which she stood. Part of her seemed to reach out and embrace it as though it alone could understand the depth of the emotion now engulfing her. This was the renunciation of hope and she accepted it as such. Now she knew Nicholas for what he was... His question came back to torment her: 'And suppose I had told you that I was in love with you and had asked you to marry me ... would you, then, have held the past against me?' So easy to feed that passionate longing with the possibility of his sincerity... But Hester's story was the indictment; hers the betrayal of his true character. Even now he was ready to make Hester believe in their final reunion, while, at the same time, adopting towards her a lover-like possessiveness ... telling her that she belonged to him, making love to her with a fervour compelling and demanding.

Her heart-beats quickened. Even Hester realized that he was attracted to her. She hated herself for the feebleness of the argument; hated herself for clinging to that as a palliative for the pain striking, so it seemed, at her very soul. Why not face the bitter truth? Nicholas *was* attracted to her ... attracted to her in precisely the same way that he had been attracted to Valerie Brown – physically. What did ties, codes mean to him ... he sought a mistress in her... To Hester he gave the dignity of wife and, even after she had divorced him, was prepared to pick up the threads of the past again. With a gesture almost of violence, she swung around and said, tensely:

'To me Nicholas is still your husband, Hester. You love him, want him back.

Nothing that he could do, or say, to me would have the slightest effect upon that attitude. For what it is worth you can rely on me absolutely never to encourage him.'

Hester experienced a sharp, almost overwhelming reaction. Her selfish, even sadistic, mind gloated over her triumph. So much, she thought viciously, for Nicholas's precious hopes and his love for Stephanie. So much for hers, too! A malevolent gleam came into her eyes. Rebuffed (and she had no qualms whatsoever lest Stephanie would not keep to her bargain) Nicholas would retreat and never betray his innocence. Such was his temperament. How like him to have kept the secret of his relationship with Valerie as he had.

Hester looked meltingly tender, dewy-eyed, innocent as she murmured:

'You're not in love with him, Stephanie – are you? I couldn't bear it if you were to be hurt.'

Stephanie lowered her gaze and then raised it again with a certain direct and penetrating candour.

'It would be impossible for me to tell you just what my feelings are for Nicholas. In any case, they are not important, Hester. You know I wish you great happiness: you deserve it after all the misery and disillusionment you have known.'

It wasn't what Hester wanted; she had

counted on hearing Stephanie utter those words that should increase her own triumph. She said swiftly:

'But you promise that you won't be horrid to him... I mean, I've told you the truth about him, but I couldn't bear to poison your mind or anything like that. Sounds contradictory, but–'

'No; just like a woman,' said Stephanie softly. 'My mind isn't poisoned, Hester. I appreciate that only your honesty prompted you to confide in me as you have. I am not Nicholas's judge, in any case. I only hope that he gives you the happiness you deserve, as I said just now.'

Hester continued to look gentle and a trifle anxious.

'I couldn't bear you not to remain our friend,' she insisted. 'After all, you will marry soon and, then, we could all have fun – the past entirely wiped out. It's wonderful to have you in my life.' She yawned prettily, got up from her chair and, stooping kissed Stephanie's cheek. Then: 'And I do so hope you marry that nice Trevor; it is obvious that he adores you. And with all your interests ... that augurs well for your future happiness.'

Stephanie smiled – a rather wistful smile.

'Life isn't as simple as that,' she said; 'but we shall see.'

Hester was satisfied. Of course Stephanie would marry Trevor; that was almost essential for the success of her own affairs. And, if Hester wanted a thing, no one would be allowed to prevent her obtaining it.

'It will be in your case,' she said smoothly. 'Good night, darling. I'm *so* sleepy ... lovely to have a fire these chilly, spring evenings, but it does make one tired. Bed will be a positive luxury.'

With that she tripped to the door well pleased with herself and called again: 'Good night,' as she reached it.

Stephanie remained in her chair and, now, the room was illuminated only by the moonlight and the glowing embers of the fire which glinted on brass and copper and cast pools of light upon walls and floor, lacing the outline of diamond-paned windows into deep shadows that gave a strange peace to the now silent room. She heard Michael's key in the lock of the front door and called out to him. He came swiftly to her and, knowing her love of firelight, made no attempt to switch on any lights. He said softly:

'What? Alone?'

'Yes ... Hester's just gone to bed. Had a good evening?'

'Wonderful.' He flung himself down in a chair opposite her. 'Life's good, Stevie... I've been missing a hell of a lot.' He smiled wryly. 'Amazing how one's life can change so miraculously in so short a time.'

Stephanie's gaze went penetratingly into the fire.

'Yes,' she said slowly, 'amazing.'

Michael, his eyes accustomed to the semi-darkness, was aware of the sadness of her expression, the listlessness of her voice. And he said swiftly:

'What is it, darling?'

Instantly she roused herself.

'What is what?' It was a question asked lightly.

'Something is troubling you.' He added in a breath: 'Hester's return. The whole thing was a shock to you, wasn't it?'

'In a way, yes.' She was guarded, hating the idea that anyone – even Michael – should guess her secret. And aware of the fact that, thus far, she had been curiously unsuccessful in concealing her feelings, since Trevor and, she knew, Hester, had been aware of them. 'One hates to know that a friend's life has been so unhappy. The whole thing...' she said and stopped as though it were unnecessary to add more.

'I may not say a great deal,' Michael murmured softly, 'but that doesn't mean I am insensible to things, Stevie.' A pause, then: 'Felice told you that Valerie Brown was coming to stay with them?'

'Yes.'

'Have you told Hester?'

'No, but she knew that Miss Brown was

back in London… She is most unlikely to meet her or any of Felice's family.'

Michael's voice dropped slightly.

'As it happens, Valerie Brown arrived there unexpectedly tonight. I met her.'

'Really.' Stephanie felt that her heart would burst; she became tensed, while yet managing to sound casual and normally interested. 'Did you – like her?'

Michael lit a cigarette.

'Quite honestly – yes. I should go so far as to say that no one could help doing so.'

Stephanie resisted the jealousy that poured over her body rather like the effects of some physical and poisonous injection.

'That type of woman is mostly very attractive,' she said shortly.

Michael stared at her.

'That doesn't sound like you.'

Faint colour stole into Stephanie's cheeks.

'I can hardly be expected to enthuse over the woman who caused Hester such misery – can I?'

Michael was not deceived by the inflection of her voice. It held, for him, a note of pathos, of misery touching the fringe of agony. And it tore at him because he knew Stephanie, her great sincerity, and just how deep any wound would go. He said, gently:

'No, my dear; you cannot be expected to do that … the thing that concerns me is that she shall not, indirectly, cause *you* that same

190

misery. A ghost can sometimes be more painful to contemplate than reality.'

And Stephanie, unguarded, wretched, cried:

'Oh, Michael! Am I as transparent as that?'

'Ah,' he murmured... Then: 'I was afraid I was right.' He leaned forward. 'I like Nicholas,' he insisted. 'There's something about him–'

Almost cynically, she interposed:

'I agree with you there ... something very deceptive.'

'I was going to say something direct and sincere.'

'The cloak of those who indulge in subterfuge,' she countered.

'I hate to hear that bitter note in your voice.'

She got up and switched a small table lamp on; it glowed like an illuminated flower, diffusing the room with a soft, orange glow. Outside the garden became no more than a soft, dark shadow. Stephanie said weakly:

'I hate it, too, Michael... Do you mind if we don't talk about me any more.' She forced a smile. 'You and Felice are far more interesting.'

'As you like, my dear; but I'm always here, you know and–'

She interrupted softly:

'I'm so thankful to have you in the world, Michael.'

They didn't speak for a second, then he said almost abruptly:

'Felice and I decided to get married next week – slip away quietly to that little church at Coleshill – you know it.'

The little church at Coleshill! Stephanie drew in her breath sharply. Nicholas .. and the tremulous happiness, the excitement she had known as they wandered through it together. The blood seemed to heat in her veins, making her hot, uncomfortable as she recalled her own emotions on that evening ... her hopes, her dreams. What a fool she'd been. And all the time he was Hester's ex-husband! Could anything be more ironical than that. Her voice was quiet, subdued, however, as she answered:

'Yes, I know it.'

Michael jerked his head up; his expression was inquiring.

'Don't you approve of the idea, darling? I know it is rushing things, but–'

She started, aware that her attitude might lead to a misunderstanding.

'But of course I approve. I think you are being awfully sensible. Why waste even precious days?... How about Felice's parents?'

'They are quite reconciled to the idea. At first there was trouble, but Felice managed to bring them round to her way of thinking.'

'And your honeymoon?'

'Portugal. A fortnight,' he said gleefully.

'Felice's father is arranging our passages with a friend of his. We'll fly, of course.'

Stephanie was making mental calculations and said swiftly:

'That means about three and a half weeks before you'll want to take over this cottage?'

Michael made a sound to suggest that such an idea was absurd.

'Of course not, Stevie; we can find a quiet hotel somewhere. No staying with mamma, for either of us – you'll understand that.'

'I certainly do! All the same, I shall be out of here and it will all be ready for you by the time you get back.'

He said earnestly.

'Are you sure about this? After all, it has always been *our* home, darling, and–'

'My share in it will be part of my wedding gift to you both, Michael. I know you love it and, should you ever want to sell in order that you can design and build your own home... I'd like the first refusal!' She laughed. 'But, honestly, I want to get away ... the rooms I have in Warwick will be quite ready. Do me good to have a change,' she added lightly.

'And – Hester?'

'Hester will understand. In any case she can stay with me there if she likes; somehow I don't think that will be necessary.' She added swiftly; 'She and Nicholas will be married again very soon, you'll see.'

193

'Do you really believe that?' Michael's voice was almost abrupt.

'Definitely. The worst philanderer has one woman in his life who means more than the others – even if he betrays her, also! Hester is, obviously, that woman to Nicholas.'

'I don't quite agree.'

Stephanie exclaimed:

'But that's ridiculous, Michael.'

'It may be,' he said adamantly. 'But it is my opinion and–' he grinned, 'I'm entitled to it.'

'Naturally! Time will prove.'

Michael leaned forward and said very urgently:

'Don't be reckless, darling; don't plunge into something you'll regret. Emotion is utterly without reason, you know; and hurt makes fools of us all, because it drives us to extremes.'

Stephanie felt the tears stinging her eyes, but she said banteringly:

'Very well, grandfather: I'll remember your good advice!'

Michael did not pursue the subject; he was well aware of Stephanie's state of mind and worried by the turn of events since Hester's arrival. In all the circumstances as they had been made known to him, he could not help the instinctive feeling that there was a missing link somewhere. Michael flattered himself that he was rather a good judge of men and he found nothing whatsoever in Nicholas's attitude to inspire the belief that the man was in any way a philanderer. On the other hand, despite his prejudice in her favour, there was something in Hester's behaviour that failed wholly to convince him of her complete sincerity. He knew, however, that it was useless voicing this doubt to Stephanie: she was far too loyal ever to listen to any adverse criticism of a friend and, in her present mood of bewildered disillusionment, was receptive to the hurt of realization that Nicholas was nothing she had, at first, thought him.

A certain desperation possessed him as he sat there... His own helplessness maddened him, but he knew that he could but hold a watching brief and, with Felice's help, pray that, in the end, Stephanie would find her happiness.

Stephanie left him some seconds later and went up to bed. It seemed to her that, as she lay awake in the moonlit room, her life disintegrated. Hester's appeal had destroyed, for her, even the possibility of future hope. Nicholas was irrevocably lost to her and no matter what her opinion of his conduct might be, it in no way affected, or lessened, her love for him. There was something about him that drew her heart to his like a magnet; something she would never find in another man, even though she might, conceivably, compromise and experience affection as distinct from love, at some future date and with someone else, that spark would be missing.

She fought against that small, inward voice which reminded her that Hester had suggested that Nicholas was attracted to her; the thought of it was both balm and torment since such attraction was, obviously physical. Now, in any case, she had given her word to Hester... Soon she would have to endure the anguish of watching them re-marry. It struck her that the sooner this happened the better. Anything to shut and barricade the door against him...

She stirred restlessly in bed; her body hot and cold in turn as emotion surged upon her. The memory of Nicholas's kiss stole upon her as insidiously as a craved-for drug.

And it was dawn before she slept.

CHAPTER VIII

Nicholas had no intention of allowing Stephanie to elude him the following day and, just before six o'clock, arrived in Warwick, striding into the show-rooms and requesting to see her.

The youthful assistant, somewhat startled

by the forcefulness of his manner, stammered:

'I'm – I'm sorry, but Miss Reid isn't in.'

'When *will* she be in?'

'Maybe not at all this evening.'

'And Mr Morly?'

'He's out, too.'

'I see.'

Nicholas said almost roughly.

'I'll wait a few minutes.' He looked at the girl very directly: 'It is quite possible that she *may* be back?'

'Oh, yes! It just depends on how long she is kept at Lady Martin's house.'

Nicholas nodded.

'If she comes I'll tell her, at once, that you are here Mr...'

'Mr Young.'

With that she retreated.

Half an hour later Stephanie, driving up to the kerb and parking behind Nicholas's car said, breathlessly:

'We have a visitor, Trevor.'

'Young,' he exclaimed disgustedly. 'What on earth does he want?'

'To see me,' she said quietly. 'He phoned last evening and wouldn't take "no" for an answer, saying he'd call at the cottage.'

'The persistent type – eh?' He looked at her very levelly: 'I'll dismiss him – with the greatest of pleasure!'

Stephanie's heart was beating at twice its

normal speed.

'No; I'll see him; but – but please come in after a few minutes, Trevor.'

He commented somewhat jealously:

'And save you – from yourself?'

'Perhaps,' she admitted.

'He certainly believes in numbers... Hester, Valerie Brown and now you! All within a radius of a few miles.'

Stephanie gave a feeble smile and went into the building, and so to the room in which Nicholas was waiting.

He got to his feet and said slowly:

'I thought it might be more convenient if I came to see you here.'

Stephanie drew on her powers of resistance, fighting to overcome the excitement and emotion his presence awakened within her.

'I'm afraid,' she said in a quiet, conversational tone, 'that I can see no purpose whatever in your coming at all.'

Nicholas frowned. All his life he had scorned retreat; now he had been driven to it against his will. His resolutions regarding Stephanie counted for nought beside the overpowering impact of his love for her and he intended to fight. Meekly to sit back and accept her rebuff, he argued, was to deserve defeat.

'You know,' he said firmly, 'the purpose of my visit.'

'I know nothing of the kind... I feel reasonably sure that it isn't to buy any of my furniture,' she added facetiously.

He moved a pace nearer to her. His expression was set, his gaze inescapable; it seemed to reach out and dissolve into hers like some powerful ray, weakening her to the point of surrender.

'No,' he murmured; 'not that. I'm here to ask you the question I intended to ask you the night of Michael's party...'

Stephanie felt that her lungs were bursting with the weight that appeared suddenly to be pressing down upon them; her heart thudded wildly, making breathing difficult.

'I never talk for talking's sake, Nicholas,' she managed to say and now she was shaking violently. 'You and I have nothing more to discuss – ever,' she finished desperately.

Almost roughly, he reached out and gripped her shoulders:

'That is where you are so wrong,' he said with a passionate earnestness. 'There is so much I have to tell you, to explain about myself, but before I begin–' His voice became hoarse with emotion as the words fell from his lips as though nothing could stay their utterance: 'I love you – love you... I'm asking you to marry me, my darling.'

Stephanie stood there, swirling in a rapturous tide that threatened to engulf her.

His declaration touched her heart with healing fingers; every nerve, every instinct, longed, ached to believe him; desire, swift, sharp stabbed at her body and a sickness crept upon her because of the force of the love she felt for him, the need his presence awakened. For a moment she was taken off her guard; there was no past, no disillusionment, no Hester ... only the magic, the thraldom of hearing words that were as music to her very soul. She was aware of the warmth of his hands through her thin frock; the tingling sensation of passion rising swiftly, urging her into his arms and seeking his kiss. She was a woman trembling on the brink of surrender, coming to life in that world of warm, sensuous delight that knew of no resistance, only the thrill of fulfilment.

She swayed and he caught her against him, his lips finding hers and knowing the ecstasy of response as her mouth, hungry for his kisses, parted to meet his and, for a second, returning the passion that held them violently in its grip. And suddenly, with the bitterness of despair, she remembered; remembered Hester and all the desperate truths of the past...

Fiercely, loathing the weakness that had made her thus vulnerable, she drew back while the promise she had given seemed to be written up in lettering of fire that danced mockingly before her eyes... *Never to encour-*

age him ... never to encourage him. Cynicism flicked across her heart like the thong of a whip ... stilling its beat, turning passion to contempt. How well Hester knew him; here was the answer. How cleverly he had built up hopes within Hester's mind for the future; making her believe he was ready to atone for the past and, all the while, seeking yet a new love, a new adventure...

Marriage! How empty the word was of meaning to him. No more than a cloak for his less worthy desires. And who would follow in her wake when the enchantment had died down and another appealed to him more ardently. Where would Hester be ... even though he, again, became her husband. Wouldn't history repeat itself? Stabbing, torturing thoughts warred within her so that only by clutching at jealousy and contempt could she escape him and, thus, keep faith with Hester. In an icy voice, unlike her own, as she drew back from him as one recoiling, she managed to say:

'You know my answer, Nicholas. Even if I believed you to be sincere, it would still be no.'

Nicholas stared at her, his eyes darkening with emotion in which burned a flame of anger and anguish. His voice was low, hoarse as he challenged her:

'Only the past stands between us – deny that if you can? Before I wipe out of your mind the whole wretched business once and for all...'

Stephanie shut her ears against the depth and sincerity that seemed to vibrate in his voice. Slowly as one who signs her own death warrant, she cried:

'I do deny it, Nicholas. My reasons go far, far deeper than that.' She added desperately: 'You flatter yourself.'

He winced as from a blow. Then:

'I see.' It was a clipped, grim sound. 'Then I will not bore you with the details of my life and the past – since nothing I have to tell you would change your attitude. Forgive me for making a fool of myself.'

And it was at that moment Trevor came into the room. Nicholas glanced at him, inclined his head politely in Stephanie's direction and went swiftly from the building.

Stephanie stood there as one transfixed. It was as if her heart had been torn from her body and she were slowly bleeding to death... She had sent him away ... without even listening to his story. Anger whipped across the misery of that truth. What story *could* he tell that wouldn't be false, in any case. She closed her eyes as misery washed over her and she knew that, but for Hester, and no matter what crimes he might have committed, or how unworthy he might have been, she would have married him because her love was greater by far than even she had believed possible.

Trevor moved silently to Stephanie's side. She felt his arm cradling her shoulders – gently, passionlessly, and was grateful for his silence. Her eyes met his in wordless appeal and he murmured:

'I'm going to take you across to the hotel for a drink.' Then, authoritatively: 'You go out to the car. I'll see Miss West and tell her to lock up.'

Stephanie mechanically obeyed him. Once in the car, with Trevor beside her, she said abruptly:

'Do you mind if we drive home, Trevor. I don't fancy a hotel lounge at the moment.'

'Not in the least... I hope this is Mr Young's swan song,' he said rather tersely.

'It is,' she replied.

'Splendid; he's caused quite enough trouble in quite enough lives without wrecking yours.' He put out a hand and touched hers. 'Believe me, my sweet, all this will pass...'

She forced a smile. Her voice came with unnatural lightness:

'Of course. I'm going to be very gay, Trevor. I've come to the conclusion that I've been stagnating socially long enough. All work and no play–'

'I agree. When do we start?' His gaze held hers.

Very deliberately and with a touch of defiance, she said:

'When I take up "residence" in my new abode!'

'I thought you weren't coming in there until the autumn.'

'I've changed my mind.'

'A woman's privilege!'

'I'm thinking in terms of next week. I want Michael and Felice to have the cottage at once.'

'May I help you?' He glanced at her swiftly.

'Quite definitely. I certainly need a man around the place. Michael won't be there to do all the odd jobs.' She laughed. 'You asked for it!'

'And I hereby stake my claim,' he said absurdly. 'I think it will do you good to leave Willow Corner and all its associations – brief though many of them have been... What about Hester?'

'That I cannot say: of course she can come with me–'

Trevor interrupted:

'Listen, Stephanie, don't for heaven's sake let her move in with you. I tell you that–'

She said with emphasis:

'If Hester wants to join me for a while she is very welcome to do so. What kind of a friend do you imagine I am? And, don't forget what I told you before: I will not listen to any of your prejudices against her.'

Trevor looked black, as though a thunder cloud were reflected in his face.

'Very well! Only don't forget that I warned you. You ask me what kind of a friend I think you are? Well, in a few words: "a blind, trusting one". And that doesn't always pay, my dear.'

'Friendships are not intended to "pay",' she countered.

He stared at her despairingly.

'You're quite incorrigible and utterly adorable in your loyalty.'

Stephanie was conscious of a flicker as of a flame touching what seemed to be her ice-impacted heart. Trevor's devotion and friendliness appeared suddenly as a lamp in the darkness. It was good to know someone whom she could trust implicitly, rely on absolutely. Now, in her state of numb misery, she needed him more than ever.

'And you are very good to me,' she said gently. 'The one person in the world to whom I have no need to pretend.'

He shook his head.

'You could never deceive me if you tried.'

'Then it is useless my trying.'

'Do you still want to go straight home?' He spoke abruptly.

Stephanie knew that there was nothing she wanted to do more. The craving had its inception in the desire to be alone and in solitude to bandage the wound that smarted and stung within her heart; but she knew that to be weak, even foolish. This was not a situation that could possibly improve. All she hoped was that Hester and Nicholas would re-marry as quickly as possible and, in the end, leave the district. Since their reunion was inevitable the delay merely created tension and suspense, and, to her, suspense was worse, by far, than knowing. She said in a breath:

'No; let's phone and go out to dinner somewhere. Hester will understand.'

They stopped at the nearest call-box and Stephanie spoke to Hester whose voice came back in a tone of purring silkiness as she said:

'But, darling, of course I understand.' A little laugh. 'As a matter of fact, Nicholas has just been through and wants me to go up to the farm with him. He's on his way to me, now... Don't wait up for me because he hinted something about running over to Stratford-on-Avon. Suits me... Had a good day, darling?' Then, a tone higher: ''Bye.'

Stephanie stood in the box for fully a minute after replacing the receiver. She knew it was hot and stifling in there, but the distance to the car seemed beyond her strength, so violently was she trembling. Her heart appeared to be beating painfully somewhere at the base of her throat in a burning, throbbing ache. So Nicholas had been through to Hester!

Trevor strode up and made faces at her through the glass panels. Then he opened the door.

'Thinking of renting the place, pet?'

She pulled herself together.

'Possibly.'

Trevor knew that she was fighting to conceal her unhappiness. He slipped an arm through hers and led her back to the car.

'Sit there and don't bother to talk: you look precisely like a shovelful of death.'

Stephanie closed her eyes, and leaned back.

Trevor, as one suddenly remembering, delved into a side pocket of the car and brought forth a flask. Then, having poured out the brandy into a small tot which constituted the top, said peremptorily:

'Drink this.'

Stephanie took it gratefully and, in a few minutes, colour came back to her cheeks.

Trevor looked at her with indulgent tenderness. Then:

'That is the second time within a few days I've saved your life with a drink, madam. See that it doesn't occur again!'

Stephanie's body seemed to stiffen; a new light flashed into her eyes as they met his:

'Don't worry,' she insisted with some vehemence. 'It will not happen again, I assure you.'

'Good for you,' he murmured approvingly. 'And now what?'

'Anything and anywhere,' she retorted glibly. 'Anywhere that leads in the opposite direction of Stratford-on-Avon.'

'Not in the mood for Shakespeare?'

'No.' It was a hard sound. 'Not even his sonnets.'

Trevor gave her a quizzical look, but made no comment.

CHAPTER IX

Hester selected her most expensive and alluring gown in which to receive Nicholas. She stood in it before the cheval glass in her bedroom and smoothed her hips, waist and thighs in complete approval. It had cost her seventy-five guineas, but she did not grudge one penny of it; it was slimming and, at the same time, lent her an air of voluptuousness. If she noticed the fact that she was slightly fatter than when last she had worn it, she ignored the fact with that blissful and incredible blindness which some women can adopt towards their defects. Hester had reached the stage when she took as many pounds off her weight when telling anyone precisely how heavy she was, as she took off her age when necessary to betray it! The older she became the more conceited she became, as is too often the way with her sex. For all that, she looked exceedingly attractive and curved in all the correct places – even if a trifle too much.

The only fact, in relation to her appearance, of which Nicholas was aware when he saw her, was that, obviously, she was dressed to go out to dinner, which was the last thing he had in mind.

She adopted an attitude of friendly casualness by way of greeting. She knew that any possessive sentimentality would defeat her ends and that, no matter how she detested the role, or how foreign it was to her nature, she must pose as being concerned only with his happiness and affairs, while placing her own secondary.

'I wondered if you might care to have dinner in Stratford,' she said lightly, realizing that having told Stephanie that lie she must endeavour to substantiate it. 'Descending upon your housekeeper might not be convenient.' A smile. 'I know you men don't think of such things but–'

Nicholas said:

'It might be a good idea. I'm sorry to intrude like this, Hester, but I want to talk to you.' There was a note of desperation in his voice.

'But, of course,' she cooed in her little girl voice. 'We could stay here, if you prefer it.' Then, conversationally: 'Stephanie has just phoned to say that she will not be back until late and not to wait up for her because she is dining with Trevor... Michael is at Felice's home... So–' She watched him carefully, noticing the manner in which his expression hardened at the mention of Trevor's name.

'No,' he exclaimed, overpowered by the memories of the cottage and aware that the very atmosphere was fragrant with the perfume Stephanie always used. 'I prefer Stratford.'

They drove the eight and a half miles almost in silence and it was not until they were seated at dinner in the Stratford-on-Avon Hotel that Nicholas began:

'It is about Stephanie I wanted to see you, Hester.'

Hester managed to curb her irritation and to look duly concerned as she said with solicitude:

'I hope nothing is wrong.'

Nicholas felt rather like a man surrounded with barbed wire having no implement with which to cut it and so extricate himself. Stephanie's attitude both puzzled and bewildered him. He was, and had been, perfectly ready to appreciate that, without knowing the truth about the past, she might find it exceedingly difficult to believe in his sincerity. Yet, against that, she had made it impossible for him to confide that same truth. He argued that Hester was her friend; that fact might, conceivably, complicate matters since, being Stephanie, she would, possibly, consider that the tie of marriage between Hester and himself, precluded her from the picture and made any future in which she herself was identified with him, out of the question. That being so, only Hester could enlighten him.

Nicholas looked at Hester very earnestly:

'Everything would seem to be.' He paused, then: 'You said, yesterday, Hester, that you would do anything to help me... I was frank with you, even if reluctant to discuss my feelings—' He paused, and Hester, her heart beating rapidly, said convincingly, sympathetically:

'What I said to you, then was true, Nicky. In me you have an ally. How could it be otherwise now that I realize how innocent you were of all you were accused and how gravely I wronged you.' She hastened: 'The fact that I could not be blamed for thinking as I did, doesn't alter things ... but we can, at least, repair some of the damage by helping each other now. And in any case, I am devoted to Stephanie: she has been perfectly sweet to me ... please don't feel any restraint and believe me when I say that if there is anything – *anything* I can do you have only to name it.'

'Thank you,' he said gravely, encouraged by her attitude, grateful for her gentleness. Then: 'Just what have you told Stephanie about me?'

Hester's mind darted about after the manner of a minnow in a stream. How to answer that and see, in advance, the repercussions of whatever might be said. Subtly, truthfully, she said, her eyes meeting his very levelly, honestly:

'It wasn't a case of my telling her anything, Nicholas. When we met again the other night Stephanie asked me if I divorced you; naturally I said yes...' She paused. 'I remember, also, that she wanted to know the name of the other woman and that also, I told her. But if I say that in doing so I in no way sought to blacken you.' Hester lowered her gaze effectively. 'Anything but that.'

He said and now he sat tensed, agonized by the suspense that held him as in a vice:

'Did you tell her the truth about me after our talk yesterday?'

Hester was at a disadvantage; she was completely in the dark inasmuch as she was completely ignorant of any conversation that might have taken place between Stephanie and Nicholas. But, instinctively she answered him:

'Yes, Nicky; I did. Don't tell me I was wrong. I wanted to redeem you in her eyes knowing how you felt.' She looked at him anxiously. 'What is it?'

Nicholas had paled. A knife seemed to split his heart.

'What was her attitude?'

Hester puckered her brows and, building up what she conceived to be an excellent support having regard to the fact of Stephanie's vow to her, went on:

'I thought it a trifle strange. Or perhaps disinterested would be a more honest description. She said she was glad I had found out the truth from you, but that she just could not regard you as wholly sincere on account of it.'

'I see.' It was a grim sound. How perfectly that tallied with Stephanie's attitude. She would not even give him the benefit of telling him she already knew the truth.

Hester simulated embarrassment.

'You may criticize me, Nicky, but since you have asked me about all this, it is only fair to you that I am absolutely honest. I must confess that I told her, also, that it was my belief you cared for her...' She paused effectively. 'I – I hate saying this–'

'Go on – please.' He spoke urgently, every nerve in his body tensing under the strain.

'She merely said that she wasn't interested in your feelings and that she could never, in any case, return them. I *tried* to plead your cause, Nicky, but–' She shook her head. 'I could see it was quite useless. I hope,' she added swiftly, 'you do not resent my having done so.'

Nicholas shook his head. A sickness was upon him; his mouth was dry, a depression seeped into his very soul. He said almost curtly:

'Trevor?'

Hester was startled by the tone of his voice; the flame of passion in his eyes.

'You know what I've felt about her regard for him, Nicky. Yes; I definitely do think it is Trevor but that, at the moment, she doesn't want to be tied to him. She's interested in her work above all else. But, of this I feel certain, that when there *is* a man seriously in her life he will be her choice.'

Nicholas leaned forward; he had forgotten Hester's past relationship to him. Now he was desperate in the cause of his own happiness; a man floundering, bewildered, as he reflected upon Stephanie's attitude; her curious response to his caress only a matter of hours before; a man not accustomed to failure or to fostering illusions and, again, that force within him cried out in its insistence that Stephanie cared; that her love for him was in her eyes, in her voice and the passionate yielding of her body... Yet, she had left him in no doubt but that she would never marry him and that her decision was irrevocable. He asked sharply:

'Hester, tell me; do you think it would have made any difference had I told Stephanie the truth about myself – told her at the very beginning? Do you think that the fact of discovering that you were previously my wife – oh the whole thing – was such a shock that, even though she is now aware of the true story, the mud has, somehow, stuck?'

Hester said calculatingly, as one appearing to be scrupulously fair:

'Honestly, I doubt it. Stephanie is a worldly person and a very just one and I should say that she is the type who, once in love, would make every possible excuse for a man's previous failings.'

Nicholas sighed.

'All that is borne out by the fact that, even knowing I had never betrayed you, she still refused to marry me.' He raised his gaze and looked at Hester very intently: 'I asked her today ... and she went so far as to tell me that she had nothing further to say to me ever. A man cannot deceive himself that a woman cares for him when she talks in that strain.' His voice was bitter, cynical. 'The past, you – neither was mentioned. She gave me no opportunity for discussion in any case. All the same her behaviour was exceedingly odd–'

'Odd,' echoed Hester fearfully.

'Yes; it is difficult to explain, but she was

215

like someone labouring under a strain; one moment drawn to me, the next, violently antagonistic.'

Hester saw danger in that summing up and said gently:

'Don't you think that you might have imagined that to be so, Nicky? You, yourself, must have been overwrought and–' She added sympathetically: 'We are such fools when our affections are involved.'

He nodded.

'There may be something in that.'

'At least, since you had that unhappy experience earlier today, nothing I have said to you now can have been any shock, for which I am thankful. You had already proved the nature of Stephanie's feelings for you. Stephanie is a strange person. She can be exceedingly hard in some ways, even intolerant; and yet, in others… We are very complex, though, aren't we?'

'Very.' It was a grim sound.

'May I make a suggestion?'

'By all means.'

'Then, when next you see her, treat her as if all this had never been. Ask no questions and, on no account refer to the past. Women are queer creatures and indifference can often achieve miracles. No–' She smiled and shook her head– 'I'm not going to advise you to adopt the hackneyed method of trying to make her jealous by turning your attentions to another woman but, rather, of sitting back for a while, and waiting. Beyond that I cannot see.' Her voice became suddenly indulgent: 'I believe I warned you, before, that Stephanie had always been flirtatious. She likes men and their attentions, being made love to by them; the physical side of life appeals to her...' She hastened as one who would hate to convey the wrong impression: 'Oh, she is above reproach, I didn't mean *that*... But, after all, she and I talk together and I do *know*.'

Nicholas felt a burning anger, a fierce and ungovernable rage consuming him. So the love he had imagined in Stephanie's very eyes was merely a sexual reaction. Inwardly, he groaned at the very thought. How different she was from anything he had supposed her to be... Doubtless his earlier attentions had amused her and she had thought in terms of a pleasant and flirtatious interlude. Her only scruples being an aversion to any kind of relationship with a married man. Perhaps, he thought cynically, the fact that he had *been* married, had offended her susceptibilities. He paused. That reasoning didn't help; it didn't remove the hurt, the searing pain and aching sense of loss... The thought came to him that, despite events, he was thankful that now she knew he was not the cad she had imagined him to be... Nevertheless, in possession of that knowledge, her behaviour and general attitude towards him was doubly difficult to understand. Doubtless, Hester's suggestion was the wisest and was, in fact, all that was left to him to do.

Hester congratulated herself on playing a very subtle hand. She had eradicated all suggestion of self, talked as one regarding the matter entirely objectively and from Nicholas's standpoint alone ... thus he would argue in those moments when he had time for reflection. Yet, at the same time, she had driven a wedge between him and Stephanie that nothing was likely to remove. If he waited... Her heart beats quickened... Stephanie would doubtless become involved with Trevor and, she, Hester would so have consolidated her position in Nicholas's life as to be invulnerable. No, every move had been faultless; Nicholas would not lower his pride by mentioning the past and, therefore, to Stephanie, he would still remain the philanderer... Hester decided, also, that in any case, Stephanie could be relied upon to keep the promise she had made ... never to encourage Nicholas. Hadn't she more than proved her staunchness that very day? Later, when she and Nicholas were safely re-married, she could impart the truth to Stephanie about Valerie Brown and, thus, the matter would die a natural death. It all became incredibly simple.

She said suddenly:

'Nicholas, if you would like, or prefer, to drive back to the farm... I understand. I know that when one feels as you must be feeling ... well, home can be a sanctuary and I am ready to fall in with anything you wish.'

Nicholas warmed to the sympathy in her voice; it wasn't a question of deceiving himself about her importance, but of being grateful to have someone to whom he could unburden his mind. Had she not known Stephanie so intimately, however, such a course would never have occurred to him. He answered quietly:

'You've been very kind, Hester. Thank you for bearing with me. I appreciate it.'

Never for an instant did it occur to him to doubt her sincerity. Hester, in her daily life, had always been far too clever to *appear* to be untruthful and, in all those matters in which there was the danger of being proved deceptive, she adhered to facts! Intrigue, cunning, scheming – yes; these were as much a part of her character as her make-up was a part of her face. She had Nicholas's confidence for the simple reason that she knew he would argue that, while she might have many failings, lying was not one of them and, thus, she did not in any way come under suspicion. The real Hester was as deep and as calculating as it was possible for any woman to be and few could even begin to understand her craftiness and duplicity.

'And I appreciate your giving me the opportunity,' she said with just the right inflection and without indulging any eye-flickering or attempts to ensnare him or resort to her feminine charms in the hope that, on the rebound, he might turn to her. Open attack would not, she had decided, be of avail in Nicholas's case; seductiveness, blatantly revealed, would completely disgust him. Appeals to his generosity, or the memory of their past associations – none would further her cause. He must be made to see her as a woman re-born; a woman changed almost beyond recognition, so that he could care for her as he might care for an entirely different personality from the Hester of old. And, with Stephanie causing him heartache and keeping her bargain, Hester had no qualms about the ultimate success of her designs.

Nicholas took advantage of Hester's offer, longing for the solitude of the farm and unable to make polite conversation which could be only an anti-climax. Hester, continuing the role she had carefully chosen, maintained a discreet silence most of the journey back to Winchcombe and was thankful that, at least, through returning so early there would be no question of Stephanie and Trevor being there.

When they finally reached Willow Corner, however, to her chagrin Trevor's car was already parked outside the wicket gate.

'So, they are back,' she said and gave a little chuckle.

Nicholas's jaw seemed to tighten.

'You will understand if I merely drop you outside – won't you?' he said grimly.

'Of course.'

But, even as the car drew up, Trevor and Stephanie – to Hester's delight – arm in arm, appeared in the front garden, obviously having strolled around from the main lawns. To avoid speaking to them was, Nicholas knew, quite impossible.

Hester greeted them gaily.

'So we are both home early! We had not expected *you* back for ages.'

They had reached Trevor and Stephanie in those seconds and stood, a trifle awkwardly, facing them. Hester babbled on:

'We've been to Stratford! I do love that place; in fact it is all so wonderful around here and *what* a heavenly evening.'

Actually, it was one of those long, spring evenings when summer had impinged its warmth prematurely and the freshness of green foliage laced a sky softly blue and shot with mother-of-pearl tints that gradually deepened with the sunset. Blossom, fragrant, heady, gleaned in opalescent splendour, fluffy, snow-like and shading to a shell pink.

The cottage seemed to have reached out and taken the sun's rays as a cloak about its shoulders, its roof and windows were as solid gold; the rest was folded into indigo shadows, gentle and caressing. The last of the tulips, forget-me-nots, wallflowers, stood in sweet confusion in wide flower beds cut out of smooth, vivid green lawns.

It was a typically English scene and its beauty touched Nicholas and Stephanie's heart so that emotion swelled within them like music in a cathedral, bearing them onwards to a spiritual exultation which was made all the greater and thrown into sharp relief by the poignance of their suffering, their longing and passionate desire for each other. Their eyes met and it was as if they understood the other's appreciation of their surroundings and for a split second, were ready to compromise after the manner of two people placing a tribute on nature's altar. It was a moment when nothing could come between them; when as it were, they stepped out of character and experienced momentary affinity.

But the moment was short lived, for Stephanie, tensed, nervous, dare not preserve it; dare not allow herself to recognize it, and she said flippantly:

'I think this is where we all need a drink. Let's go in.'

Nicholas's voice came almost sharply and

very decisively:

'Thank you all the same, but I must get back.'

Trevor again slipped his arm through Stephanie's – this time deliberately.

'The trials of a farm – even at this late hour!'

Hester chipped in as one seeming to leap to the defence of Nicholas.

'Just because you can laze, Mr Morly, in the rarified atmosphere of an antique *salon*, shall we say... Your day could hardly be called strenuous!'

Trevor flashed Hester a very penetrating glance:

'And you are suddenly interested in farming, Mrs Wincott?' His words were faintly cynical and not altogether without a certain contemptuous ring.

Hester frowned; she was quick to sense a potential enemy and was well aware that Trevor Morly was both suspicious and antagonistic towards her. She made a mental note that he was the one person of whom she must beware and, if possible, placate; although she was not so foolish as to imagine that any feminine wiles would assist her and, thus, influence his opinion.

'I do not feel,' she said, quite seriously, 'that one can truly be interested in anything until one understands it. At the *moment* I do not profess to do so but ... I can learn.'

Nicholas inclined his head in Stephanie's direction as he said, with studied politeness:

'Good night, Stephanie ... 'night, Morly.'

Hester made it quite obvious that she was going to walk to the car with him, which she did, and her attitude was that of quiet confidence allied to a certain possessiveness; it was subtly done as to convey the impression of harmony and understanding and even of intimacy.

'How welcome he is to her,' Trevor said tartly. 'Did they *have* to return so early?' He paused, adding meaningly, 'But, then, obviously, they did not expect *us* to be back so soon.'

Stephanie did not speak. There was a tightening of the muscles at her throat; she felt beaten, defenceless, beside the emotional forces ranged against her. The sight of Nicholas and Hester together caused her an intense and overwhelming anguish. Her affection for Hester, while reducing in intensity the jealousy she felt, nevertheless, complicated the entire issue... She was torn and shattered, bound by a promise which, in effect, could only wreck her life. Easy, in the beginning to employ scorn, derision, cynicism; to condemn him as a cad ... but that in no way killed the love she felt for him. Like thousands of women before her, she would have prayed that the force of her affection for him might have been instrumental in his reformation. She was wretched without him; even were she wretched *with* him, she would have lost nothing, while having much to gain from his presence. Yet ... she drew upon her natural hatred of deceit as a weapon with which to fight such reflections... How swiftly he had sought solace in Hester's company, and how obvious it was that there was a silent bond between them.

Fool, to allow her thoughts to dwell, even for a moment, on the possibility of his sincerity, and the supposition that his declaration of love for her was true. Yet, as against that, what had he hoped for by asking her to marry him? A relationship which might have borrowed the intimacy of marriage long before the legal tie had been established... Had it been in his mind that an 'engagement' would have enabled him to persuade her to become his mistress? It was, she decided, finally, exceedingly doubtful that he had any more intention of marrying her than he had of marrying Valerie Brown after his affair with her.

Hester rejoined them; she was radiant, well pleased with the evening's work. She had even persuaded Nicholas to take her to see his accountants the following day. That would show Stephanie just how the situation was, and negate any romantic illusions she might cherish because of his proposal. The very idea of that seared her, awakening a bitter and vindictive jealousy. It wasn't enough that Stephanie had remained loyal to her; she loathed the thought that, even for a second, she had been given the crumb of comfort embodied in Nicholas's proposal. She must manage to have a few words with Stephanie that night, solicit her confidence. Being Stephanie, however, she would probably tell her about Nicholas.

Trevor left the cottage within ten minutes. He found that Hester was repulsive to him; she irritated and annoyed him and he could not rid himself of the hateful feeling that she was not really Stephanie's friend, but using her in some way best known to herself, for her own ends.

Alone with Stephanie, Hester began confidentially:

'Did you have a nice evening with Trevor, darling?'

'Quite, thank you ... and you?'

'Heavenly.' A smirk. 'But your being here rather cramped our style... Oh, Stephanie—' She stretched herself after the manner of a slinky cat— 'Nicholas really is the most devastating person.' She leaned forward as one imparting a confidence such as some women wallow in giving. 'And no one – just *no* one can kiss as he does...' She paused to mark the effect of her words, amazed at the vicious delight she derived from the pain that flashed into Stephanie's eyes and inwardly furious because she, herself, needed to fight and scheme in order to succeed.

Stephanie felt suffocated, almost nauseated. It didn't seem possible that any man could be quite such a hypocrite as Nicholas obviously was. Yet she knew that to argue with Hester, tell her all that had transpired that day could but serve to hurt her the more. She wanted Nicholas back and there was nothing that anyone could do to protect her, since she was fully aware of his fickleness and philandering. She said, trying to keep her voice steady:

'All I pray is, Hester, that you will not be hurt again.'

Instantly, Hester was suspicious.

'Why should I be?'

Stephanie said gently:

'My dear, knowing Nicholas as you do–'

Hester retaliated with:

'I've already told you that, given the chance I can change all that. Nicholas knows his weakness and admits the fact – he even confessed it to me tonight – that he is a perfect fool over women. But, being in his confidence, knowing that I am the one person who really counts outside his philandering, I am sure of our future.' She added, knowing that her remark could not fail to sting: 'They say that women adore bad men, don't they? And I suppose that Nicholas isn't too keen to tie himself down again. Marriage, to him, is just a very tempting bait to be used to persuade his victims to do as he wishes.' She laughed. 'Do you think it dreadful of me to talk like this? But, at *heart* I know he is far, far better than he appears and that, in the end, he will be quite different. He's exactly the type who, at forty, becomes the convert and most moral.'

Stephanie felt sick.

'Meanwhile I suppose it doesn't matter how many women he deceives, or leaves?'

'Don't be hard, darling. Really, you know, they do ask for it, half of them. They have always thrown themselves at his head.' A sigh. 'That is why it is such a comfort to know that you are on my side and–' She paused significantly.

Stephanie's voice rang with a contempt she could not conceal as she said:

'You certainly have no need to fear that I shall fling myself at his head, Hester – quite apart from my promise.'

'I know, darling.' A beaming smile. 'You are as staunch as a rock, bless you. By the way, Nicky and I are going to town together for the day tomorrow. Probably stay in town.' A yawn. 'I must get some beauty sleep... He noticed my frock tonight and said I was a very attractive woman who had not forgotten how to kiss!' A little giggle. 'Darling, you don't mind my talking like this – do you? I know it must sound awfully foolish, but there is just no one else I can discuss anything with and I shall burst if I don't share my happiness.'

Stephanie said swiftly:

'On the contrary ... I'm interested.'

That night, mentally, she wiped Nicholas out of her life. She could, she argued, have kept her promise to Hester and still nurtured the love she felt for him, she could have striven to allow her thoughts of him to lose all bitterness; excuse the defects which, since Hester could find in her heart to overlook, were not for her to hold against him. But there was something in his attitude to Hester that nauseated her... And so far as she was concerned it was the end. Now she would begin on very different lines. Resolutely she got up from her chair. If there was anything on earth she despised it was a lovesick woman sitting about looking dejected and wearing a martyred expression. In actual time, her relationship with Nicholas had been exceedingly brief, but the experience she had gained as a result of it, was far reaching and disastrous. This was, she decided, where she began to live it down. All her preconceived notions of love and romance were as nought. She thought of Trevor: he was at least honest; he certainly didn't drag marriage into the picture as a sop, or an inducement for purely physical satisfaction. No one would be deceived by him.

A little, bitter expression played about her mouth. Nicholas Young... She could hear him telling Hester that she was 'a very attractive woman who had not forgotten how to kiss' ... and picture the whole, sordid business.

She prayed that Hester might never come to realize exactly how debased he was, or how little he had, or would ever, have reformed.

CHAPTER X

Michael and Felice were married at Coleshill Church as they intended. To Stephanie the wedding was in the nature of an ordeal and only her thankfulness on account of Michael's happiness saved her from collapse.

Hester, realizing that Valerie Brown was to be there, made a convenient excuse not to attend. Now, Valerie was the last person she wanted to meet, for Nicholas's confidence about the divorce had robbed her of both weapons and power. Nicholas, himself, pleaded a business appointment and remained out of the district all day to avoid the strain of being with Stephanie on such an occasion.

The inevitable moment arrived when, back at Felice's home, the few guests were introduced to each other and Valerie Brown held out her hand to Stephanie:

'Felice has talked a very great deal about you and if I fall back on the atrocious remark that I feel I know you – well! It will but be true!'

Stephanie studied the face now smiling into her own, fighting down prejudices, striving to cut off that section of her brain which reminded her that this was the woman whose lover Nicholas had once been... She knew that, despite herself, it was a face she liked, with a high, intelligent forehead, clean cut, artistic features and a friendly, generous mouth. The eyes were direct, without being challenging, and there was a light of kindliness and understanding within them as of one who would never judge harshly. Yet ... it was also the face of a woman who had betrayed her friend. She realized immediately that Valerie Brown had personality and vivacity without any wearying 'good spirits', that were but a cloak for nervous excitability exhausting and unutterably boring to endure. There was a quiet restraint about her, allied to an infectious sense of humour. Stephanie said, without in any way realizing the pointedness of the remark, or wishing to commit a *faux pas:*

'And I have heard a very great deal about

you, Miss Brown.'

Valerie held her gaze for a second, then:

'I'm sure you have,' she murmured good naturedly. She added with an appealing and confidential air: 'Don't quite believe *all* you hear, will you? The black sheep are never *quite* so bad as they are painted, you know!'

Colour flamed into Stephanie's cheeks and she stammered with genuine regret:

'I didn't mean it that way at all.'

'I'm sure you didn't! I was just trying to stake a small claim to your friendship... May I call you Stephanie?'

Stephanie wanted to dismiss all that as pure 'gush'. Valerie was an actress and they were all the same, she told herself fiercely. The 'darlings' meant nothing... And yet–

'Of course,' she found herself saying involuntarily.

Valerie turned to look in the direction of Michael and Felice.

'They make an attractive pair... I like your brother enormously. Felice is a singularly fortunate girl.' She added swiftly: 'She will – unless I'm very much mistaken – never have to wait up half the night wondering where *he* is!'

Stephanie could not resist saying:

'You evidently haven't a very good opinion of men.'

Valerie showed a row of perfect teeth in an attractive smile.

'I have the very highest opinion of some, but of others – there is nothing low enough to justify a comparison.'

Stephanie felt suddenly cold... How obvious that Nicholas had inspired the latter such opinion.

'We agree on that point.'

Valerie took in the details of the room in which they stood.

'This is a beautiful house, isn't it?' she said appreciatively.

'Very beautiful,' commented Stephanie with enthusiasm. 'I love the colour scheme of off-white and that shell pink; it throws the lilacs into such wonderful relief; exquisite taste.'

'Yet Felice much prefers Willow Corner for all that,' Valerie exclaimed. 'I, too, adore old houses.'

'And I,' said Stephanie.

'To say nothing of old furniture... May I come and browse around your antiques before I return to town? I'm looking for a Bacon settle.'

'I happen to have one.' Stephanie stopped and then laughed. She had forgotten her antagonism towards this woman. 'How unforgivable of me to talk business at my brother's wedding!'

'I began it!' Valerie moved away a few paces and glanced back over her shoulder. 'I'll look in on you during the week.'

A voice said:

'Didn't I say she was attractive?'

'Michael!' Stephanie gazed up at him. Then: 'I must agree.'

'You can,' he said steadily, 'rely on my opinion – particularly now that I am a married man.'

'Happy?' Stephanie ignored his remark.

'Gloriously!' He drew Felice – radiant in soft blue chiffon – to him and looked down at her. 'May we want to stand as close as this fifty years from now,' he added earnestly and then laughed to hide his emotion.

'I feel,' said Stephanie, 'that you will. I shall, by then, be a dear, old great aunt with her knitting and mittens.'

'And a family of your own,' Felice insisted, her face beaming, her whole body appearing to glow as though illuminated within from some secret fire.

'That,' said Stephanie stoutly, 'is highly improbable. Spinsters do not have children – at least not so that you'd notice them!' She tried to sound bantering.

'Rot,' Michael said tersely. 'You, a spinster!' He smiled adoringly at Felice, saying: 'Darling, it is time for us to go if we are to reach London in respectable time.'

Felice's parents, doting, indulgent, joined them in that instant. Mrs Morgan, a woman of fifty, slim, elegant, exquisitely gowned in dove grey, and wearing the minimum of jewellery, believed that the essence of smartness was simplicity and, with her still perfect figure, had all the charm of a woman half her age. Edward Morgan, no less than his wife, was exceedingly youthful for his years; tall, spare, and dark. Wealth became them both and they neither indulged ostentation. Not for them the vulgar display that sought to advertise their possessions, but rather the dignity and discretion of understatement and modesty. Their generosity to the town was responsible for much of its well-being. But they gave by stealth and sought no applause.

'I must confess,' Felice's mother said with a warm, gentle smile, 'that I had pictured my daughter in veils and ivory chiffon! But, now that it is all over, I think they were so wise to have that quiet and lovely ceremony.' She looked at Stephanie very earnestly: 'I do hope, my dear, that you will come to see us here as one of the family. We love Michael as a son and you are his sister. So far, there has been little opportunity for us to become acquainted! Trust my daughter to choose a whirlwind wedding, after assuring us that she would never marry at all!'

They all laughed together – friendly, understanding laughter that is a bond. Valerie slipped an arm through the older woman's and then, looking at Stephanie said:

'Wherever Hilary Morgan is, there also is

home and happiness.'

'I can well believe that,' Stephanie murmured softly.

Edward Morgan smiled down at her.

'I'm always delighted to welcome pretty girls to the family circle – aren't I, Hilary?'

'Always,' she retorted gaily.

It was all informal, intimate and without any trace of strain. It seemed to Stephanie, looking back on it, that going there had been like wearing a pair of exquisitely comfortable shoes! And she thanked God that Michael had found such happiness and that Felicity had known such a home: she would most surely carry on its proud tradition in her own.

Beyond that, she refused to be subjective. Her world at the moment was fantastically unreal and thus she wished it to be. No time for thought; the numbness inducing a certain forgetfulness. She refused to allow her mind to dwell upon the fact that Valerie had been co-respondent in Hester's divorce suit. And no disloyalty to Hester was intended because she could find it easy to understand how such a situation arose. Loving Nicholas as she, herself, did she was honest enough to concede how great the temptation must have been. And how agonizing his subsequent betrayal.

Hester declined Stephanie's offer to stay

with her at the flat in Warwick.

'It wouldn't be fair to you, my dear,' Hester said considerately. 'Here, at this cottage, it is rather different and no business is involved.' She paused subtly: 'As a matter of fact Nicholas has suggested that I stay at Wilderness Farm for a bit.' She giggled. 'Servants to chaperone us! But–' She nodded her head wisely. 'I think that, much as I adore it, a hotel would be safer and more discreet. I know Nicky, and I know myself! I'd never resist him if we were living under the same roof and then, afterwards, he would not be so keen on re-marrying – and I fully intend that it shall be nothing less than marriage.'

Stephanie tried to remain calm, but her heart beat sickeningly as though it were thudding in a void and had nowhere to rest. There was something faintly distasteful to her in Hester's frankness and in the whole sordid situation.

'I suppose,' she managed to say helpfully, 'that the hotel – or rather it is really an old inn – near Sedgeberrow wouldn't help?'

Hester beamed.

'Darling, how clever of you! That is exactly where Nicholas suggested after I'd put my foot down about staying with him at the farm.' She looked suddenly appealingly: 'You do agree with my attitude – don't you? I mean, one just must be cautious and not ask for trouble!'

Stephanie knew, as she listened, that she would be very thankful to be spared Hester's continual confidences and that she was relieved and grateful that the move to the flat would put an end to their continual intimacy and daily contact. It wasn't a question of liking Hester any less, or of any increasing jealousy; merely that constantly to hear repeated all that Nicholas said made it impossible for her to shut the door on her own experiences with him. She said genuinely:

'I think you are being very wise. After all, now you do know the character of the man with whom you are dealing and forewarned is forearmed!'

Hester smiled, a slow, calculating smile.

'How right you are, my dear... I shall miss you, Stephanie; I mean,' she corrected herself, 'miss not having our chats every day. But I know, or at least hope, that I may pop in at any time when you are settled at the flat... Trevor will help you with the move, of course?'

Stephanie exclaimed lightly:

'It will all be very simple; I'm leaving quite a bit of furniture here – stuff that Michael particularly loves.'

'You're being very generous – aren't you?' Hester was far from generous herself and seldom, if ever, gave without an ulterior motive.

'Not in the least,' Stephanie said. 'There's nothing generous in any act that gives me great pleasure.'

Hester felt irritated. She was fully aware of her own greed and the contrast in Stephanie's character emphasized it. She detested having to be made aware of virtues in others which were lacking in herself.

'The philanthropist, in fact,' she said, and her voice had an edge to it.'

Stephanie glanced at her swiftly.

'Don't be absurd, Hester.'

Hester smirked.

'All right, darling! Don't be touchy.'

Stephanie frowned; but she maintained a discreet silence. She was in no mood for any fatuous play on words. A second or so later, she said:

'Of course Hester, your trunks can remain here until the honeymooners return – that is if that will help you.'

Hester looked smug.

'Thank you, darling; but Nicky has already offered to keep the bulk of my luggage at the farm for me.' It was an absolute lie as was her reference to Nicholas's suggestion that she stay at his house, but she knew that it created the illusion in Stephanie's mind that her relationship with Nicholas was becoming daily more intimate and successful. Also, she enjoyed the belief that she was causing Stephanie suffering. The sadistic streak in her found delight in the power to inflict pain.

Stephanie tried to keep her voice steady.

'That will save you a great deal of trouble,' she said swiftly.

'I doubt,' Hester commented, 'that I'll ever need to remove it... Stephanie? I think I'd like to be re-married at that little church at Coleshill, you know.'

'Why not?' It was a clipped utterance.

Hester felt a pang of jealousy. Obviously Coleshill had some associations for Stephanie. She said:

'I suppose they would re-marry us – not like an ordinary divorce case where they refuse to marry any divorced persons.' A smile. 'It's quite romantic, when you come to think of it. And amusing to go off on a honeymoon with one's former husband.' A significant laugh. 'Expedition of rediscovery since we know each other so well.

Stephanie felt that every pulse in her body was throbbing as with an abcess. She could not master the weakness that assailed her at the very mention of Nicholas as a husband ... the thought of his attentions to Hester at the moment agonized her. She said flippantly:

'Do we any of us know the other person *well?*'

Hester, to curb her annoyance, said patronizingly and with faint indulgence:

240

'You don't quite understand, darling. When one has been married to a person for a number of years there's that *something—*' She sighed; a sigh of self-satisfaction: 'Impossible to describe.' A smile. 'You'll know what I mean, one day.'

Stephanie's voice was hard as she retorted:

'I think I've seen enough of marriage to avoid it. Your experience has hardly encouraged me, my dear.'

Hester, in that second, loathed the fact that Stephanie was aware of the truth. Now, she wanted to build up the illusion of success and happiness – quite impossible in the circumstances. With Stephanie as a potential danger, Hester was ready to play any part in order to enlist her help and sympathy, but with that same danger finally removed, she resented being at a disadvantage. And the knowledge that only her own scheming and cunning had prevented Nicholas marrying Stephanie, goaded her to fury. She said, and there was an edge to her words:

'When two people are divorced and then come together again, theirs is probably the greatest devotion and romance of all.'

Stephanie gave her a swift glance.

'Sincerely I hope you will prove that to be so, Hester.'

It struck her that the entire situation was fantastic. What would Hester say were she to tell her of Nicholas's proposal... She dismissed the thought; that was one thing she would never learn and, thus, her peace of mind would be safeguarded.

Hester altered her mood. Only when she was safely back in Nicholas's life could she afford to sever her friendship with Stephanie... She said wheedingly:

'Any news from Michael? He really is a charming person. And I like Felice much better than I did at first...'

'Yes, I heard from Michael this morning. They are at Lake Maggiore and seemingly in Paradise!'

Hester smiled.

'Ah me! Nicky and I spent our honeymoon in Italy...' A pause. 'You haven't told me what you thought of Valerie Brown, by the way. I've intended asking you before but, somehow, the opportunity just hasn't arisen.'

Stephanie said very honestly:

'She was nothing I imagined her to be. Michael had expressed his liking for her before I met her. She just doesn't look the type of woman—'

Hester said with a deadly calm.

'Deliberately to ensnare a friend's husband? Smash an otherwise happy marriage... No, my dear; she doesn't. That is precisely why she is so dangerous.' She hastened. 'Don't think I'm bitter; don't misunderstand me, darling. You'll probably have to meet her socially, for I was right inasmuch as I believed she was very friendly with the Morgans and, for that reason, you are bound to run into her from time to time. It may even be my lot.' She resorted to her faintly simpering tone which was beginning to get on Stephanie's nerves: 'I shall treat her with friendliness... Forgive her the grave wrong she did me.' A sigh. 'One can afford to be generous when one regains one's happiness.' That, she thought, was a decidedly clever move for, should it so happen that Stephanie was ever present when she and Valerie met, she would not be made suspicious by such an attitude!

Stephanie studied her with great intensity:

'That is true,' she said slowly.

'What were you thinking?' It was a breathless utterance.

Stephanie raised her eyes.

'I couldn't quite explain, Hester. It was just that it struck me that you are very difficult to type.'

Hester's heart missed a beat. If ever Stephanie should see through her... She hastened:

'I know I am ... and I know, too, that my greatest failing is that I just can't bear grudges against people for long.'

'I hardly consider that a failing.'

'Oh, but it is... I ought to hate Valerie ... I did hate her; but now I don't. Such an attitude might easily be misunderstood.'

'Why should it?' Stephanie didn't quite know why she felt a sudden resistance.

'Darling! Don't be so difficult! Wives are not usually forgiving towards their husband's mistress now – are they?'

Stephanie replied:

'They might be, Hester – when that same mistress has been discarded. Human nature being what it is.'

Hester laughed.

'Trust you to delve into the psychological aspect.' A pause. 'But I hope you approve of my attitude. I simply had to face the possibility of running into her. Nothing like schooling oneself in advance.'

'I agree,' said Stephanie.

'All the same – and this is perhaps odd to you! Although I've said what I have about your knowing her, I should be horribly jealous if you ever really became even acquaintances! I know it's horrid of me but–' She sighed. 'There it is; I wonder if you can understand.'

'I think so,' said Stephanie, adding: 'But you need have no fear: we are not likely to see much of her although–' Stephanie paused: 'She did say something about claiming a stake in my friendship?'

'What!' It was a fearful sound.

'Probably the champagne,' Stephanie laughed.

'Just like her,' Hester said disgustedly. 'So gushing and insincere always.'

'I just can't think of her as that type – it's no use.'

'That,' and now Hester was roused, 'is because you don't know her, my dear.' She pulled herself up sharply and convincingly: 'Which goes to prove how true my words were about being jealous!'

'Has – has Nicholas seen her?'

'No.' It was a harsh sound. 'And has no desire to do so. One day I shall have all the facts, although I think I know just what happened. Nicky lost interest in her the moment he became her lover. Just like a man. She's probably suffered quite a bit over it all, so I suppose I must be charitable.'

Stephanie found herself saying involuntarily:

'She certainly didn't seem in need of any sympathy when I met her at Michael's wedding.'

Hester flashed:

'Darling! She's an *actress!* That vivacity is her stock in trade!'

Stephanie fought down the desire to defend Valerie Brown, realizing that it was quite absurd and nothing whatever to do with her. But the agonizing jealousy she had expected to feel for her was, to her amazement, now completely missing. While that same sensation was growing with a deadly significance towards Hester, much as she hated the idea and fought against it. She managed to say coolly:

'I suppose so. I'm afraid I am out of my depth when it comes to all this posing, insincerity and intrigue.'

'"Intrigue?"' It was a breathless cry. 'Why "intrigue"?'

Stephanie gave a half laugh.

'I don't know really why I used the word ... but the two usually go hand in hand, don't they?'

Hester experienced a sharp relief.

'How right you are,' she agreed. 'Darling, I must *rush*. I'm meeting Nicholas in half an hour and I've simply got to change... He's taking me to see that inn.' She looked coy and foolish.

It struck Stephanie sharply and bitterly that Hester was the last woman on earth to whom she would have thought Nicholas would have been attracted. At least, not to re-marry... She stopped, uneasy at the reflection... She despised jealousy above all things, but she knew that it was already insinuating itself into her relationship with Hester with all the strangling force of bindweed.

CHAPTER XI

During the following week, Stephanie absorbed herself completely with the arranging of her new flat, deriving intense satisfaction from its artistic embellishment and amusing Trevor by her repeated claims upon their own store of furniture on sale! The result, however, more than justified the extravagance. Every room was in harmony with the period of the building and the deep blues and tudor rose chintz gave to the atmosphere a charm and restlessness for which she was noted.

Trevor stood and gazed about him when the lounge was finally finished.

'It looks like a photograph taken from *Country Life*,' he said enthusiastically. 'Stephanie, you are a wizard at this kind of thing. It positively glows and there's just the right amount of brass ornamenting that chimney corner and the flowers – the blues and golds! Full marks.' He glanced down at the light sapphire carpet. 'That is perfect against the panelling.'

'In fact, you like the place!' she teased.

'I knew what I was doing when I became your partner,' he said facetiously. 'Particularly since you are our best customer at the moment!'

'I have been extravagant – haven't I?' She spoke self-critically.

'Makes it excellent for trade, and this flat will certainly be a good advertisement among our customer-friends.'

Stephanie looked at the wide chimney corner with its side cushioned-covered settles.

'I'm going to light a fire there tonight,' she said enthusiastically, 'even if it *is* too hot.' She glanced out at the rather grey day, the scudding, slate clouds, and listening to the wind shrieking about the building. 'You cannot say that nature isn't obliging,' she added. 'Hilda is on my side, too.'

Trevor sat down on the velvet upholstered settee – a perfect reproduction of an early couch – and lit a cigarette.

'You know they *had* something in the old days. This is comfortable,' he said approvingly.

Stephanie smiled.

'I hate the modern settees: you want legs as long as a giraffe to sit back in them; they are so square and ugly, somehow. Ah well,' she sighed. 'I'm glad you like my new home.' She glanced out to where Warwick Castle rose majestically against the dark clouds. 'I feel that I belong here, at any rate.'

'No regrets about leaving Willow Corner?'

'None; it is right that Michael would have it now. He and Felice will love it as it should be loved.' She met Trevor's eyes very earnestly: 'I sometimes wish I didn't love things quite so much,' she said reflectively.

Trevor held her gaze.

'I wish you didn't love people quite so much, Stephanie,' he said quietly, tentatively.

She looked swiftly away from him and moved to a gate-legged table on which stood an exquisitely arranged posy of forget-me-nots, sprigs of Japanese cherry blossom and golden wallflowers. She gave them special attention, moving their stems to alter the effect. It was a nervous gesture and she knew that Trevor was in no way deceived.

'I wish that, too,' she murmured. 'But I am making progress.' She flashed him a defiant smile. 'I hate hang-dogs!'

Trevor's voice was a trifle unsteady as he said:

'Have you made sufficient progress to invite me to dinner tonight, so that I can share that glorious fire you've talked about?' he finished, trying to infuse a note of lightness into the request.

Stephanie knew that the question held far more than the usual significance; she knew that she had reached a moment in her life, and in her relationship with Trevor, when

249

running away in no way solved it, or even offered escape. Her mind caught at the remembrance of something Trevor had said to her a short while previously: 'The finest antidote for one man is another'. Could she disprove that without giving it a trial. What was to be gained by wrapping herself in solitude? She had fought to live up to her resolution of putting Nicholas, mentally as well as physically, out of her life; and, never for a second, had she any hope, or the slightest illusion, that theirs might be a story having an unexpectedly happy ending. The situation between Nicholas and Hester was perfectly obvious and allowed of no alteration except a mere legal ceremony. Why, then, waste precious time. She and Trevor were two, free people fully justified in enjoying each other's company and widening their already considerable interests. She said firmly:

'I'd love you to come to dinner, Trevor. We'll eat a great deal; drink enough to create an atmosphere of gaiety and not enough to spoil anything...' She paused.

'Is that all?' His gaze was steady, challenging.

'Can one conjure up a mood in advance?' she asked shakenly.

Trevor smiled.

'A man can perhaps – a woman...'

'A woman lives far more in a mental world

and interprets that world in physical expression. A man lives in a physical world and is far less concerned with the mental.'

He smiled again.

'You understand my sex pretty well.'

'I should hate to feel completely ignorant of your eccentricities. All the same, a woman longs most to find a blending of both mental and physical: that is ecstasy at its height.'

'A man can desire that, also,' Trevor said with unexpected gravity. 'But when he feels that it is too much like sighing for the moon, he compromises.'

'Ah,' said Stephanie, 'a woman hates having to compromise.'

'She just goes on sighing.'

'Sometimes.'

'Do you intend–'

She interrupted him somewhat harshly:

'No; I do not intend to sigh, Trevor. I detest flabbiness, indecision. A state of negation.'

Trevor got to his feet. Deliberately, he crossed to where she was standing and, equally deliberately, tilted her head backwards with the aid of his finger and thumb, then bent his mouth to hers. She made no attempt to draw away.

'Until tonight, my sweet,' he said softly as, after a brief second, he lifted his lips from hers. 'Meanwhile, I'll be on duty down

251

below… Sevenish?'

'Cocktails at seven,' she said lightly. 'And I shall wear a long frock.'

'Splendid! May I be allowed to bring the champagne?'

'My guests never bring their own champagne,' she countered.

He looked at her.

'I rather thought I'd been elevated from the "guest" stage, darling.'

She hesitated, then:

'Very well… You shall bring the champagne.'

'Thank you.' He gave a mock bow. 'And if anyone calls–'

'I shall not,' she hastened, 'be in.'

Trevor lifted the latch of the oaken doorway and stepped out into the narrow corridor, the floor of which was polished as a mirror.

'Not an ideal spot after a party,' he chuckled. 'Those Persian rugs may be wonderful to look at, but how easy to break one's neck.'

'The floor is *not* polished beneath them!'

'I'll take your word for it,' he said putting his head around the door and smiling across the room at her.

Stephanie gave him a friendly little chuckle.

'All the same, be careful of the champagne tonight!'

'In other words, break your neck, but

don't smash any bottles.'

'Naturally.'

There was, he thought, with a quickening of his pulses, something more than usually attractive about her as she stood there smiling at him. A certain defiant appeal as of one taking life in both hands and shaking it vigorously; if her expression had hardened a little it was only to be expected, but she had lost that strained, anguished look and he congratulated himself that the advent of Nicholas Young would not have any too serious repercussions. Actually, although he would not openly admit it, he felt that there was something a trifle odd about the situation and he was more than ever convinced that Hester was, in some way, the 'nigger in the woodpile'. The trite saying served to sum up his reactions. Be that as it might, he reasoned, he had to be grateful to her for appearing so conveniently upon the scene and, thus, in effect, delivering Stephanie into his keeping.

Stephanie went straight to Hilda, in the kitchen – the plan of which followed American lines and was as perfectly modern as the rest of the flat was old.

'A guest for dinner tonight,' she announced with a friendly smile. 'Now what can you conjure up, Hilda.'

Hilda beamed:

'Melon; salmon mayonnaise; baby

chicken… And, perhaps a chocolate mousse?'

Stephanie glanced at the large, built-in "fridge."

'All there–' She clicked her fingers – 'just like that?'

Hilda's face was as beaming as a full moon; her expert hands itched to get busy.

'Just like that, Miss … I felt as you'd be havin' company… Mr Young, Miss?' It was a question asked without inquisitiveness, but with a certain amount of hope.

Stephanie's heart dropped, it seemed, a few inches.

'Good gracious no, Hilda. Why ever should it be Mr Young?… As a matter of fact it is Mr Morly.'

Hilda pretended to be occupied at the sink.

'I see, Miss … you'll be wanting the fire lit.' She was far too discreet to make further comment, but she was disappointed, nevertheless. In her opinion, Mr Young was the man for Miss Stephanie. Mr Morly was *nice* but not in the *street* as the other one!

Stephanie made a certain ceremonial occasion of that evening, dressing very leisurely after her bath and trying to lux-uriate amid the newness and the beauty of her surroundings. Her bedroom, with its rich damask of softest blue and pink, was, she knew, a perfect replica of what it might have been hundreds of years before. The bedstead had a needlework panel of exquisite design in the head-board, and the quilt that adorned it was of the same damask as the hangings – heavy, yet of such artistry in colouring and pastel delicacy as to put to shame the most luxurious materials used to emphasize the modern trend. Between two quaint, latticed windows, stood a bow-fronted chest of drawers and large, oval mirror; its simplicity threw into relief the magnificence of the bed... The carpet was off-white and unobtrusive, but offering a perfect background upon which to paint the picture. An atmosphere of romantic history permeated it all and, in the distance, Caesar's Tower rose above the dark tapestry of trees which enveloped the castle and dipped its shadow in the shimmering light of the river.

Stephanie stood immobile, gazing out upon the scene, feeling the tug of its beauty at her heart and the longing for Nicholas came back sharply, poignantly, so that, swiftly she turned, and almost violently drew a frock from the deep, fitted cupboard. Not to *think* ... not to be subjective. Trevor was coming to dinner... Concentrate on him, inflame the imagination with thoughts of his devotion and desire. Colour touched her cheeks. Why not? Now, she had nothing to lose; there would never be another

Nicholas and, since that was so, Trevor would give her greater happiness than any other man. What love was left to her to give she might just as well give to him and, in fact, had already done so. Time wouldn't alter that beyond, possibly, increasing its measure in the purely physical sense.

Compromise, he had said, and she knew that was the only thing left to her.

The dress she had chosen was of sapphire silk velvet; tight fitting to the waist, outlining her perfect figure and cut into a deep, low, heart-shaped neckline that revealed the exquisite moulding of her breasts. A single string of pearls was her only ornament and no other adornment could have enhanced the picture she finally made as she stood at the chimney corner, while the leaping flames from a log fire played on her dark, chestnut hair and caught avidly at its sorrel tints and seemed, then, to reflect themselves in her large, passionate eyes.

'Stephanie!' Trevor came towards her, appraising her as he moved. 'You fit into all this so wonderfully ... it is a long while since I saw you look so lovely.' His voice was quietly subdued; there was no flattery in its inflection, only a somewhat awed realization of her beauty and vibrant personality. She had, he knew, matured in the face of suffering; the light-hearted, often naïve, girl had become a woman of depth and greater charm; and in that transition was the more desirable.

She made no attempt to deprecate his words, but inclined her head and said graciously:

'Thank you, Trevor...' There was an imperceptible pause. 'How strange this all is and how little I dreamed that I should be installed here so soon, or that Michael, of all people, would marry almost at a moment's notice!' She crossed to an antique cupboard, and drew out the crystal glasses and cocktail shaker.

'This,' she said gaily, 'is where we come back to earth. Cocktails in this room!'

Trevor flashed her a smile. It registered in her mind that, in his evening clothes, he was more than usually attractive and she endeavoured to be moved by that same attraction; to foster it within her mind, see him as a man in whose arms she might find both forgetfulness and sanctuary and an experience that would soften the blow of Nicholas. He moved to her side, took the glass she offered him, raised it and, looking into her eyes, murmured:

'To this night and – us, my darling.'

For an imperceptible second she hesitated and the silence of the room became heavy, almost unbearable in its suspense. The grandfather's clock ticked on ... as it had ticked through several centuries and would go on ticking … reality poised in time, making everything material insignificant; every hope futile; and all human emotions ephemeral. Stephanie was conscious of a certain mesmerism about that moment; conscious of its inevitability and its far-reaching implications. From this hour with Trevor there could be no turning back: she was crossing a bridge between two worlds and leaving Nicholas behind... The heart, the soul of her resisted the journey; but the anguish and pain saturating her mind in longing for him, cried out for the palliative of forgetfulness – even forgetfulness in the arms of another man. She had thought herself strong, invulnerable, but the torment of jealousy, disillusionment, love unfulfilled, had left her bereft of weapons with which to fight and, now, fiercely she rebelled.

Defiantly, she drank to Trevor's toast, her eyes meeting his above the rim of the glass, their expression dark, promising and breath-takingly beautiful. After a second or so they sat down before the fire, talking easily about the day's work, individual problems of a minor nature and then:

'I have to go to Kilnorth Grange next month, by the way,' he said suddenly. 'The Orwells' secretary phoned me today.'

Stephanie sipped her drink.

'We should be able to get some wonderful pieces from that Orwell collection.'

'Will you come with me?' His voice was low.

And her answer came steadily:

'Yes; we could make a long weekend of it. Take it as part of a summer holiday.'

'Excellent idea.' He relaxed. 'We'll run down to London. Time we went gay and did a few shows.'

London! She had imagined Nicholas taking her there and had felt, in advance, the thrill of seeing it again, after many months absence. A thrill no less great than that which came with the return to the country after the whirl was over.

'I'd like that.'

'Good. We're going to have fun, you and I, my sweet.'

Stephanie leaned slightly forward and held out her hands to the blaze, then:

'Trevor?'

'Yes?' He raised his gaze questioningly.

'Quite seriously ... are you honestly not interested in marriage?'

Trevor sat back and, for a moment, became solemn in his reflections. He had told himself for so long that marriage was not for him that he had come to believe it. He said:

'Frankly, Stephanie, my answer is still "no". And, quite contrary to the impression I usually convey, that isn't really cynicism or even evidence of a philandering spirit. *If* I could meet the woman, fall in love with her, find in her the things that I firmly believe are essential in marriage, then I would, quite truthfully, be only too glad to reverse my ideas. But, I don't want less than that or to be shut up in that cage of so-called respectability. I value my freedom far too much and it would have to be "all" before I was prepared to relinquish that freedom. I don't think,' he went on naturally, 'that I have the temperament, or the character, if you like, wholly to fall in love. At any rate it hasn't happened yet.' He looked at her very steadily. 'You are the only person I've ever met that I can bear to think of seeing every day of my life; but that doesn't mean that I am in love with you in the sense that *you* mean. I admire you and love you and you know I desire you; but I would never pretend that my feelings were other than as they are in order to persuade you to make a decision you might regret.'

Stephanie said, and again there was pain in her heart:

'How I admire you for being so frank; for *not* pretending: if you only knew how I've come to despise men who do–' She drew in her breath sharply. 'But one of these days, you will met that "one woman"… I suppose sooner or later it happens to us all – inevitably – that we find what we believe to be our affinity. Whether or not the result is happiness or – or anguish–' A sigh. 'Only fate can decide that. Nevertheless, I do hope that you will meet–'

'I don't particularly want to do so, you know!' He laughed. 'I'm very content as I am. This being torn and agonized and ecstatic in turn seems too much like hard work for me! There is so much *without* that degree of intensity.' He drew her gaze to his. 'This, for instance ... being here with you. A certain excitement, understanding; physical attraction. Those things count a very great deal. Emotion in the frame of freedom; pretty thought,' he added.

'Better by far that than a disastrous marriage. But what of the heights?'

'I believe that one can reach them even without that suffocating love, my darling.'

'I wonder.' Her voice was low. 'Can there be forgetfulness without absolute surrender and can there be absolute surrender without that spark?'

'Between some people – yes,' he insisted.

'Again, at the risk of repetition,' she countered, 'I would say it is much more likely for a man to find it, rather than a woman ... women are so complex; so much a victim of their imagination and, if a certain type, so incurably romantic–'

Trevor leaned out and took her hand.

'Words, my sweet,' he said softly. 'What I mean is a matter of moods, and the man, and the moment. You cannot argue a relationship out of existence before it has begun.'

Her cheeks flushed and her eyes seemed to brighten for that reason.

'No,' she said tensely. 'I suppose that is true.' She relaxed, her head resting against the back of her chair. 'You–'

'I surprise you!'

'Frankly – yes!'

'I surprise myself!' He laughed, 'but what can you expect – being here like this with you, in this setting? Time stands still and one is carried along as on some magic tide.'

Dinner (served faultlessly and eaten by candlelight; the table twinkling with its discreet adornment of crystal and Georgian silver) was a long, lingering meal over which Stephanie and Trevor sat discussing generalities with always the trend leaning towards business. Their common interests were of a practical turn and Stephanie welcomed such conversion. But, reluctantly, and inevitably the moment came to return to the lounge and the coffee that awaited them there.

'That was the height of perfection,' he said. 'Hilda is certainly a wizard and you the–'

'Grateful employer. I'd be absolutely lost without her,' she admitted. 'I can do all that is necessary in a house and I can cook but – not from choice! And to pretend otherwise would be dishonest.'

'Not, in fact, out to ensnare a husband!'

'Definitely not.'

'Personally,' he said, taking the coffee cup she handed to him, 'I am not impressed by the over-domesticated woman who never seems to think of anything outside the oven and the sink! If such misery is forced upon her, through circumstances, I admire her intensely for doing the job cheerfully and expertly … but if I had married, or if ever I were to marry, I'd prefer to be entertained by my wife than merely fed by her! I could pay a cook to satisfy my appetite, but *not* to be gay and amusing and susceptible to my moods – both mental and physical.'

Stephanie smiled.

'That seems to be the general opinion of men. The day of the "little woman" wallowing in the chores is over. I think the war did much to bring that attitude about. No servants and the man realizing the ghastly drudgery entailed in "this domesticity"!'

He laughed.

'How right that is! I was left alone in a place for a week once and, at the end of it, I'd used every cooking utensil and piece of crockery in the place! And,' he added absurdly, 'swept the dust under the mats!'

Stephanie chuckled.

'You'd be a riot as a husband and a poor man!'

The hours went by; the fire burned to glowing embers; the softly shaded table lamps threw a golden light upon the rich panelling.

Trevor reached out and drew Stephanie into his arms as they sat together on the settee; drew her to him with a certain demanding possessiveness that was gentle even in its passion. Before his lips met hers, he looked down questioningly into her eyes without receiving wholly his answer. Fiercely he bent his mouth to hers and now her head was cradled on his shoulder, her body resting across his knees. For a second she lay stiff, almost resisting, and then, suddenly, as one struggling and fighting some invisible enemy, she relaxed against him and, as the pressure of his lips increased, her arms stole up around his neck...

'Darling...' His voice was thick, hoarse; desire leapt from him touching her with faint, but unmistakable caress.

Stephanie knew that this was not what she had asked for from life; knew, that were Nicholas holding her, the world would already have died, thought have been deadened, while only her love and need of him would have remained to plead the cause of an immutable devotion... But Nicholas was not holding her and he would never do so. Probably at that moment he was making love to Hester. Her heart seemed to be split in half by the impact of the idea. She heard Trevor's voice; felt the touch of his hand upon her breast...

The clock ticked on ... the fire burned to a white ash...

CHAPTER XII

Stephanie awakened the following morning in a state of suspense as, for a moment, she tried to reconstruct the events of the previous night and suddenly, consciousness stabbed and she remembered... Trevor...

A strange, unreal sensation stole upon her in the light of reflection; a certain inability to feel either elation or regret but, rather, a certain numbness of acceptance. Emotionally, she remained untouched, but she was psychologist enough to know that thus would it ever be. In love with Nicholas, it was sheer folly to expect that the caresses of another man could enthral her. Why, then, she argued with herself, accept those caresses... And she knew that the alternative would have been a somewhat grim virginity, a barren sense of unfulfilment, as though life were passing her by. What was more, the longing for escape from the perpetual ache in her need of Nicholas, urged her on towards the acceptance of Trevor's attentions.

For all that, a faint pang shot through her: it was not what she had intended to do with her life; what she wanted... Always the thought of marriage – a romantic, sincere marriage – had been her ultimate goal. The fact that she had refused several proposals in her short life, proved the intense power of Nicholas's attraction. Hers was not the nature to indulge indecision. As she knew that, almost at first sight, she loved Nicholas, so, also did she know even as she lay there, that nothing, and no one, would ever take his place. It wasn't her idea of things to cling to this belief, or build up the illusion of any undying devotion; rather was it a fearless acceptance of a grim and unpalatable fact.

She looked at herself in the mirror and her eyes – reflected back at her – seemed to express the words repeating themselves in her brain... Trevor is now your lover... And it suddenly seemed absurd that a single act could thus establish and label a human relationship. And, almost violently came the echo of Nicholas's words: 'You belong to me, my darling ... never forget that, for I never shall'.

'You belong to me'... Colour mounted her cheeks. How like him in his arrogant self-confidence! Well! She had given him his answer!

She dressed in a severely tailored grey flannel suit, with a crisp white blouse and, as she went down to the show-room, the faint, but unmistakable fragrance of bath soap, powder dusted on a fastidiously clean body, followed in her wake. Her slender figure moved in perfect rhythm – smoothly and with grace. Her hair shone, her skin glowed with cleanliness and health, without in any way having the hardness that too often accompanies the ultra vigorous and healthy woman's appearance. Stephanie had a delicacy about her, a certain frailty beneath the glow that enhanced her charm and gave her an essential sensitivity.

Miss West, the assistant, came forward with a smile in greeting. She both liked and respected Stephanie, whose friendliness and consideration for her held all the dignity and kindliness that inspired devotion and loyalty.

'A Mr Young phoned,' she said swiftly. 'I didn't disturb you because he explained that he would be calling in later on as he had to come over to Warwick.'

Stephanie kept her voice casual.

'I see.' But her thoughts began to race. Nicholas! What did he want with her; would he never realize that all she asked was to be left in peace. The voice of sincerity rose plaintively: how false that was… Her heart was already thudding in anticipation.

Actually, Nicholas, no matter how he cursed himself for a fool, had deliberately contrived to see her, even though he lashed himself as behaving after the manner of an adolescent. He might know that Hester's explanation for Stephanie's attitude was correct; he might appreciate that her decision was irrevocable, but that in no way damped the fire of his love for her, or negated the overwhelming desire to see her. Feebly, he had decided that he needed a set of Charles II chairs for his dining-room and why shouldn't he be business-like and order them from her? It might be amusing and helpful, even as Hester said, to behave quite normally and not to refer to the past. A baffled woman was most intrigued by a situation and, in her curiosity, became vulnerable, he reasoned.

He arrived half an hour later. Stephanie had returned to her flat and was informed of his presence by house telephone.

'Please ask Mr Young to come up,' she said smoothly. And with that she made her way to the flat door, opened it and awaited his arrival, hearing his footsteps upon the polished oak stairs and saying lightly the moment he appeared in view:

'I think I shall have to carpet those stairs, after all. Far too noisy.' And in that second, she decided to behave as though he were merely an acquaintance – politely, affably

and on no account to flatter him by antagonism. He was just the kind of man, she
argued with all a woman's illogical absurdity, to regard such antagonism as proof of
regard!

'It could be more discreet that way,' he
said with equal carelessness. He reached the
top. 'There is no need for me to intrude in
your private suite,' he went on: 'I'm here as
a customer.'

They had reached the lounge and,
although instantly it appealed to his artistic
sense, he refrained from comment.

Stephanie studied him. This was not
anything she had expected: he might have
been no more than a prospective buyer
judging by his attitude... Just what was in
his mind?

'What can I do for you,' she said, borrow-
ing his mood and impersonal manner.

'I'm looking for a set of Charles II chairs,'
he said slowly.

She offered him a cigarette from a chased
silver box and indicated a chair, sat down
herself, and said:

'I know where there are some – Kilnorth
Grange, Coventry. But they are not being
sold until next month when they go up for
auction.'

'Could you get them, then?'

'Certainly, if you want them.'

'Then I'd be grateful if you'd make the

purchase for me,' he said pleasantly. For a second he forgot his resolutions: 'I seem to remember that we first met on account of a piece of furniture.'

'The card table you refused to sell.'

'So you do remember?' His eyes held hers with all the old fascination and mastery, weaving their spell upon her, making her heart quicken its beat and her body thrill with the memory of his kisses. How ridiculous it was to imagine that any other relationship could lessen the degree of her need of him. As he sat there, in riding breeches and hacking coat, he had all the careless grace, the virility of manhood of which he was, physically, an excellent specimen. The tan of his skin was smooth, the firm line of his jaw, dominating; the light in his eyes both fearless and fascinating. Looking at him she reflected that he appeared to be the very last man on earth whom one would suspect of deceit, lies, or sensuality. The sweep of his forehead, the set of his dark, fine hair, gave him a certain intellectual intensity emphasized by the level brows and well-spaced eyes. In those seconds, she studied him as she might have studied a stranger, critically and carefully and knowing that, despite her love, she liked that which she saw. She said evenly, giving him no quarter:

'I have an excellent memory, Nicholas.'

'I'm sure you have.' He got to his feet as he spoke, cursing himself for coming on such a fool's errand and feeling the stubborn inflexibility of her will creating a barricade between them.

At that second the door was flung open and Trevor called gaily:

'Hallo, darling! How about playing truant today and–'

He caught sight of Nicholas and paused abruptly.

Nicholas said coolly:

'Good morning, Morly.'

Trevor stepped over the threshold and took up a position at Stephanie's side, receiving her smile and warming to it, although the flame of jealousy burned fiercely. Couldn't that damn fellow keep away!

Stephanie explained Nicholas's visit. Finishing with:

'We could get those chairs from Coventry – couldn't we?'

'Easily.' He looked at Nicholas very levelly. 'They would cost quite a bit.'

'Whatever you feel to be a fair price,' said Nicholas, 'will satisfy me.'

'Very well.' Trevor spoke in a business-like tone.

The phone interrupted them. Stephanie answered it.

Hester said:

'Darling ... would you tell Nicky that I'm

271

waiting for him at the Leycester. He'll understand... May I pop in, later? Around six! 'Bye.'

Stephanie replaced the receiver, her heart was beating in a sick and suffocating pain. So Hester was waiting for him at the hotel. How well she knew his every movement. She gave him the message and, although it was, in fact, wholly unintelligible to him, he said:

'Thanks.' Why waste time explaining that he had no idea Hester was even in Warwick, and less desire to see her! Stephanie would merely be bored and was, obviously, interested only in Trevor. His attitude of possessiveness towards her made Nicholas writhe. He fought against the stinging bitterness of the memory of Hester's words about Stephanie being flirtatious. It seared him to think that, could he have taken her in his arms even then she would have responded – as she had always done. Yet, did that knowledge take the edge of his love for her, his longing for her... He recoiled from the truth that it was not so. Standing there, radiant, appealing, it was as though she drew from him both strength and all resistance. The cool, freshness of her appearance; the tailored suit and the careless grace with which she wore it, gave her that elegance which he admired so intensely, because it was without obvious display; a natural characteristic and not one studiously acquired.

He wanted to stride forward and take her by force, demand that mental and spiritual response which, so far, he believed she had denied him. It was as if some power within him still refused to accept defeat, as though he would not reconcile himself to the belief that such defeat was entirely her wish.

Trevor asked, the mood of truculence passing as his pride of possession made him expansive and subdued his jealousy:

'How's the farming going?'

'Reasonably well. I detest failure and I'll make it a success if it kills me.'

Trevor laughed, but without rancour:

'It probably will! But I sympathize with your point of view.'

Stephanie added to that:

'Failure seems always to be such a personal slight – no matter how great the effort made.' She glanced at Trevor and Nicholas recoiled from the obvious intimacy of the gaze, which held that strange and elusive quality eloquent in itself. 'We were terrified when we started in business here.'

Trevor laughed and confided in Nicholas:

'Stephanie has been our very best customer this month! Simple way to do business!'

Nicholas could not endure the atmosphere of easy and polite friendliness a moment longer. Stephanie contemptuous, scornful… Stephanie relaxing in his arms … but never Stephanie casual and conversational and it was as though Trevor, when he spoke, included her in every word uttered. He moved to the door.

'I must be going.' It was an abrupt sound.

Trevor smiled.

'Even ex-wives hate to be kept waiting!'

Nicholas started: he had completely forgotten Hester and wondered what on earth she wanted.

'True,' he said, without trace of the annoyance he felt at having his former relationship with Hester emphasized thus. 'Good-bye, Stephanie. Thank you for your help.'

Trevor put in easily:

'That's all right, Young; leave it to us…'

Stephanie longed to say something that would prevent Nicholas going just then. There was a certain finality about it that sent a pang of regret over her body. She struggled with the conflicting thoughts of Hester, Nicholas's proposal and her promise… And, then, as one coming back to reality, glanced at Trevor… She had chosen her path and there could be no compromise, no turning back from it. She wandered over to the door and met Nicholas's steady, but inscrutable gaze:

'Thank you,' she said with mock seriousness, 'for your custom!'

Nicholas's laugh was forced and hollow.

'I'll see myself out.' For an imperceptible moment his eyes darkened with a passionate intensity, then: 'It is not entirely strange to me.'

Stephanie looked at him and emotion quivered between them. How vividly she recalled that evening when they explored the flat together and he had kissed her for the first time... It might have been centuries, instead of weeks, ago.

Trevor stepped forward.

'I'm coming down.' He smiled over his shoulder at Stephanie. 'Be back in a moment.'

Nicholas fought the depression that assailed him; fighting the hateful suspicion that had taken shape within his mind when he heard that 'darling' on Trevor's lips as he had greeted Stephanie believing that she was alone. And dismissing it with the reflection that endearments to a man of Trevor's type would mean precisely nothing.

Trevor saw him off the premises with affable farewell. Then, he went swiftly back to Stephanie who awaited him.

'Queer customer that,' he said, as one who had no intention ever again of regarding him as a rival, or of remembering all he had meant to her. 'He can be pleasant when he likes. I think I feel indulgent towards him because it is obvious that he is going to be drawn into Hester's net again!'

Stephanie turned around from the window at which she had been standing, looking out into the cobbled street below.

'That is, of course, absurd! He is a perfectly free agent and doesn't *have* to be with Hester unless he wishes!'

Trevor was careful not to foster the wrong impression.

'True! I wasn't, for one moment, suggesting that, at this stage, he doesn't *want* to be drawn into her net ... only of how bitterly he will regret it afterwards.' He reached her side and drew her close to him, his lips within a few inches of her own. 'But don't let us waste precious moments talking about him, my sweet.' He kissed her gently. Then, almost gravely, drew her to the settee. 'Sit down ... there's something I want to say to you.'

She glanced up at him as he remained standing beside her.

'What is it?' she asked breathlessly. 'You look very solemn – for you!'

Almost restlessly, he sat down beside her and, holding her hand in his began slowly:

'I've done quite a bit of thinking since I left you last night, my darling.'

Stephanie didn't lower her gaze, or betray embarrassment; her attitude was natural and encouraging.

'Was that – necessary?' she asked gently.

'Yes.' He looked down at the hand he held,

smoothed it and said: 'Stephanie let us get married, darling.'

She stared at him aghast.

'Married!' It was an incredulous sound.

He smiled.

'My sweet, what is so outrageous about *that?*'

'Nothing, of course, but... Trevor, we went into all this and you admitted that you had no desire to marry – unless, of course–'

He interrupted her.

'I haven't forgotten a word of all that,' he said truthfully. 'But I realize that you are so different from everyone else and–' He paused. 'I'm not making a very good job of this – am I?'

'I think,' she said softly, 'that you are making a wonderful job of it.'

'Then you will marry me?' It was an eager sound.

She shook her head.

'No, Trevor.' Her voice was low, firm. 'Oh, I appreciate beyond measure your asking me, but – no.'

'Why?' It was a faint, questioning sound.

'Because nothing fundamental has changed since last night, my dear. And I am fully aware of the reason that prompted you to make this suggestion.' She looked at him very frankly: 'I know that you respect me, Trevor; that *you* know my life and that anything promiscuous is hateful to me...

With that knowledge I can accept you as my lover without qualm or loss of dignity.'

He said with a deep sincerity:

'I could not bear you to imagine that I held you cheaply. I know that, in the beginning, my attitude was gay, even irresponsible... Somehow, with you, that seems an insult to all you have to give. My dear, it would be no – no sacrifice, or act of generosity on my part if–'

She interrupted him.

'I realize all that ... but we should do no more than borrow the cloak of marriage to conform to a purely conventional idea. We are not two people madly *in* love and, therefore, we could bring nothing *to* marriage, while accepting from it a certain, even hypocritical, protection.' She paused: 'What is more, Trevor, while I have everything to gain from the legal tie, you have everything to lose.'

He stared at her.

'In heaven's name how do you make that out?'

She didn't prevaricate as she answered him:

'You admit that you have never been in love ... you know I have. I, quite honestly, have no desire whatsoever to marry because I cannot compromise, as I told you before, and accept less than the heights merely for the sake of *being* married. You, on the other hand, may fall in love tomorrow … and even though you know I would release you, it wouldn't be the same and cause a great deal of upheaval.' She added quietly: 'At this moment, we are two free people, answerable only to ourselves for our actions and hurting no one. If we can find happiness, and an emotional outlet, in each other's company, all well and good. Only let us not confuse the issues.' She entwined her fingers more closely in his. 'I should never forgive myself if that happened. But … bless you for looking at all this as you do.'

'Bless you, for understanding how I feel, my sweet.'

She subjected him to a very steady scrutiny:

'Only honesty between us, ever! You know you are free, Trevor, and should you want to alter your life and change all this, you have only to say so. No strings, my dear. I hate them unless they are tied voluntarily with an undying love. Anything less than that is, to me, sheer mockery and vile hypocrisy. I have no intention, whatsoever, of indulging secrecy, or sneaking around corners. Neither do I intend to shout my affairs from the house-tops.'

'And – Michael?'

'He will see it my way and, even if he didn't, my life is my own.'

'I'd hate to cause trouble.'

279

She smiled.

'You won't do anything of the kind.'

He looked at her earnestly:

'You're about the loveliest person any man could wish to find.'

She shook her head.

'I can't agree with you, of course, but ... how strange it is that we cannot fall *in* love where we best *love*.'

'I could have persuaded myself that I was in love with you last night,' he admitted honestly.

She spoke on the breath of a regretful sigh.

'The falsity of emotional thraldom that borrows the mirror of love in the hope of finding there its own reflection,' she said softly. 'How easy to deceive oneself.' Her gaze was earnest.

'I suppose so.' He chuckled softly. 'Most women imagine every man they meet to be in love with them; you go to great lengths to prove to the contrary!'

Stephanie said sagely:

'When women adopt that attitude, and imagine that every man is in love with them, it is only because no man is – and they are sadly and bitterly aware of the fact.'

Trevor's laugh was low and appreciative.

'How right!' He added: 'You're a pretty wise person.'

She shook her head.

'Wisdom is something a woman has when

dealing with the lives of those around her: never when she is dealing with her own.'

'Quite epigrammatical!' He admired her with a glance. 'You, at least, would always emerge gracefully from any situation, my sweet. Folly can be redeemed by a dignified exit – always. I don't suppose there is anything on earth a man loathes more than a woman – no matter what her position in his life may be or may have been – who doesn't know when to write *finis!* Or, for that matter, the woman who deliberately angles for him in the first place. I think we men definitely have the scent for that type!'

'And, like the devils you are, egg them on, flirt with them in order to scorn and ridicule them behind their back.'

'Sounds grim,' he confessed. 'But you are about right. You must admit, though, that they dam' well ask for it.'

Stephanie laughed.

'Just where has this conversation got to – such *perfect* grammar!' she finished apologetically.

And all the time she was talking she was, in truth, thinking of Nicholas and struggling to deaden the echo of his voice in her ears. Wherever she looked it was as though that same thought were visual and she could picture him standing there ... he was far more real to her than Trevor's physical presence. She said suddenly, jerkily:

'Trevor, let's play truant and go out somewhere today. There's nothing on that Miss West cannot handle and I'm in the mood!'

He jumped to his feet.

'Precisely what I was going to suggest to you when I found Young here,' he said blithely. 'Where shall it be?'

'Let's wind our way to Kenilworth and Hampton-in-Arden, then to Temple Balsall. Oh, just anywhere!'

'That will do to start with.' He drew her to her feet.

'I must be back to see Hester about six,' she exclaimed.

'Damn Hester!'

'Trevor!'

'Oh, very well, darling... Meet me downstairs, I'll have a word with Miss West.' He held her against him and kissed her lingeringly. Then: 'Happy?'

She met his steady gaze without flinching.

'As happy as I possibly can be – like you!'

'Cleverly put.'

'No; honestly put.'

'I can't win – can I?'

She moved away from him and threw him a little smile over her shoulder.

'I don't think you've made such bad progress,' she said lightly.

And with that she vanished into the bedroom. Trevor ran down the stairs; he felt singularly gay and carefree. Trust Stephanie never to take advantage of a situation. All the same, he felt the better for having asked her to marry him. She would know, at least, that his regard for her was invested with esteem and importance such as any wife might inspire. He was, he knew, a singularly fortunate man and he prayed fervently that nothing might transpire in the future to change this very excellent and satisfactory relationship.

CHAPTER XIII

Hester arrived at the flat immediately after six, coming into it with an air of approval and admiration calculated to win favour.

'But this is quite perfect, darling,' she cooed and, sensing that Stephanie was not impressed by her particular tone of voice, reverted to her normal thin, and somewhat cold, tones. 'You really have the most amazing flair for colour; and furnishing!' A laugh. 'I shall have to call you in to do Wilderness Farm when the time comes ... thank you for giving my message to Nicky.' She sat down as she spoke and drew off a pair of long, black suede gloves. It registered in Stephanie's mind that she looked overdressed in black with a rather too massive fur cape that was anything but slimming. 'We've been to buy a car,' she volunteered. 'Found just a snip: Talbot. Nicky has a nose for bargains. I simple had to have a car; his was not enough, even though he has been very generous over lending it to me ... darling, you look very alluring tonight!' Her somewhat greedy eyes fixed themselves into a deliberate gaze until Stephanie found herself colouring – much to her own annoyance.

Stephanie busied herself with pouring out the drinks.

'I've been out all day – the country is too good to miss at this time of year.'

'With Trevor?' Hester took the glass and looked up from her position on the settee as she spoke.

'Yes.' Stephanie was wrestling with the problem of whether or not to tell Hester the truth and her reluctance to do so was in no way indicative of a desire for secrecy but, rather, because she hated the thought lest Hester might introduce a bantering note of cheapness into her comments. On the other hand, she and Hester were very close and Hester might well be hurt at what could, at a later date, appear to be lack of trust, or confidence, should she not be made privy to the facts.

'All I can say is, my dear, that you should

repeat the outing more often. I've never seen you look quite as you do tonight.' A smile. 'Something *about* you–' Hester paused. She was feeling her way. For days she had it fixed firmly in her mind that Stephanie and Trevor would, eventually, indulge in some romantic association. The moment Stephanie realized that Nicholas was lost to her (quite apart from her own dismissal of him) she argued to herself, Trevor would inevitably come into the picture as comforter. Yet, in her selfish, perverted mind, she hated the idea that while Stephanie could attract two men she, herself, was having to fight desperately hard to secure one. And while, for her own ends, she wanted Stephanie safely installed in Trevor's life she, nevertheless, resented the idea that she might, in the process, find happiness! Hester was prepared only to allow the other person the reflection of her *own* happiness, never that actual happiness itself: hers was the prerogative of gaiety, of success and even of popularity.

Stephanie still could not bring herself to the point of confidence as she exclaimed:

'I think a day away from business and the peace of the countryside is about as good a tonic as anything.'

Hester laughed.

'That, my child, is positively naïve... I love that frock; blue is definitely your colour and

I was always addicted to an accordion pleated skirt. You're a most attractive person, Stevie – truly you are.' She wanted to ingratiate herself; to inspire a cosy, confidential air and, giving Stephanie credit for her own weakness, imagined that flattery was an excellent stepping stone. 'By the way, are you going to the Charity Ball at Castle Grange next month?'

'I hadn't given it a thought; we're only just in June; the ball isn't until the end of July.'

'Not the end, Stevie – the twelfth. I was talking to Nicholas about it today. He's going to take me... I expect Trevor will take you – won't he?'

'Probably.' Stephanie felt a sudden disinclination to discuss Trevor.

Hester, crossing her legs and gently swinging one while she looked down first at her toe and then at the ceiling with an expression of faintly mocking challenge, said:

'Very evasive all of a sudden, my pet. You wouldn't be hiding anything from little Hester, would you?' A hard-done-by look: 'And after the way I've confided in *you*, too.'

Stephanie said quite steadily:

'There is no question of my being secretive, Hester or wishing to keep things hidden from you. But–' She paused significantly, 'we all have some events in our lives that–'

Hester became suddenly bold and made a shot in the dark.

'It's Trevor, isn't it? He's your lover?'

The question was direct, inescapable and Stephanie had neither the wish, nor the intention, of lying about the matter. All the same, a slight irritation possessed her that Hester should be so inquisitive.

She said quietly:

'Since you ask me – yes.'

Hester overcame her first, tingling jealousy and switched over to the gloating relief. Wait until Nicholas heard that! She beamed and purred the words:

'But, darling! I'm so glad for you! I just knew there was something.'

'You mean you – hoped,' Stephanie could not resist saying swiftly.

Hester dared not reveal her intense annoyance, but she exclaimed:

'Darling! What a funny thing to say!'

Stephanie stood her ground, goaded by an instinct she could not understand.

'I don't think it funny. After all, Hester, you've always been most anxious that I should marry Trevor and–'

'I've,' Hester interrupted, 'always been most anxious to see you happy. I don't think you quite understand me over all this.'

Stephanie overcame her irritation.

'Suppose we forget it, my dear.'

'By all means.' A laugh. 'I must remember in future that you are rather touchy on the subject, mustn't I?'

Stephanie ignored that and the matter was dropped. But a shadow seemed to fall upon her heart and, although she hated having to admit the fact, she knew she was more than glad when Hester, some two hours later – and after dinner – said she must be going.

Hester had been itching to get away. Excitement surged within her. That final victory was hers. Now, she had nothing more to fear from Stephanie and could, therefore, gradually break away from her. Her thoughts gathered momentum. Stephanie wasn't anything she had imagined her to be... She scratched around to find faults hitherto undreamed of. Of course it was *her* business if she chose to take a lover, but she really couldn't be expected to hold her in quite the same regard, or high esteem. It wasn't after all, the thing ... and there was nothing whatsoever to prevent their being married. She caught avidly at that. Marriage would have been far more satisfactory from her own point of view ... although Nicholas would hardly tolerate Stephanie once he knew about this. A hateful gleam of malicious delight came to her eyes. But she'd had to drag the truth out of her... Trust Stephanie; the dark horse, concealing everything connected with her intimate life. No, she concluded, from now on she would be very guarded and have as little to do with her as possible ... just enough to allow her to be conversant with the facts of her life. But, at least, she had succeeded in removing her from Nicholas's path. She congratulated herself. It had, after all, been a pretty clever piece of work.

She dare not intrude on Nicholas again that night, although deliberately she drove past the farm, longing to go in, yet fearful of being obvious. It was at about ten that she decided to walk down the by-lane leading to it. Often Nicholas took the dog out at that hour and it might well be that they would meet. Which they did.

'And so I'm caught trespassing,' she said apologetically.

Nicholas craved solitude, but felt no irritation at her presence: she wasn't important enough for that.

'Hardly trespassing. This is my land, but everyone enjoys the right of way over this particular spot.'

'And *what* a spot!' She took in the view of the Cotswolds as she spoke, their dark, sombre ridge flung against a sky bannered by the pastel shades of the afterglow, like a multi-coloured sea. 'Could anything be lovelier?'

The farm lands lay dark beneath the approaching night; the air was laden with the sweet, sharp fragrance of dew-drenched earth, crisp bracken, giant firs. The sweep of newly turned acres, the olive green of woodland rising from deep valleys...

'No,' said Nicholas and even as he gazed the picture dissolved and became Stephanie's face.

Hester fell into step beside him.

'I've been to see Stephanie, as you know.'

Nicholas was arrested by her inflection.

'That sounds almost portentous.'

'It is, really. I'm foolish perhaps, but I'm so fond of her that I hate to think of her doing the wrong thing. It isn't easy to advise a person, is it?'

Nicholas felt a growing impatience. What was the woman gibbering about. He said tersely:

'Doesn't that rather depend on the kind of advice needed?'

Hester looked up at him without smiling.

'I suppose so; but when it comes to romance–' She sighed. 'I never feel I've said quite the right thing.'

'Romance.' Nicholas spoke sharply. 'Does Stephanie need advice on that subject?'

Hester played her hand with care and craftiness:

'I should have given it to her, had I known, whether she had asked for it or not.'

'This,' said Nicholas, 'is all very mysterious.'

Hester changed her attitude.

'The fact is, Nicholas, that I had a shock tonight.' She gave him a meaning look. 'As you know, I've always felt that Trevor and Stephanie were more to each other than she would ever admit, but I'd no *idea* that it had gone as far as it has.' She paused to lend drama to her words and extract the last ounce of suspense from them.

Nicholas's face paled. His question came almost challenging.

'Meaning just what?'

Hester sighed regretfully. Then:

'Just that Stephanie told me herself that Trevor was her lover. Odd, I'd never thought along those lines; never had the faintest suspicion.' She raised an innocent gaze to his. 'Had you?'

Nicholas felt as though he had received a severe kick just beneath the heart; sickness stole upon him.

'I don't believe it,' he exclaimed, as one talking to himself.

Hester kept a very cool head.

Ironical if he should refuse to believe the truth when she imparted it, while having previously believed the lies she had told him!

'That is hardly flattering to me... Why *ever* should Stephanie confide a thing like that unless it were true? She wasn't in the least squeamish about it and involved me in no promise of secrecy. In fact, to be honest, it seemed to me that she wanted me to tell *you*, particularly, about it.'

'Really!' It was an icy sound. 'It would have been very much better if she had told me the truth *herself* in the beginning,' he said harshly. A glimmer of hope pierced the anguish. 'How – how long has this been going on?'

Hester sighed.

'She didn't, actually, say; but she conveyed the impression that it was quite some time.' Her brain conjured up a perfect alibi. 'She spoke of moving to the flat because it made it so much easier for Trevor to come to her there; whereas, at Willow Corner, well ... there was Michael. So, it... Oh, Nicky; I'm sorry: this has hurt you – hasn't it?'

Nicholas was wrestling with a dozen demons each more damnable than the last. So, all the time, Stephanie had been fooling him... Even lying. How well he recalled her words about Trevor almost on their first outing together: 'He is not my lover if that is what you mean!' It seemed utterly unbelievable, fantastic, that she could be guilty of such absolute deception. And he said involuntarily, as one unable to bear his own suffering:

'Are you *sure*, Hester?'

Hester did not lose her temper, although she was perilously near to doing so, as her jealousy and hatred of Stephanie mounted in face of Nicholas's obvious reactions.

'Oh, Nicky, *is* that the kind of thing one imagines? You know I've always linked them together.' She struck another blow. 'Think back – I can remember every word now: one is always so wise after the event – didn't I, on the first night I met you again, suggest that they would marry? I sensed something, but in all truth, never for a *moment* that he was her lover. Although again, as I told you, I knew that Stephanie was the flirtatious, physical type ... well, that's different.' She hastened: 'Don't think I'm condemning her: it is her life and she is free to do what she chooses with it. I've told you simply because I know that, even though nothing was said, she wanted you to be told. Were that not so, she probably wouldn't have confided in anyone – not even me.'

Nicholas clenched his teeth for a fraction of a second, then:

'Thank you for enlightening me, my dear, and for sparing me further humiliation.' A sensation of acute embarrassment over-whelmed him as he thought of his pathetic ruse to see her only that very day; his insistence that, despite her rejections of him, somewhere that spark burned within her in love of him. Poor, blind fool! He cursed inwardly. And all the time... That very morning... Incidents came back to sear him. The way Trevor had come into the room, not knowing that he, Nicholas, was there ... the 'darling' and the manner in which he spoke for her; the intimacy of their friendliness. How easy it was to piece together and realize the truth. He said, with a certain defiant anger that made his voice rough, uncompromising. 'I think I need a drink – how about joining me?'

Hester glowed.

'Very well,' she agreed. 'If you like.'

She wasn't deceived: she knew why Stephanie had behaved as she had, just as she had a very strong suspicion that this relationship with Trevor was of a very ,very recent nature. She was madly in love with Nicholas – it stood out a mile – and Trevor was to assuage her wounds. She sighed inwardly. What a brilliant move it had been on her own part to extract that promise from her... Stephanie was just the kind of fool to keep it and even to take a lover as guarantee!

Hester slipped her hand surreptitiously through Nicholas's arm. He didn't withdraw, or convey impatience. They walked on in silence.

CHAPTER XIV

The night of the Charity Ball at Castle Grange followed, for Stephanie, weeks of reconstruction, when she endeavoured to accept life, and her own position and to make the best of both. Michael, while understanding the situation between her and Trevor, nevertheless, regretted it because knowing Stephanie, he appreciated the significance behind such a decision and deplored the fact that she could not have found happiness with Nicholas whom, he knew, she still loved.

During those weeks, Stephanie saw Nicholas only once and then the meeting had been on strictly business lines, and when the chairs he had ordered were delivered. His attitude of terse, polite coldness had stabbed her, but she had returned it and remained in his company less than ten minutes, vowing to avoid him, at all costs, in future.

'I have no desire,' she said to Trevor, 'to go to this ball tonight. I'd far rather you take me out to dinner somewhere – quietly.'

'Darling,' he insisted, 'we cannot back out, now. Michael and Felice are calling for us and it will be their first real "family" outing since their marriage. And Felice's people expect it of you: you did *say* you'd go, after all.'

'I know.' It was a weary sound.

Trevor smiled.

'No use; you cannot get out of it, my sweet: all you can do is to look your most glamorous for my sake! How about it?'

She smiled back at him.

'You're a very nice person, Trevor.' She

paused thoughtfully. 'We'll always be friends, whatever happens – won't we? I mean, even if you should marry later on?'

Trevor crossed to her and placed a hand on her forehead.

'What on earth is that for?' she demanded.

'To make sure you haven't a temperature,' he said comically.

They laughed together.

Stephanie bathed and dressed that evening rather after the manner of one in a trance. Only when, finally, she stood before the panel mirror in a shimmering white chiffon frock, embroidered in silver thread, did she come back to the awareness of her surroundings and the possibilities of the evening ahead. At least, the gown was, in itself, beautiful, with its masses of material which flared out when she moved, like a giant umbrella which, nevertheless, closed to an exquisitely slender line when her body was still. The bodice, a wispy affair, off the shoulder, revealed the gentle curves of her breasts and, against her white, velvety skin a single string of small diamonds – left to her by a maternal great-grandmother – gleamed like stars, twinkling, fiery. No other jewellery, apart from a diamond ring, spoilt the picture she ultimately presented as she made her way down the three steps and so to the lounge where Trevor awaited her.

At the sight of her, he exclaimed:

'Darling! That's absolutely perfect.'

She swirled around, childishly pleased with the manner in which the skirt revolved, until it was a vast circle in a line with her waist. For a split second she felt young and gay. Then, abruptly, she stopped, as depression seeped back, hating the weakness that made her heart ache for Nicholas and detesting the feeling of disloyalty that engulfed her because of Trevor.

He helped her into her ermine jacket as the sound of Michael and Felice's voices were heard outside the door.

'Hallo there!' Trevor went forward, taking in the details of Felice's pencil slim, scarlet crepe frock which suited her particular type of beauty. 'Michael, old man, we shall certainly have the belles of the ball tonight.'

Felice, starry-eyed, happy beyond her wildest dreams, cried:

'Stephanie! That dress is heavenly! Honestly, you've never looked lovelier.' Her voice was deep and sincere and Stephanie warmed to it.

'Good! Then I can forget it,' she said naturally. 'If there is one thing I loathe it is having to think of one's clothes after one leaves the house!'

Felice said quietly:

'The essence of being well dressed is never to *have* to do so! My mother impressed that on me in my teens. "Choose the right thing to begin with, my child, and forget it! The well-dressed woman is one who has the minimum of clothes, but always the garment for the occasion and is never 'overdressed'!'" She laughed. 'I've never forgotten it and tried to live up to it... We're nice and early.'

Trevor poured out the drinks.

'And it is a fine, warm night, too, thank heaven. Fairy lights, rain and cold do not go together.'

They chatted easily and with understanding friendliness. Felice said:

'I saw Hester this morning; she was in very good spirits, but lamenting the fact that she just couldn't find the right shoes for her evening frock! You know, I just can't like that woman, or feel that she's sincere.'

Stephanie didn't speak. She had seen very little of Hester during those weeks and while not antagonistic on that account, was shrewd enough – even in her generosity – to realize that Hester, having immobilized her and made quite sure that she was no threat to her future with Nicholas, had very little use for her as a result. She tried to still the voice within her which deplored such conduct and to stem the tide of her disillusionment and, up to a point, succeeded; but the bloom had gone from the friendship. In the circumstances, since she imagined that Hester and Nicholas were on the verge of re-marrying, it was the best thing; but a nasty taste had been left in her mouth, all the same.

Castle Grange – home of Sir William and Lady Graceton – stood on the outskirts of Warwick and was set against tiered, woodland slopes which rose above its Elizabethan turrets and loomed as a magnificent canvas on which the old stone walls were painted. Its moated grandeur gave an atmosphere wholly medieval so that, as one passed through the massive, spiked gates, over the drawbridge, and so into the central archway, one slid back into the mists of time and breathed the romance of another age. Every year the ball was held in aid of hospital funds; every year, garlanded, festooned with fairy lights and lanterns, the grounds were opened to the public and people converged for miles around.

Within the Grange itself, in the lofty, vaulted ballroom, with its rich tapestries, exquisite maple panelling and priceless chandeliers, friends and acquaintances and all civic personnel, were invited to a special dance which began at nine-thirty and went on until the early hours of the morning. The event was the highlight of the summer season and proceeded yearly with a minimum of restriction and without incident. Stage and screen stars mingled with the crowds, selling their autographs for the charity, and finally joining the dances. Sir

William and Lady Graceton, were a beloved couple fast approaching their seventies, but with a spirit of youth unquenched; their happiness and the success of their marriage shone in their bright, friendly eyes, and they gave to their home an atmosphere, of simplicity and warmth.

Michael and Stephanie had known them for many years for they were life-long friends of their parents. Actually, Stephanie, while loving, normally, the gaiety of that particular evening, much preferred her casual visits to them, especially in winter when the grounds lay white under their covering of frost rime and the countryside, stark, even grey, took to itself all the grimness and splendour which not even the lushness of summer could improve. To Stephanie, Castle Grange was a winter home; the stone walls seeming to be a part of the sombre skyline and stand, rugged, invulnerable against the shrieking, north winds.

On this night, however, as she felt her feet sinking onto the dry, springy lawns, a certain excitement possessed her, making her shiver in anticipation. As far as eye could see, twinkling lights shimmered among the trees; from the uncurtained, open windows, beams of amber flooded the grounds like giant fans of light pouring from a stage. Music came hauntingly, romantically from the ballroom; the swirl of dancers, the soft swish of perfumed skirts, the subdued murmur of voices... All went to make up the glorious and incredible scene.

She glanced around her when, finally, Trevor insisted that they must have the waltz just beginning. She knew for whom she was looking, but she had been dancing for quite some time before her gaze rested upon Nicholas who, with Hester at his side, stood by the entrance as one appraising, or criticizing, the picture that met his eye. His tall figure, handsome in evening dress, appeared to lift itself from the rest of the gathering and Stephanie's heart lurched painfully with the realization that time, in its passing, in no way lessened her love for him, or the yearning that love awakened.

Trevor followed her gaze and said disgustedly:

'That woman is like a very large black beetle!' A chuckle. 'Can't say your friend looks exactly bursting with happiness. Wonder if they're married again yet?'

Stephanie said, hating the very idea so much that she could not keep the impatience from her voice:

'Of course not! Hester would have told me.'

'Yes ... I suppose so. They've seen us and... Michael and Felice have joined them. Suppose we'd better go over. The music *would* stop now!'

Stephanie seemed to walk without volition; her figure moving with such grace and litheness as to create a fascination in itself.

Nicholas watched her, unable to remove his gaze from her slim, supple body, conscious almost to the point of madness of Trevor's claim upon her and of his own humiliation at her hands.

Hester gushed.

'Stephanie, my dear, you look enchanting ... doesn't she, Nicky? That frock, so – so simple and–' She smoothed her hips as she spoke, as one waiting for the compliment to be returned and unable to find the words with which to finish the sentence.

Stephanie did no more than smile; she thought Hester's dress anything but becoming and far too tight and she could not be hypocrite enough to compliment her. She glanced at Nicholas:

'I cannot imagine your liking all this,' she said pointedly.

'You imagine correctly; on the other hand I appreciate the setting enormously and I think Sir William and his wife are the finest couple one could ever wish to meet.'

Hester chuckled.

'Dear Nicky; he really should have been born in the age of ruffles and knee-breeches!'

'Heaven forbid,' groaned Trevor. 'I'd hate to have missed this particular century.'

Nicholas looked at Stephanie:

'And you?' He spoke almost coldly, but

there was an expression in his eyes that baffled her; an expression of anger touched with passion; a challenging gaze that left her breathless and excited.

'I wish it were possible to go back and live for a brief while in all the ages,' she replied. 'They each have so much on the credit and debit side.'

Nicholas tensed.

'A very typical feminine reaction. In short, you want to have your cake and eat it.'

'I don't think,' she countered swiftly, 'that your simile is a particularly good one. Or that my reactions are so feminine: in fact it is mostly the man who wants that privilege.'

Felice cried gaily:

'If you two intend starting a debating society why not slip into one of the ante-rooms and enjoy yourselves!'

Nicholas forced a laugh. Hester frowned and, tugging at his arm, said:

'This is our dance, Nicky … we mustn't miss a moment of it.'

Nicholas could not escape and he knew it but, before taking the floor, he said to Stephanie:

'I claim the privilege of continuing our debate with the next waltz.'

Hester said as she and Nicholas were out of range of the others:

'I thought you would be glad to escape, Nicky.'

Nicholas was both thankful and, contradictorily, sorry. The sight of Stephanie with Trevor, in the light of his present knowledge, could but be a torture; yet in her presence all the old yearning and need crept back to reinforce his love for her. He knew that, for the past weeks, he had moved after the fashion of an automaton; nothing had been quite real to him except the pain that turned and stabbed at his heart like a knife. Hester during that time had been, he reflected, more than kind and sympathetic. Never obtrusive; but, somehow, had always managed to be there while in no way conveying the impression that she was endeavouring to plead her own cause.

'I suppose I was,' he said quietly.

Hester looked up at him as they danced:

'I somehow resent the feeling that Stephanie is mocking you and pitying me,' she said cunningly.

He stared at her.

'That is absurd!'

'Is it? She seems always to be hitting out – even if slyly – at you. I thought, at least, that once she knew the truth about you and our divorce, she would have been different. I'm terribly disappointed in her, Nicky: she just has no understanding of my feelings and regards me with a kind of contemptuous pity.'

'Really!' Nicholas looked grim. He glanced

to where Stephanie and Trevor were dancing across the ballroom and, in that instant, saw Trevor's lips touch Stephanie's cheek in a swift, surreptitious caress. Every nerve in his body seemed to become taut like a violin string; a sickness enveloped him. And, suddenly, as a man fiercely resolved; a man realizing that only by fighting could he hope to recover from the madness that consumed him, as he said almost tersely:

'Suppose I were to sell up the farm, Hester and—' He paused while emotion after emotion flooded his body in nauseating rapidity... All his hopes, his plans ... his fight against Stephanie; his ultimate capitulation as he realized how deeply he loved her... The first ecstasy of believing she cared... Her attitude after Hester's return; her falseness, when all the time Trevor was her lover... The whole story flashed through his mind like the back projection in a film. And he knew he had come to the end of his resistance that from now on, he must carve a new life; escape, somehow, from himself. Warwick, Winchcombe, the continual proximity; the continual frustration and anger – all were futile and effete. This was where he did something practical about it.

Hester's pulse quickened. Now ... now was the moment when, without being aware of it, Nicholas was going to propose to her.

'I think,' she murmured helpfully, 'that it

would be a very good idea to leave this district. I know you are not happy here... Why not a trip abroad somewhere?'

Nicholas experienced a sudden longing to get away.

'It might be a good idea,' he said reflectively. 'Although alone–'

Hester pressed closer to him.

'Must it be alone, Nicky?'

He stared down at her.

'I see no way of–'

She cut in:

'All this time, Nicky, I've watched you, realized that your feelings were very much concerned with Stephanie ... but that hasn't changed me, or my feelings for you. I know how you feel about Stephanie, so that there would be no question of misunderstanding between us... And I know, too, that at the moment, all you want from me is just, well, friendship shall we say? Don't you think that might be a very good basis for something stronger. I'm alone; and so are you.' She pleaded, her eyes meeting his. 'Must I say more?'

Nicholas felt suddenly grim and at war with life. Why not seek escape that way. Hester had, after all, changed beyond recognition and she had been ready to stand by him, help him all this while. He said, after the manner of a man plunging recklessly, knowing that only by such a method would he have the necessary courage:

'No.' He spoke as one challenging some invisible enemy. 'And if you are prepared to face the future with me, having no illusions about the nature of my regard for you.' He paused and added: 'Perhaps we may still make something of our lives.'

Hester wanted to hear the actual words on his lips.

'You mean for us to re-marry.' She hardly dare breathe so great was the tension and suspense.

Nicholas had a curious sensation as though all this were happening to someone else and not him; it was quite unreal and yet, in some strange, unfathomable way, he was goaded to action.

'Yes; just that.'

Hester said:

'Oh, Nicky... It will all be so different; I've learned so much.'

He didn't want to discuss the matter and she, wisely, did not pursue it beyond saying:

'May I ask that it be soon? It has been rather a strain for me, and I honestly believe that the best thing would be for us to get right away – from all the old associations, even as you suggested just now.'

'I leave the date to you,' he said casually. 'As for leaving the farm; it will take some while to get rid of and there is quite a bit of my capital sunk there.'

Hester said, making the admittance openly for the first time:

'I am rather a wealthy woman, you know, darling.'

Nicholas frowned.

'That doesn't affect *my* position, Hester.'

'But, *darling*–' She looked up at him with a melting tenderness: 'Between us, isn't it rather absurd?'

Nicholas stood his ground.

'I'm not *concerned* about the financial aspect,' he insisted, 'merely that I would like to sell out before leaving England.'

'That might take some time.' She dared not be persistent, but having won her case, she wanted, instantly, to dominate him.

'We shall have to see.'

'So long as we leave the district,' she said. 'In any case, Nicky, I've been so disillusioned in Stephanie that I cannot feel the same friendship for her and I hate being insincere. She was very good to me when I returned to England, but so much has happened since then.'

'Don't worry,' he assured her somewhat sombrely. 'I am just as anxious to get away from the district as you.'

Hester beamed at him.

'I'm so terribly fond of you,' she whispered. 'I'm glad, Nicky, that I've always cared ... it makes this somehow right – doesn't it. And, in time, I know you will feel differently.'

'Yes,' he murmured dubiously, 'I suppose I shall.'

The music ended and as they were making their way to a quiet ante-room, a voice behind them said:

'Good evening.' The tone was both light and yet somehow challenging.

Nicholas swung round.

'Valerie,' he said in obvious and unmistakable delight.

Hester looked sickly.

'Oh, hallo,' she murmured in a thin voice. 'I heard you were staying with the Morgans.'

Valerie, natural, and at ease was smiling up at Nicholas, feeling a glow of pleasure as she did so. He hadn't change and the years of their friendship became suddenly very precious to her. How much they had once been through together; how staunch and reliable he had been. She glanced at Hester ... and how damnably treacherous *she* had been ... and, just, raced her brain, what was she doing here with him?

Before anything further could be said, Trevor and Stephanie, Michael and Felice joined them. Stephanie found herself staring at Valerie almost in mesmerized fascination while the blood chilled in her veins ... seeing her there with Nicholas, remembering their relationship... How completely master of the situation Nicholas was; no embarrassment; no awkwardness; just that calm, smooth manner, that determined and decisive voice with its low, attractive tones. She said to Valerie:

'We have met.'

Nicholas arched his brows.

'At Michael's wedding,' Valerie explained. She added almost apologetically: 'I'm so sorry, Stephanie, I couldn't keep my promise to look you up and get my precious settle, but I was called back to London for rehearsals and have only just got away again.'

Hester stood there, tensed, predatory, waiting for the perfect opening, aware of Stephanie's gaze somewhat apprehensively and sympathetically upon her and she began in a slow, impressive tone:

'You *couldn't* have chosen a more opportune moment to come back, Valerie.' She moved to Nicholas's side, slipped her arm possessively through his, glanced from face to face, her gaze lingering for a second longer when it came to Stephanie, then: 'You see, it just so happens that Nicky and I have, only this evening, decided to re-marry.' A little laugh. 'So all's well that ends well – eh?'

Stephanie longed to escape; the colour went from her cheeks; the strength from her legs. She had waited for this moment in an agony of suspense, told herself that she was quite prepared for it but, now that it was an established fact the shock stunned her. She felt Nicholas's eyes upon her and managed to raise her own, fought to draw a blind down upon the pain she was afraid might be reflected there and, before anyone else had time to speak, said gaily:

'Congratulations to you both.' She could not resist adding: 'Although we have all expected it, you know.'

Trevor came forward, his gaze was upon Valerie and it seemed that hers leapt to his.

'Since no one will introduce us,' he said deliberately, changing the subject for Stephanie's sake and much to Hester's fury, 'my name is Trevor Morly ... we ought to have met at the wedding, but I couldn't leave the grind-stone... You're Valerie Brown.'

'Yes,' she said, breathlessly.

'Shall we dance?' He crooked his arm as he spoke and, with a challenging glance at Hester and Nicholas, and a warm little smile in Stephanie's direction, led her away.

Hester said, aggrieved:

'Well! What extraordinary behaviour!'

Stephanie squared her shoulders; no one must suspect her hurt.

'Trevor is nothing if not tactful,' she exclaimed.

Instantly, Hester realized that they were on dangerous ground. Stephanie, from Nicholas's point of view, was supposed to know the truth about the divorce and of both his and Valerie's innocence ... why, then should tact

311

be necessary. She cried hastily:

'The charm of the actress … they make a wonderful pair – don't they? Valerie always was a perfect dancer, I must admit.' She looked up at Nicholas who was frowning after the manner of a man slightly confused and uncertain of what to do.

At that moment the orchestra struck up a waltz and, without another word, he moved to Stephanie's side:

'This,' he said tensely, 'is ours.'

Stephanie allowed him to guide her into the ballroom; she was incapable of coherent thought and her heart was beating so madly that she could hardly speak. His arms went around her swiftly, surely and closely; they moved away as one person.

Neither spoke for some minutes, then:

'Our first and our last dance together,' he said hoarsely.

'Swan song,' she countered.

'Swan song', the words caught at his imagination, swirling him back to the days of their first meeting when he had insisted that it should be the 'swan song' of his association with her.

She added swiftly:

'I hope you and Hester will be very happy, Nicholas.' Her voice was unsteady and no matter what restraint she fought to maintain she could feel her heart pounding against him and, in return, his thudding as though in her own breast.

'Thanks.' It was a clipped, uncompromising sound.

'I seem to remember saying to you once, "They always go back".' She struggled to be faintly cynical and bantering. 'And, thus, once more the theory is proved correct.'

'Circumstances play a very great part,' he said grimly.

'Of course.' Now her eyes met his in faint bitterness.

'Suppose,' he went on coolly, 'we mention your affairs for a change.'

Stephanie's heart stopped, so it seemed and, then reduced the swiftness of its beat. Pain, anguish, a sick depression came upon her like a pall. Only by hitting out, taking the fight to him, appearing hard and sophisticated, could she hope to get through the ordeal of that dance. Never, never should he have the satisfaction of knowing she cared; or of feeling that she was in any way affected by his decision to re-marry. Deliberately, without flinching, and in a calm, casual tone, she said:

'Why not? I feel reasonably sure that Hester has told you about Trevor and me...'

Nicholas's voice was a trifle hoarse:

'Yes,' he admitted; 'she has told me.'

For a second the words hung between them seeing to quiver in dramatic suspense.

'You were surprised?' She fought to keep

her voice steady.

'Yes.' It was a sharp sound.

Stephanie was perilously near to breaking down, but she managed to say, inducing a tone of lightness, even banter:

'And so, our respective love affairs come into line. Yours in re-marriage; mine–' She paused, 'by avoiding marriage.'

He cried, almost as though the words were wrung from him:

'Why, Stephanie – why?'

For a second eyes met eyes in mute inquiry; passion, stark, unmistakable flamed to life. His arms went more tightly about her so that there was no escape, only the torment of a nearness that mocked at their desires. She managed to answer him:

'Why not? I think I despise marriage.'

'That,' he said, 'is no answer, or excuse.'

Instantly, she challenged him:

'Is there any reason why I should give you an answer – *or* an excuse?'

He recoiled from that and, looking down at her said quietly:

'No; none, if you feel like that.'

She was trembling, violently, feeling faint with an emotion that surged upon her in a sick, paralysing wave; she knew that any tenderness from him, any inflection of voice (which, in different circumstances, she might have been justified in regarding as love), would defeat her. She drew fiercely, almost wildly on the memory of those weeks of anguish... He was going to marry Hester... He had, in fact, gone straight to Hester after pretending to *her* that he cared ... and, across the ballroom, waltzing with Trevor, was Valerie Brown whom he could greet so airily... Anger surged within her and she said, scornfully:

'Don't tell me that *you* are shocked, or that your moral susceptibilities are offended!'

Nicholas was too tense, too overwhelmed by the force of his own emotion rightly to grasp the full implication of those words. And he said almost curtly:

'Your actions are no concern of mine.'

She said cuttingly:

'Exactly.'

And the moment she had uttered the word she wanted to retract it. This was probably the last time she would ever be with Nicholas alone; the last time they would have an opportunity of talking together. She had sent him out of her life and Hester had won him back... Yes, could any power on earth say just what fate would have decreed suppose her attitude towards him had been different when he asked her to marry him. She despised herself for the weakness of the thought. What man professing to love a woman would go straight from her to the arms of his ex-wife – as he had done.

They danced in silence for a few seconds,

then, quietly she said:

'I hope everything will turn out right for you, Nicholas. Ours has been a strange relationship but–'

He looked down at her and that look silenced them both; and without their being conscious of the fact they clung together after the manner of two people who could fight no more.

'"Ships that pass in the night"!' There was a sombre note in his voice. Then, jerkily and as one drawn back to the thoughts he had vowed to ignore, he said tensely: 'Will you marry Trevor?' He added, 'eventually.'

Her reply came swiftly and decisively.

'No – never!'

He puckered his brows.

'But – *why* not?'

She held herself in check.

'I think that is just as much my business, Nicholas, as why you are re-marrying Hester is yours.' She spoke with a quiet dignity. 'Although, of course, in your case the reason is obvious.'

Still he held her gaze:

'Is it?' His voice was hoarse.

She plunged recklessly:

'Some relationships do not need iron bars.'

Solemnly, almost as though the words were wrung from him he said:

'How well you must love him, my dear, or – how little.'

Stephanie started and the colour flamed into her face.

Nicholas's jaw line tightened; a muscle just above it twitched through the sheer force of the strain under which he laboured.

'Do you think I am the type of woman to accept a lover without love of any kind?' she demanded.

And he replied, his voice tearing at her in its inflection of regret:

'I don't think, Stephanie, that I am qualified to know anything whatsoever about you … you made it quite impossible for me to do so.' A sigh. 'Suppose we leave it at that?'

Her eyes flashed him a spirited glance:

'And do you imagine that I know any more about *you?*' Her voice rang with disdain.

'You know all there is to know about me,' he said quietly.

She glanced up at him and her answer came:

'All and – nothing, Nicholas.'

He said, little knowing how open to misconstruction his words were:

'Hester has told you all there is to tell. Now I can add nothing to her story that would interest you.'

Stephanie stared at him. His quiet acceptance of the fact left her speechless and bewildered.

'I'm sure you can't,' she murmured.

'Why do you look at me like that?'

She smiled as one who realized that it was beyond her comprehension even to try to understand him.

'No reason,' she replied, then, changing the subject abruptly: 'You will live at the farm still?'

He said instantly:

'No; I'm selling out.'

Consternation showed in her face.

'But you loved the place–' Her voice was incredulous.

'One can love many things,' he answered slowly, 'but one cannot always keep them, Stephanie.'

Colour flooded her cheeks.

'But, after all you've done there – all you've planned to do?'

He held her gaze:

'I'm flattered by your interest.'

'It would have been such a perfect old house when it was really renovated,' she said. 'And the atmosphere – oh, everything!'

'We shall go abroad,' he said stiffly, feeling depression seeping upon him at the very thought of it and longing for the music to end so that the torment of her nearness would be no more.

'Any particular spot in mind?' She endeavoured to sound interested in a careless fashion.

'No.' He added: 'It never does to plan too

far ahead.'

She remained silent, as one bereft of speech and, suddenly the music stopped.

Nicholas looked at her with a direct and penetrating gaze.

'Thank you,' he said almost stiffly.

She walked beside him to where their party was gathered in an ante-room – Hilary and Edward Morgan, Sir William and Lady Graceton among them. Stephanie wasn't conscious of anything taking place around her; it was as though she were struggling in some strange, isolated world, where only her thoughts were real. Nicholas was going away...

Sir William, aristocratic, but friendly, with a Vandyke beard, held out both hands to her in welcome and exclaimed:

'Quite the fairy princess tonight, my dear.'

And his wife commented.

'We shall not wait much longer for that prince, Stephanie. Your brother cheated us of a big wedding; don't you dare to the same!' She smiled, her pale, faintly flushed cheeks and silver hair, presenting a picture of old-world charm. 'I will not be cheated of giving you a party here.'

Stephanie felt a hateful pang. Suddenly her life seemed complex and difficult, but she said gaily, knowing that Lady Graceton was understanding and exceedingly broad-minded:

'Marriage is not for me... I believe in being very gay and quite free!'

'Not a bad idea,' said Hilary Morgan with a twinkle in her eye.

Trevor said suddenly and in a rather serious tone:

'We all feel like that until someone takes us by storm.'

Stephanie glanced at him swiftly. Something in his manner arrested her attention, and she found herself transferring her gaze to Valerie Brown's face, aware of the faint colour that was stealing into Valerie's cheeks.

There was, she argued, nothing whatsoever to indicate that Nicholas and Valerie were other than excellent friends; their attitude was natural, without even the faintest embarrassment when, even had they been the most worldly of people, surely some faint strain would have manifested itself in the circumstances. She drew on a certain self-contempt. How naïve she still was. What did infidelity mean to either of them. Meeting an ex-lover in the presence of his ex-wife was a commonplace event... One fact stood out above all others: Nicholas had, obviously, not parted from her in any anger, or left within her mind the feeling as of having been disgracefully treated. Probably, she had no desire to marry him after the divorce any more than she, herself, had any desire to marry Trevor. Her mind went back over much of her conversation with Nicholas during their dance... How calm and unmoved he had been when he suggested that Hester had told her the story... One might almost have imagined him to be proud of it!

She watched him carefully as he approached Valerie for the next dance, while Trevor claimed her for his partner.

Valerie seemed curiously preoccupied as she gave her assent and Nicholas said banteringly, as they reached the floor:

'Would you mind coming back to earth, my dear! It is years since we met and I'd like to get a little sense out of you!'

She started almost guiltily.

'Sorry, Nick! I feel a bit odd tonight!'

He grinned.

'Meeting me again, no doubt!'

'Meeting you again, after two, or ten years makes it seem that we saw each other less than ten minutes before.'

'That,' he said smoothly, 'is friendship.'

She raised her eyes to his.

'And so you are re-marrying Hester!' Her sigh synchronized with a shake of her head. 'That simply staggers me.'

Nicholas said defensively:

'Hester has changed a very great deal.'

Valerie grunted.

'She would need to!' She hastened: 'Sorry, Nick, you know me well enough to realize that I can't mince matters and Hester is red rag to a bull to me.'

Nicholas said almost impatiently:

'A great deal has happened since those days, Valerie. It just isn't worth worrying about.'

'You don't expect me to believe that you have suddenly fallen madly in love with her!'

'No,' he admitted. 'And she has no illusions on that score, either.'

She glanced up at him.

'Then you must be mental,' she said coolly. 'Quite, quite batty, my dear man.' She drew her brows together in puzzled inquiry. 'Don't tell me you are doing that favourite masculine act: escape from one woman by marrying another.'

Nicholas's face became etched in shadow; the light went from his eyes, the banter ceased after the manner of one weary of dissembling.

'You always were far too discerning,' he said with an intonation of one resigned.

'And you always were far too quixotic.'

His laugh came cynically.

'You should tell Stephanie Reid that – it would amuse her.'

Valerie raised her gaze.

'Why Stephanie, particularly?'

Nicholas hastened, too casually:

'Stephanie, or anyone else. Don't be so

damned precise.'

'Does that mean you are out of favour with Stephanie?'

Nicholas said warningly:

'It means that if you ask any more questions, *you* will be out of favour!' A pause. 'You always were a menace at interfering with people's affairs – oh, yes you were! Charmingly, I admit. Tell me, Valerie–' His tone altered to a warm interest. 'How are things with you and how have they been since last we met?'

'Perfectly and gloriously neutral,' she admitted. 'I've enjoyed a complete respite from all romantic entanglements!'

Nicholas's voice was rather rough as he said:

'And I, until recently. In fact I'd come to enjoy a hermit-like existence.'

Valerie glanced across the room to where Trevor was dancing with Stephanie. She knew she was suddenly, violently sex-conscious for the first time for a very long while. She tried to keep her voice steady as she said:

'An attractive pair.'

'Very.'

'She's lovely and most attractive.'

'Yes.' It was a harsh sound.

'Are they – are they engaged or anything?'

Nicholas couldn't tell even Valerie the truth.

'No such announcement has been made. As you know they are in business together.'

'Yes; Mr Morly was telling me.'

'What did you think of him?'

'Is this a cross-examination?'

'Have you any objection?'

'None.' She paused. 'I liked him,' she admitted simply.

'I don't,' Nicholas countered.

'Prejudice or – jealousy?'

Nicholas met Valerie's searching gaze:

'Both – wholly unpardonable.'

Valerie said:

'We always were a couple of fools, Nick. Why on earth couldn't we have fallen in love? Been so damned simple!'

'Too simple; life doesn't hand out favours so easily.'

'And I come back to find you going to re-marry Hester! That kills me.'

'I'm leaving England,' he said tensely. 'Selling out. Restless as the devil, don't care for my own company, either.'

Valerie said comically:

'Move over; I've caught a similar bug tonight.' She hurried on. 'I love it in South Africa ... why not make that your first stop?'

'It's an idea...'

'Hester knows about us, now – doesn't she?' Valerie spoke firmly.

'Yes; I told her when we met again. She was–'

'Terribly upset to think she had misjudged us?'

'Yes, exactly. Why do you look at me like that?'

'Merely thinking how charmingly dumb you are.'

'Thanks! Not a scrap of improvement in you, woman,' he said, trying to forget his own problems in the whimsical banter that had always been the keynote of his friendship with Valerie. 'Suppose we are honest enough to admit that, though we were guiltless, we allowed people to think us guilty for our own ends. We cannot, therefore, condemn people for taking us at our word – can we? Least of all Hester?'

Valerie looked him very directly in the eyes.

'I couldn't agree with you more on that particular issue,' she said generously.

'Then what else is there?'

'Nothing,' she said swiftly. 'Nothing... Will you come to the opening of my new play next week? I've Wickham Masters playing opposite me.' A sly smile. 'You can be certain of one good performance at least – from him!'

'It's a date,' he promised.

'I'll send you the seats.'

He shook his head.

'Oh no, you won't! I detest being the dead-head. I'll get them through an agency.'

Valerie laughed.

'You really haven't changed a bit, Nick.'

'And it is in no spirit of flattery that I say you haven't *altered* a scrap,' he insisted.

'I'm thirty,' she exclaimed.

'Great age. I'm thirty-three. So what?'

'I want to grow old gracefully in my theatrical career,' she said slowly. 'Never to play daughters when I should be playing mothers.'

Nicholas looked at her meditatively.

'You should,' he said quietly, 'get married again now, my dear. One disastrous attempt isn't any reason why one should not try again.'

'Are you trying to convince yourself on that point, or to influence me?' she demanded bluntly. 'When I marry again – if ever I do – it will be because I cannot resist the man. Argue how you will, only being really in love makes marriage worth while, Nick.'

He said sombrely:

'I refuse to be drawn into an argument... Are you down here for long?'

'Only until Monday; but I shall sneak up every week-end if I can. The Morgans are perfectly sweet to me and now that Felice is married they seem particularly glad to have me. *What* a nice person Michael is! She's lucky, isn't she? And she is terribly fond of Stephanie. Such a lovely atmosphere in the family. Makes all the difference, especially in this casual, hard-boiled age.'

Hester had only a few moments alone with Valerie during the evening and she fixed her gaze boldly, challenging upon her, saying:

'I hope Valerie that you bear me no grudge about the past. Nicholas told me the truth and I've wanted to see you to–'

Valerie met those cold, merciless blue eyes without any light of compromise. She said:

'You couldn't, on the face of it, be expected to think other than you did, once we decided not to defend the case.' She paused significantly. 'But I happen to know, Hester, how very well it served your purpose to believe us guilty at that time, and to refuse to accept Nicholas's word.'

Hester went a sickly, parchment shade.

'What *are* you talking about?' she gasped.

Valerie's answer came scathingly.

'If you could look in the mirror the pallor of your cheeks would provide the answer.'

'You must be mad!'

Valerie glanced deliberately around her.

'I am the only person here who really knows you for what you are; the only person who, in an emergency, could prove you a liar and a cheat,' she said with a brutal frankness. 'And I'm warning you, Hester, if ever I have cause to believe that you are endangering Nicholas's happiness – whether you are remarried or not – then I warn you: I shall have no mercy for you whatsoever.'

Hester gave an inane, hysterical giggle.

'I think,' she managed to say, 'you must be reciting something from your very extensive repertoire... Really, Valerie, you theatrical people are a bit – *theatrical*,' she added.

'But we are seldom moral cowards,' Valerie hit back.

'I wasn't aware that you understood the meaning of the word "moral"! My dear, do you mind if we put an end to this boring conversation. I'm afraid you must be very much mistaken if you imagine for one moment that threats impress me. Nicholas and I intend to re-marry and pick up the threads of our happiness once more. Nothing that you could do, or say, would alter our very great devotion. Perhaps that irritates you?' She smiled, a slow, cunning smile. 'We are leaving England, too ... but perhaps Nicholas told you. I doubt very much if we will ever return.'

'I should make quite sure that I *left* before I talked of not coming back,' Valerie retorted.

Hester began to tremble. She was unnerved, the more so since she was completely ignorant of Valerie's power; what she knew, or, as was more than likely, that which she was guessing. Of course, it was obvious that she wanted Nicholas for herself and had hoped to renew their friendship and take it to a romantic conclusion the moment she returned to England after her African tour. And she had been thwarted. Hester regained her composure and her sadistic instinct fed on the sweet delight of Valerie's possible suffering and annoyance. Trust little Hester to come along and take the most eligible male in the district right from under the noses of other women.

Hester moved away as the rest of the party came into view.

'Thank you for a most amusing few minutes, Valerie,' she said quietly. 'We must have a talk again sometime... Ah, Nicky ... how about our having some champagne, darling?' And, leaving him no alternative but to take her to the buffet, they moved away.

It was just before one o'clock that Hester decided that she wished to return to her hotel.

Michael protested:

'But you cannot break up the party yet! I was counting on you both joining us at the cottage for bacon and eggs afterwards.'

Hester began to put on her little girl face and, then, aware of Valerie's critical, even contemptuous gaze, thought better of it.

'I'm awfully sorry,' she said regretfully. 'But I have a simply splitting headache. I know Nicholas won't mind driving me back – will you, darling?'

Nicholas was grateful for the chance of escape.

'No,' he said quietly. 'Not at all.'

Stephanie, noticing that Hester was unusually pale, even strained, exclaimed:

'Would you like to come back to the flat with me, Hester? We're so *near* that–'

'My *dear*, I wouldn't dream of spoiling things ... no, I'll be quite all right and the drive will do me good.' She smiled a trifle wanly at the others.

Nicholas, having spoken to each person in turn, said to Valerie:

'It's a date for the opening night. Dinner afterwards.'

Michael took that up.

'I've an idea we're going to gate crash at that party, Nicholas. Felice is itching to get down to London and Valerie's new play is the perfect alibi. We ought to make a night out of it.' He glanced at Stephanie and Trevor as he spoke.

Trevor found his gaze going very directly to Valerie; there was a strange and unfamiliar sensation just under his heart as their eyes met. And he knew that he wanted to see her again more than he had ever wanted to see any woman in his life. So powerful, in fact, was the emotion that he dared not analyse it. But he said:

'Count us in, Mike.' And for the first time he was aware of the significance of that 'us'.

Stephanie added her voice to his and it seemed that nothing could prevent her gaze leaping to Nicholas. Another evening when she would, at least, see him, she thought, and blushed for her own weakness.

Hester stood pale and trembling, hardly daring to speak lest her words became a vitriolic outburst. How she hated Valerie in that second; loathed the idea that Nicholas might be drawn into her friendly, Bohemian circle where, doubtless, contact with Stephanie would become more frequent and her own influence infinitely less powerful.

Afraid lest she might attract undue attention to herself by her silence, she purred:

'It will be wonderful to see you acting again, Valerie dear. A red-letter day, in fact, won't it, Nicky?'

Nicholas said, irritated by her overdone effusiveness:

'Of course... Will you get your wrap?'

She hated the idea that he would be left with these people, each of whom she had come to detest. Adroitly, by pleading a complete lack of any sense of direction and suggesting that she would never find him again once she wandered off alone, he was forced to accompany her. Once outside the house and in the car, she looked at him with adoring tenderness:

'I knew you wanted to get away, darling... I *have* a beastly head, but I wouldn't have said a word if I'd thought you were enjoying yourself...' She waited, tensed for his answer.

Nicholas spoke mechanically; he was thinking of Stephanie.

'I was quite ready to leave.'

Hester frowned. His casualness was beginning to madden her. Even after a matter of hours, having won her victory, she was creeping back to her old possessiveness, forgetful of her previous suspense and anxiety lest he night not ask her to re-marry him. She pressed her head against his arm.

'A night to remember, darling ... Castle Grange... The Charity Ball when we decided to re-marry. We must make all the rest of the years memorable, Nicky. I do so want to make up to you for – you know.'

'Forget it,' he said briefly and lapsed into silence. 'Looking back is always so futile.'

CHAPTER XV

July merged into early September and the fragrance of the countryside became sharper and more earthy. The sun deepened its golden hue and fell with a curious mellowness upon trees and hedgerow. Fields lay bathed in heavy dews from which mushrooms sprang with a certain perkiness, having been denied the privilege too long. Neat haystacks appeared miraculously upon farms, dotting the landscape with reassurance and fulfilment. The pungent, nostalgic smell of bonfires hung like incense in the cool, fresh air. Cottage gardens were thick with dahlias and asters. Autumn, with her gentle shadows, her early morning mists, her softening outline, was slowly stealing towards a final supremacy.

Trevor found that, for the first time in his life he was acutely conscious of the changing seasons and that it was as though the beauties around him held a special message, drawing him into their secrets and imparting a feeling as of *belonging* and understanding. His blithe, inconsequential manner changed to a more sombre and impressive calm that made it seem he was a man living within himself.

If Stephanie noticed it she said nothing and although his friendly attitude and gentleness in no way changed, she was aware of a subtle difference in his love-making and, with a certain sensitive appreciation of his mood, avoided creating any situations which might place him in that position which demanded passionate expression. She wanted to be absolutely certain of her facts before she discussed their relationship with him.

Valerie had been up to the Morgans practically every weekend, during that time, had been a continual visitor to the flat –

always at Stephanie's invitation. Then, suddenly, however, her visits ceased and, to Stephanie, the excuse of work keeping her in London failed to ring true. It was one evening when the day's work was done and Trevor said almost apologetically: 'I've quite a bit to do, darling: I'll take the accounts home tonight and work on them,' that Stephanie said quietly:

'Come and have a drink first, Trevor: I want to talk to you.'

He glanced at her swiftly, almost fearfully. Then:

'Very well,' he murmured.

They went up into the familiar lounge where, now, in the evenings a log fire always burned. She poured out two sherries and, sitting down opposite him began:

'Do you remember our conversation when we became lovers, Trevor … to the effect that there must be no strings; no hesitation when the time came to write *finis?*'

She saw him start almost guiltily.

'I remember,' he said in a low, rather hoarse tone.

Stephanie didn't hesitate.'

'I think that time has come now – don't you?'

Trevor stood restlessly with his back to the fire. Turning to the window as a man seeking guidance and uncertain of what angle to take, he finally said, and now, his attitude had strength, fearlessness and infinite gentleness.

'So, you know.'

She gave him a little, indulgent smile.

'That you are in love with Valerie – yes, my dear: I know.'

'Out of character – isn't it?' he exclaimed. 'Oh, I talked of the possibility of falling deeply in love–' He made an impatient gesture– 'but it was no more than words. Damnable part is that I cannot do anything about it.'

'Perhaps that is the loveliest part,' she said softly. 'Oh, Trevor, you knew that I should understand.'

Trevor sat down beside her.

'I knew that,' he agreed; 'but I hated having to tell you and–' He gave her a half smile. 'The courage of the male; hah!'

Stephanie met his gaze very steadily:

'You've never been deceived about my feelings for you, Trevor. Possibly I was wrong in the first place in doing as I did; but there are times in life when, even without acting on impulse, the forces propel one forward towards recklessness. The longing to escape one's own hurt; to find forget-fulness–'

'And have you found that forgetfulness?'

She shook her head and sighed.

'No. That will not surprise you now – will it?'

He looked tense.

'No,' he echoed, 'that will not surprise me now. I've tried it – without success.'

Stephanie put out a hand and grasped his.

'Then we both talk the same language ... and Valerie?'

'I think she feels the same; I've not allowed myself to find out.'

Stephanie said swiftly:

'Then I suggest you take the night train to London and find out, my dear.'

Trevor stared at her.

'Just like that?'

'Just like that! I would, in your place.'

'You're wonderful, Stephanie... I could never pretend to regret these months.' He looked suddenly grave. 'My fear is whether Nicholas is still – at least mentally – in the picture.' There was a grimness in his tone.

Stephanie said emphatically:

'Definitely – no!'

'Has she told you?' It was an eager, almost boyish, sound.

'I can't say that; in fact the subject of Nicholas and Hester has never, somehow, arisen when Valerie and I have been alone. Naturally, I shouldn't appear to be curious and her attitude has always been ... *casual*. That is hardly the word, Trevor; but on those rare occasions when I've seen Valerie in Nicholas's company there has been nothing suggestive of anything deeper than–'

'Than we've known,' he said encouragingly.

'In a way – yes. Probably in the past it was so. In any case, Valerie obviously bears him no grudge.' Stephanie added tensely: 'One can never fathom the relationships between two people without knowing all the details of what prompted their actions in the first place.'

'How true that is and how apt we are to forget it.' He looked at his wrist watch as he spoke. Then: 'Did you know that Wilderness Farm goes under the hammer next week? And that Nicholas and Hester are being married this coming Saturday?' He spoke in a low, understanding tone, eyeing her anxiously; aware of the strain, the tension of her life and able, now, to imagine some of its anguish.

'Yes,' she said slowly. 'I've seen the posters announcing the sale and, a few days ago, Hester told me about the wedding. Apparently, it is to be very quiet and in London. No one to attend it; and the honeymoon is to be spent, so she said, in Italy – where they went the first time.'

'You've come round to my way of thinking about Hester – haven't you,' he asked sharply.

She countered:

'Not that, Trevor. Hester is just selfish – perhaps her experiences have made her so.

And, now, having won Nicholas back, she hasn't any time for friendship.'

'You hardly ever see her – do you?'

'Only by accident. Although the other week she did ring me to suggest we had a coffee together as she would be in the town.'

'And – Nicholas?'

'I've seen him only once since the night of the ball.'

Trevor explained:

'It was never indifference on my part because I didn't ask you, or mention him, Stephanie.'

She gave him a warm, affectionate smile.

'I know that.'

'What are you going to do, now?' There was anxiety in his voice.

'Go on as before, my dear. The question is: what are *you*? I cannot imagine that you will want to live in Warwick and Valerie in London! All I want you to know is that, whatever you decide upon, I shall–'

'I shall certainly not cease to be your business partner,' he said stoutly. 'That is, while you want me here.' He looked at her very earnestly. 'I wish I could say something helpful.; but words have a beastly knack of sounding trite or smug, or both... Of course, if Valerie should turn me down–'

Stephanie shook her head.

'She will not do that!'

'Are you sure?'

'Absolutely ... you will tell her about us?'
Her voice was subdued. She stared at him.
'All that happened to her in the past makes
no difference to you, Trevor?'

He gave a little incredulous exclamation.

'Good heavens, no! Better to have one's
experiences when one is young and profit by
them!'

Stephanie managed to laugh.

'Then I am all right,' she said.

'In any language,' he added, and looking at
his wrist watch, exclaimed: 'I'd better get
that something-to-nine train, hadn't I?'

'You would reach Valerie's flat about the
time she gets back from the theatre, then,'
Stephanie agreed. 'She told me she is
seldom home until half-past eleven.'

'I feel just like a kid about to sit for an
examination,' he said absurdly.

'Butterflies in your tummy!' She gave him
a little indulgent smile, feeling almost
maternal towards him. 'Or don't men admit
to such weaknesses.'

'I do,' he confessed readily. 'If that deprives
me of my sex – so be it!' The laughter died
on his lips. 'Oh, darling, if I could see *you*
happy. That isn't mawkish but–'

'I know how you mean it, Trevor. But
please do not worry about me or you will
make me unhappy. I'm so glad for you.' She
added solemnly: 'I could never really be
cynical about marriage or the real things

that go to make it up ... just that, some-times, one has to compromise with life. I have said that I would never do that–'

'But you did – with me?' A pause. 'Do you regret it?'

'No; I've learned a great deal about myself, Trevor.' She looked at him very earnestly. 'I'd like you to know that ours is an experience I shall not repeat – ever. Friendship, Trevor, from now on – never anything more.'

He looked at her as one trying to sum her up.

'You are a very gallant person, my dear.' He added: 'You've changed, you know.' A faint laugh. 'That sounds a bit odd, but you know what I mean.'

'That I'm not gallant because I've changed!' A smile. 'I've grown up, Trevor. Falling in love, in the true sense, has that effect on a woman. The exquisite sadness of watching that first careless rapture of youth fade.' A nervous chuckle. 'Thus speaks the dear, old lady ... and, now, I'm going to tell Hilda to put dinner forward.' She stopped. 'Why not go to London by car, or don't you want the effort?'

'I was just turning the idea over in my mind,' he said thoughtfully. 'I could be there in about two and three-quarter hours – less, with luck. Don't bother about dinner, my dear: I'll start right away.'

Stephanie got to her feet and he followed

immediately; she leaned towards him and kissed him on the cheek. It was a passionless, affectionate gesture almost of renunciation. No regret stirred within her because their intimate relationship was over; if anything, a certain relief stole upon her. Nicholas would hear of Trevor and Valerie's engagement (and she had no doubt but that Valerie was in love with him) and know that... She dragged her thoughts away. What would it matter to him!

A curious sensation of loneliness stole upon her as she watched Trevor drive away. She felt that she was standing back from life and watching it as one might watch a play or a film – but never really taking part in it.

CHAPTER XVI

Trevor reached London and Valerie's flat in Portland Place some half an hour before she returned to it. He waited in a state of feverish apprehension until, after what appeared to be an eternity, she came swiftly into the lounge to greet him. Her attitude was friendly, welcoming, but impersonal and a certain uneasiness took the place of his former hope, as she said:

'Trevor! How nice of you to look me up. I

341

could hardly believe it when Martha told me you were here. I'm going to have sandwiches and coffee – will you join me?'

Trevor felt that both would choke him at that moment, but he said swiftly:

'Thanks; I'd love to join you.'

She threw off an exquisite mink wrap which revealed a soft powder blue crepe frock, embroidered with diamante.

'That's better!' A sigh. Then taking a cigarette he offered her and bending to the flame of his lighter, she said conversationally: 'Tell me all the news from Warwick.'

It was nothing Trevor had expected, or rehearsed in his mind. He had visualized himself going swiftly into the room and, almost before a word had been uttered, finding Valerie in his arms while he stammered some incoherency about his love for her. This quiet, unassuming friendliness both baffled and disconcerted him.

He plunged; better to know his fate than to wait in an agony of suspense.

'I'm not here to talk about Warwick,' he said almost abruptly.

Valerie looked at him swiftly and then lowered her gaze. For weeks she had fought against the insidious power of her love for him, refusing to visit the Morgans and risk the danger of seeing him. She distrusted emotion and her own in particular and had steadfastly resisted, for several years – even as she had told Nicholas – all romantic contacts. Her neutral state had been satisfying and free from suffering and, thus, she insisted to herself, she fully intended it should remain. Trevor had smashed into her peaceful reverie and, after their first meeting, she had found herself concentrating upon him to the exclusion of all else – her work included – and that in no way pleased her. She was, in fact, highly indignant and annoyed with herself. But time had not worked any miracles and she was still in that state of tension and excitement, particularly when she allowed her mind to ponder the possibility that he might care for her in return. Without conceit, she had every reason for knowing that there was ample evidence to support such a belief.

Trevor watched her, his nerves taut, his heart thudding violently. He was wholly incapable of grappling with the emotions that swirled upon him in rapid succession; emotions vastly different from any he had experienced before.

She turned swiftly from the mantlepiece, picked up an ashtray, put it down on a table nearby and exclaimed, breathlessly:

'There's nothing wrong – is there?'

'That depends!'

'On what?' She was trembling.

'You.' He moved close to her. 'I'm in love with you, Valerie,' he said, and nothing could have stayed the words. 'I wanted to tell you before, but–' He broke off desperately, feeling wretched and inadequate and unnerved by her stillness.

Then suddenly, like a sigh on the breeze, her words came:

'Oh, Trevor!'

He stared at her, not daring to move, or even to hope. Her voice, with its deep, perfect modulation, echoed through the silence like the throb of muted strings.

He wasn't conscious of having reached out and drawn her into his arms, but the next second she was there, held fiercely against him, her head on his shoulder, her lips warm and soft against his while the weeks of denial and doubt vanished before the ecstasy of possession and avowel.

'You love me?' He lifted his mouth from hers and looked deeply into her eyes. His own were dark with the passionate devotion engulfing him. Before, a caress had lacked all spiritual significance, all mental appreciation. As he held Valerie, however, he felt humbled before the force of his own love and the wonder of her surrender.

'Yes,' she breathed. 'From the first ... I didn't want to love you. I fought you – terribly hard.'

'And I you!' He added gravely: 'I've not taken all this very seriously until now, Valerie, I'm afraid.'

Valerie, with her characteristic honesty said:

'I did, Trevor – once; it didn't work out and I vowed that never again would I give any man the chance to hurt me ... now, here I am, helpless against you.'

Trevor felt a pang of jealousy which, he argued, he had no right to indulge. It would be sheer hypocrisy on his part to condemn her for the weakness of which he, himself, had been guilty. But he said in a rather strangled, unnatural tone:

'Nicholas?'

She stared at him somewhat incredulously, while knowing what was in his mind despite the fact that the question had rather lost its sequence.

'Do you mean was Nicholas the man for whom I once cared?'

'Yes.' He moved with her to a cushion-piled settee and, still holding her hand in his, turned upon her a tense, wondering gaze.

Valerie sighed.

'No, darling; the man happened to be my husband.'

'Your *husband!*' Trevor's voice was shaken.

'Is that so strange?'

'No, but–' He stammered: 'I mean, I thought that Nicholas was the one and–'

'So did a great many other people,' she murmured. 'Although I rather imagined that everyone in our intimate circle knew the truth of all that by now.'

Trevor felt his heart miss a beat; the sickness in the pit of his stomach was increasing; he would never have believed that the past could tear at his emotions quite so deeply. He hated even the idea of having to tell her about Stephanie, fearful lest she, too, might share his present reactions. But he plunged:

'I imagine they do ... the same thing might be said about me, Valerie.' He looked at her very levelly. 'I appreciate that all this business about self-confession is, between two people who understand each other, quite unnecessary but – well, since I have the advantage of knowing your life, you must, also, know mine.' He lowered his gaze for a fraction of a second and then raised it fearlessly; 'Stephanie and I, for the past months–'

'I guessed,' she interrupted simply. 'Stephanie didn't *tell* me in so many words, but neither did she make any attempt to conceal the truth.'

'She knows that I am here,' he added simply. 'And I have no need to tell you that the past, in that way, is dead.'

Valerie felt a tremor go over her body.

'I'm glad it was Stephanie,' she said softly. 'I like her so much.'

'This will not change things between you?'

She shook her head.

'Never.'

Trevor studied her intently.

'May I ask you something?'

'Anything.'

'Then, since you were so fond of your husband ... why the divorce and – Nicholas?'

Valerie sighed as one looking back over years that had ceased to be more than a rarely recalled memory. She answered quietly:

'There comes a time in all human relationships, Trevor, when one can suffer no more and when one knows that, at no matter what the cost, one must escape. I reached that stage and fate threw Nicholas and me together in circumstances that provided perfect evidence... We were both sick at heart, wretched in our respective marriages and ... we let the case go through without defending it.'

Trevor became rigid; his heart began to beat at seemingly twice its normal pace.

'You mean that you and Nicholas were never–' He could get no further so great was his excitement.

'Never anything more than the best of friends,' she said quietly, but firmly.

Trevor stared at her in utter amazement, while relief and bewilderment flooded over his body.

'But ... oh *darling!*' It was a husky sound

of thankfulness. 'I was so afraid lest you had cared deeply for him and–'

She interrupted, her brows were wrinkled in puzzled inquiry:

'You should have *known* the truth. Nicholas told Hester the facts when they met again.' A sigh. 'Although, of course, it was not likely that she would redeem us in anyone else's mind. She couldn't be generous enough for that. And certainly neither Nicholas nor I would broadcast it. Somehow, when one is innocent one just does not worry, or seek to explain to people... But Stephanie! Surely *she* knew.'

Trevor stared at her, while a wave of excitement surged upon him; excitement that dissolved into a fierce agitation:

'No,' he exclaimed in a breath as of one making an important discovery. 'That is just the point – she didn't, or doesn't know.' He stared at Valerie. 'Darling! I'm asking myself just what difference it would have made to her life had she done so.'

'Why should it affect her?'

'Because she happens to be in love with Nicholas!'

Valerie shivered, as a wave of apprehension enveloped her body. The thought of Hester came insidiously. And she recalled Nicholas's conversation and attitude on the night of the ball. He might have just decided to re-marry Hester, but he was far from being a happy man. 'I remember,' she said hastily, 'suggesting to Nicholas that he was not in love with Hester and he admitted I was right and that she was aware of the fact.' She added: 'I, also, said something to the effect that he was escaping from one woman by marrying another.' Valerie paused impressively. 'I felt, somehow, that there *was* a woman in his life and, come to think of it, he did mention Stephanie, but I cannot recall in what connection.'

'I think,' Trevor said firmly, 'that this is where we take a hand, darling. I have never trusted Hester, although Stephanie believed in her.'

'Hester,' said Valerie quietly, 'is the sugar coating on a poison pill. She's plausible, cunning and quite unscrupulous and she will stop at nothing to get what she wants.'

'And,' said Trevor grimly, 'she is being married to Nicholas on Saturday ... this is Thursday night. If any of my suspicions are correct, we haven't a great deal of time to lose, my darling.' He added earnestly: 'Are you prepared to come up to Warwick with me and see this thing through? Knowing the truth, I am convinced that Nicholas is just as much in love with Stephanie as she is with him, but that, somewhere, there is a missing link.'

Valerie gave him a tender and adoring smile.

'I'm with you every inch of the way. Oddly enough, I warned Hester that if ever there was any trouble I'd expose her. I know so *much*, darling, believe me, and it is far too long a story to begin now … and we've other things to talk about, anyway.' She relaxed in his arms. Then, after a few seconds, exclaimed: 'Darling, how do you feel about starting for Warwick now? I must be back here for the evening performance at the latest by seven tomorrow evening and–' Her eyes met his in excited happiness. 'The drive through the night would be a wonderful beginning… I can go straight to the Morgans. I'll ring them to expect me. Or are you too tired?'

He smiled and held her more closely.

'You know the answer to that question… Valerie, you will not want a long engagement?'

She studied him thoughtfully. Then:

I really do think we should wait at least until you can get a special licence,' she said softly.

'Darling!'

'Could you bring me back tomorrow and – stay until we can leave for our honeymoon? There is a highly respectable hotel close by where all the best bridegrooms stay,' she added amusedly.

'Thank heaven for that! I can keep an eye on you and see that you do not escape me!'

'Optimist! Just try to escape *me* and see how far you get!'

They got to their feet and he held her against him for a few seconds.

'I cannot believe we are together like this,' he murmured hoarsely. 'I've almost ridiculed the idea of falling deeply in love and, now, here I am completely at your mercy!'

'And I told Nicholas, such a short while ago, that I was neutral – or had been,' she hastened.

'Meaning that you were not completely indifferent to me after that first dance?'

Valerie said emphatically:

'Meaning that I knew I hated saying good-bye to you.'

'And I, you,' he added. Then, to cover the intense emotion he felt, he gave a little, nervous laugh.

It was much later, when they were driving through the misted country lanes, where rabbits scuttled in the glare of the headlights, and woodland and valley lay shrouded in purple darkness, rifted by the gold of the moon, that Valerie asked:

'What are you plans when we reach Warwick?'

Trevor said swiftly:

'I shall go straight to Nicholas. He can only tell me to mind my own business if our surmises are not correct. If they are correct, then everything will follow in natural sequence.'

'I'll look in to see Stephanie.'

Trevor said gently:

'And say nothing to her, my darling. What-ever there is to tell she would rather hear from Nicholas's lips.'

'Of course,' Valerie agreed. 'I am quite the tactician, my sweet.'

'You're the woman I love,' he said hoarsely.

CHAPTER XVII

Trevor reached Wilderness Farm soon after nine o'clock the following morning, having phoned Valerie at the Morgans and deter-mined their ultimate meeting place at Stephanie's flat.

Nicholas greeted him somewhat curtly and in that uncompromising manner which, tacitly, suggested that he was about as wel-come as smallpox.

Trevor said firmly:

'I want a word with you, Young. It is very important and urgent.'

At that Nicholas started anxiously. Then:

'Come into my study,' he said swiftly and, once they were settled in their respective chairs, their cigarettes lit, he added: 'I'm listening, Morly.'

Actually, Nicholas's composure was entirely feigned. His pulse had quickened and fear possessed him. He dare not relax sufficiently to undergo questioning but the thought came that Stephanie might be in danger ... a hundred and one things at which the mind grasps avidly in moments it conceives to be those of crisis. For no ordinary reason would Trevor Morly visit him.

Trevor began with an impressive forcefulness and directness:

'I'm here to suggest that you have a very serious talk to Stephanie. I'm also here to tell you that I am engaged to marry Valerie Brown. That fact may help you to understand my motives in coming to you.'

Nicholas stared at him incredulously.

'Engaged to *Valerie!*' A somewhat accusing expression crept into his eyes. The thought of Stephanie came swiftly and although her relationship to Trevor had always seared him, now he felt indignant that she should thus be dismissed from Trevor's life.

Trevor said with a quiet impressiveness:

'Look here, old man, there has never been any love lost between us and I can read, pretty well, the thoughts that are now going through your mind. I can, however, assure you that Stephanie is fully aware of my regard for Valerie and that the whole thing is above board.'

Nicholas relaxed and absorbed the fact

that Stephanie was again free. He said evenly:

'I appreciate your concern, Trevor; but you are aware that I am marrying Hester tomorrow. Your suggestion that I have a serious talk to Stephanie ... I have no delusions that she would be interested in such procedure.'

Trevor made an impatient sound.

'Isn't that your pride talking,' he said stoutly.

'Pride!' It was a scornful utterance.

Trevor got up from his chair. His nerves were taut and he was uncertain of how to continue, then:

'Has it occurred to you that Stephanie knows nothing of the truth of the past where you are concerned,' he burst forth.

Nicholas came back:

'Stephanie knows all there is to know about the past.'

'Because you, yourself, told her?' Trevor challenged him.

Nicholas hesitated, then:

'Because Hester told her,' he said firmly.

'Exactly!'

'What are you inferring?'

'That Hester told her only those things calculated to help *her;* certainly not to smooth the path for you or Stephanie!'

Nicholas gasped:

'Good heavens, man, do you realize what you are saying?'

'I realize it well enough.'

'And you think that Hester would be capable of–'

'That and more,' said Trevor grimly. 'That is why I am suggesting you go direct to Stephanie, yourself, and find out just what she *has* been told.'

Nicholas allowed his thoughts to dwell upon recent events. Stephanie's strange attitude: even at the ball, her suggestion that she knew all and nothing... It struck him, sharply and insistently, that she had never made reference to the fact that there had been nothing between him and Valerie... He grew hot with a surging suspense; tiny episodes came back to haunt him... Elation mingled with incredible tension. Suppose Hester had lied...

Trevor watched Nicholas carefully in that second, seeing a man wrestling with doubt, suspicion and suddenly, a grim and almost frightening determination stamping itself upon his face as he said:

'I'll do as you say.' He paused. 'Why have you waited until now before coming to me, Morly?'

'Not for the reason that might be apparent,' Trevor countered, 'but because I learned only tonight the truth about your relationship with Valerie. And while that truth, in itself, may be insignificant, I can appreciate how, in the circumstances, the concealing of it might well ruin not only your happiness, but Stephanie's.'

Nicholas spoke tensely:

'If Hester has dared to do this–'

'You'll see,' came Trevor's complacent reply.

'She is due here at any minute: we were going over to Broadway–'

'Then get away before she arrives.' Trevor added: 'She'll follow you!'

Nicholas was a man who found it exceedingly difficult to distrust even an enemy and the possibility of Hester deliberately scheming to wreck his happiness with Stephanie became abhorrent to him. Yet should Trevor's accusations be correct... He felt contempt, disgust, even hatred rising within him at the idea. To have been *fooled*, deceived... It seemed a slur upon his judgment, even his manhood.

Trevor walked to the door.

'I must get back,' he said swiftly.

'I'll follow,' came the instant response. A pause. 'Thanks, Trevor. Damned decent of you to come to me.' He pressed a bell as he spoke. 'I shan't forget.' Then, as his housekeeper answered the ring: 'Tell Mrs Wincott, when she calls, that I have gone into Warwick and ask her to wait for me.'

Trevor smiled to himself. He could just imagine the effect of that message upon Hester!

Nicholas covered the distance to Stephanie's flat in record time, the accelerator flat down while people stepped back from roads and pavements to allow of his progress, almost as though they were aware of the urgency!

Stephanie saw him and stared at him aghast. Then, trying, fighting, to maintain composure said:

'Good heavens, whatever brings you here at this hour?' A pause, then anxiously: 'Nothing wrong? Hester, she–'

'Is perfectly well.' He looked at her steadily and earnestly. 'I want to talk to you, Stephanie.'

'About – what?' Her tone was uncompromising.

'About us,' he said deliberately.

'There is nothing whatever to be said about us,' she retorted. Then, aware of her own weakness, added: 'Please, Nicholas, I have neither the time, patience, nor interest to listen to you. Tomorrow you will be remarried to Hester. Can't you be loyal to her even at this eleventh hour?'

'You still despise me, don't you?' he said and waited, tensed for her answer.

'Have I any reason to do otherwise?'

'That depends.' He was feeling his way, seeking an opening. 'You made the remark at the ball that night to the effect that you knew all and nothing about me.'

'Isn't that true?' She added swiftly. 'But what does it matter in any case?'

'It matters a very great deal,' he said slowly. His gaze met and held hers masterfully. Then: 'Just what *has* Hester told you about me?' he asked with an impressive calm.

Stephanie sighed impatiently. Her nerves were jagged; his presence tore open wounds that she had struggled to heal; she was afraid of betraying her love for him; afraid of the weakness which would make her accept him on any terms should he plead again. The memory of her promise to Hester came back mockingly. She managed to say:

'Hester has told me very little, Nicholas. The story is, after all, simple enough. You and Valerie ... the divorce; the fact that you had always cared, *really* cared, for her, Hester. And that you had wanted her back, and since I know,' she added scathingly, 'that when you last came here and asked me to marry you – *such* a convincing act, Nicholas – you went straight back to make love to her. You could not possibly expect me to do other than despise you. Heaven knows I'm not narrow-minded, but there is nothing lower, to me, than a man who plays upon the emotions of women without caring deeply for any of them. Did you imagine that I was so blind as not to realize just why you asked me to marry you?'

Nicholas, with a superhuman effort, maintained an attitude of calm; he wanted to hear all that Stephanie had to say because it was, in itself, an indictment against Hester, revealing to him a story as sordid and diabolical as any he had ever heard.

'Suppose,' he said slowly, 'you tell me why I asked you to marry me.'

Stephanie paled; she was unnerved by his inflexibility, his general behaviour, his stern calm.

'I was to be just another mistress – wasn't I?' She poke scornfully. 'With marriage the bait. Oh, I didn't flatter myself that I was so attractive to you, merely that, in your conceit, you hated the idea that after Hester returned I refused to accept your earlier attentions. Hester was never disloyal to you, but she left me in no doubt as to your weakness where women were concerned. It just so happens that, as I told you once before, I hate being one of a crowd.' She was trembling violently as she spoke and her heart was suffocating her.

Nicholas moved until he was within a few inches of her.

'But, for all that, you were, and are still, in love with me, my darling,' he said tensely and now passion flamed between them like an unquenchable fire.

'And even if that were true,' she cried fiercely, relying on anger to prevent a pitiful surrender, 'do you think I would tell you? Tell you, when tomorrow, you are to marry Hester!'

He picked up her hand and held it in his.

'Your eyes tell me, Stephanie,' he murmured hoarsely, 'your trembling body tells me and if I were to take you in my arms your lips would tell me–'

For a second they stood, quivering, their defences down, their love finding expression in the lingering gaze they exchanged. Stephanie caught at her breath on the note of a sob as she murmured:

'If you've any pity left–'

He reached out and drew her against him, holding her firmly, tenderly, as he cried:

'Oh, my darling … how we have both suffered.'

She stared up at him, arrested by the tone of his voice. Conscious, instinctively, that something had still to be told.

'Why do you say that?' Her voice cracked. 'Nicholas, why are you here?'

'To tell you the truth at last,' he said heavily; 'the truth I fondly believed that you knew – that Hester had told you.'

'You mean–'

'I mean that Hester has lied and deceived us both,' he said grimly.

An icy shudder went over Stephanie's body; her lips felt stiff, incapable of movement.

'Oh, *no!*'

Nicholas took her to the settee and sat down beside her, almost alarmed by her pallor. He was grave, impressively calm as, drawing her gaze to his, he said tensely:

'Before I begin, my dearest ... I want your trust. Without it, I'm not interested even in beginning the story I have to tell. Look at me ... do you honestly think me capable of all the things you have been led to believe about me?'

A tremor went over her body. And her voice broke in a passionate whisper as she said:

'No ... *no*, Nicholas.' Her eyes were suspiciously bright as she added: 'It's all been so difficult, so impossible for me.'

He did not remove his gaze from hers:

'And Hester did not tell you about Valerie and me?'

'Only the facts about the divorce and that she had forgiven you.'

'But not that there wasn't anything *to* forgive, or that I had told her I'd never been unfaithful to her?'

Stephanie cried sharply:

'No. Never that.'

'I see. So all this time you have imagined me guilty; believed that I was trying to crawl back into Hester's life while making love to you as a pleasant form of amusement!'

Stephanie answered him and there was a

note of exquisite tenderness in her voice as she murmured:

'Yes... I had no alternative, Nicholas, and the thought was utter agony.'

His hold of her hands tightened.

'And you are in love with me – aren't you?' There was something very real in the manner of his asking the question; a depth and sincerity greater than the mere exploitation of words.

'Terribly in love with you.' It was a whisper.

'My *darling*... And you believe, now, that I love you?'

Stephanie's heart seemed to stop beating and in that blessed second to feel the miraculous healing of the wounds inflicted during the past months. It was as though she moved from complete darkness into soft, radiant light, coming to life again, finding a reality that had so cruelly eluded her.

'Yes... Oh, yes,' she murmured huskily.

He drew her into his arms, cradling her head against him, bending his lips to hers and seeming in a single kiss to draw from her mouth the very essence of the love and passion he gave in return. Ecstasy, the sharp, sweetness of a thankful relief, held them in a spell of enchantment, so that they clung together, quivering at each other's touch, seeking a desperate fulfilment in the hunger of desire so long denied. Her lips were soft and parted beneath his own; her arms reaching up and encircling his neck as her body moved in rapturous surrender against him and, then, as one exhausted by the emotion that engulfed her, she relaxed and was still... Lifting her mouth from his and looking down into her eyes, he whispered:

'It's been hell without you ... these past weeks–'

'I know ... the night of the ball. I didn't understand, darling; your attitude to me...'

He put her gently back against the cushions at the other end of the settee.

'We've a great deal of talking to do,' he said firmly. 'But we shall never do it if you remain as close to me as this.'

Stephanie said absurdly and her eyes were like stars:

'I was never very fond of talking.'

Nicholas got to his feet and went and stood by the mantelpiece. Then, without further comment, he began the story of his marriage and its ending in divorce.

'I had no illusions about Hester's selfishness,' he went on, finally. 'But I never had occasion to believe other than that she told the truth; that her word could be relied upon. When she realized that there had been nothing between Valerie and me, her attitude was that of genuine regret that she had done me such injustice. In all fairness, she could not have thought other than that

I was guilty in the circumstances. From the beginning of our meeting again, she was anxious that we should re-marry, although for quite a while – I can see this now – she avoided mentioning it.'

Stephanie said urgently:

'Did you tell her anything about your feelings for me?'

Nicholas said steadily:

'She knew that I was in love with you and posed as the sympathetic friend anxious to help my cause all she possibly could.'

Stephanie gave a little painful cry.

'Oh, Nicholas! It is all so horrible. And all the time she was stressing the fact in my mind that you were the philanderer, but that knowing you truly cared for her, she was ready to risk anything in order to win you back. She even told me that she was aware that you were attracted to me and asked me not to encourage you so that you both might have a chance of happiness together.'

'So that explains your attitude the day I told you I loved you and asked you to marry me!'

Stephanie nodded.

'Yes; I could not believe you were sincere and, even had you been, I had given her my promise and felt that your future was linked with hers. I couldn't even begin to explain the subtlety of her insinuations... Even to telling me how beautifully you made love to her and how attractive you thought her.'

Nicholas groaned.

'I could,' he said fiercely, 'kill her for all this.'

Stephanie asked shakenly:

'What made you suspect her?'

'Trevor ... he came to see me this morning.'

'This morning!' Stephanie gasped: 'But he only motored to London late last evening to see Valerie.'

'Nevertheless, he was at the farm by nine this morning, to tell me that he and Valerie were engaged and to suggest that you and I, my darling, had a heart-to-heart talk. I didn't even stop to wonder where he had come from!'

Stephanie became suddenly silent.

'Have you forgotten – Trevor?' Her voice was jerky. 'I wonder if you could understand just why I did as I did.'

Nicholas returned to her side.

'I think so, my darling. That sense of desolation and despair that made anything better than the gloom of one's own company and one's own tormenting thoughts. In much the same spirit I agreed to marry Hester again – although she realized I had no love to give her and nothing more than friendship to offer.' His voice was hoarse as he added: 'When I knew about your relationship and realized I'd lost you ... it didn't seem to matter what I did with my life in future. On the face of it, Hester appeared to have vastly improved from the old days and to be very anxious to redeem the failure of the past–' He shrugged his shoulders expressively.

'And you forgive me?' Her eyes were solemn, appealing.

'I'm asking for your love and the future, my dearest,' he murmured softly. 'Not holding a post-mortem about the past.'

Stephanie said huskily:

'It was always you, Nicholas – never anyone else and never the pretence of it being anyone else. Trevor understood.'

For answer, Nicholas drew her into his arms, his lips seeking hers in a lingering kiss of tenderness. And it was during that moment, when they were oblivious of the world around them, that Hester, having crept stealthily up the stairs, came equally quietly, and unnoticed into the room. Her voice, harsh and accusing, broke the silence.

'A most effective and touching little scene,' she cried, stridently.

Nicholas and Stephanie made no attempt to break instantly away from each other, then slowly Nicholas rose to his feet.

'So you've added snooping to the long list of your crimes.' He said curtly: 'I'm glad you're here, Hester, it will save me the un-pleasant necessity of getting in touch with you, later.'

Hester's face was crimson with fear and rage. Hers was the nature to know of no defeat. She had raced from the farm to Warwick in a frenzy of apprehension but, never at any time, allowing herself to face the possibility of her treachery being discovered. Whatever the situation, she told herself, even as she stood there, she would bluff her way out of it... No one at this stage should rob her of Nicholas.

'I'm not here to talk to *you*, Nicholas,' she said ingratiatingly. 'But I most certainly have something to say to Stephanie.' She turned like a tigress to the settee where Stephanie sat, calm, contemptuous; 'I suppose this is your idea of loyalty and friendship.'

Stephanie answered very composedly:

'I hardly think that you are qualified to know the meaning of either words, Hester.'

Hester rapped out:

'Very clever! And just where do you think this will get you since Nicholas and I are to be married tomorrow?'

Nicholas said harshly:

'There will be no marriage tomorrow, Hester.'

Hester's face appeared to swell to twice its size as anger, fear, insensate jealousy consumed her.

'I don't think you realize what you are

saying,' she gasped. 'What do you mean, "No marriage"?' She added venomously. 'What lies has she been telling you? Can't you see that her one object has been to part us; can't you see that she'd stop at nothing to get you herself.' She gave a little cry as the words poured forth and she realized that they were an indictment against herself.

Instantly, and in a voice cold, merciless, Nicholas said:

'Thank you, Hester ... for condemning yourself! Stephanie was not supposed to have the slightest interest in me, according to you, but always to have been fond of Trevor ... that, being so, isn't your present accusation rather feeble?'

Hester, desperate now, cried:

'You don't understand. Nothing is as you think it. I–'

He interrupted her and scorn lashed his words:

'You've lied, cheated and conspired to keep us apart, distorting every simple truth. You knew we were in love with each other. You even professed sympathy for me, made me believe you had changed. And I was fool enough to take you at your word.' He added fiercely: 'You disgust me; never would I have thought you could stoop so low.'

Hester said wildly:

'You've allowed Stephanie to poison your mind against me. And just how long do you imagine that she will be faithful to you? Or don't you mind sharing her with Trevor?'

Hester knew, then, only the blind fury of the woman scorned; her bitter, vindictive mind could grasp the significance of only one word: revenge. How to be revenged upon Stephanie, whom she hated with an almost homicidal hatred.

It was at that juncture when Trevor and Valerie arrived. At the sight of them Hester seemed to cringe and a new fear leapt into her eyes. But she refused to give in as she shouted:

'So you hunt in packs – eh?' She turned to Nicholas. 'Are you going to stand by and watch me suffer – after all that has happened?' she cried pathetically. She gained courage, her unbalanced mind still clinging to the belief that, in the end, she would win. Failure wasn't possible for her; she who had always had her own way and so arranged her life as always to defeat her enemies.

Nicholas said sternly:

'I have nothing further to say to you, Hester, and it is not worth going over the old ground. You know all there is to know of your lies and deceit during the past months; let it just be understood that we are, also, aware of every mean, despicable trick.'

'That,' said Valerie briefly, 'is where you are wrong, Nicholas. You don't know the half of it.'

Hester's face lost every scrap of colour: she rushed to the door, but Valerie impeded her.

'Oh, no,' she said, and her voice rang with contempt, 'you don't leave here until you've heard all I intend to say. Had it not been for this, your secret would have died with you. As it is, I want Nicholas to know the exact extent of your vileness so that he may never again be victimized by you.'

The room had become heavy with suspense as, for a second, Valerie paused. And suddenly Hester cried and her voice was low, breathless and afraid:

'Listen Valerie, you don't understand … please–'

Valerie cut her short with a contemptuous glance.

'I understand; I understand too well, Hester,' she rapped out. 'You're rotten – just that. You divorced Nicholas knowing him to be guiltless and the fact that he was so weary of his life with you that he allowed you to do so, is quite immaterial. Never, for a second, did you even wonder if we were lovers – you knew we were not.'

'That's a lie!' Hester's voice rose frantically.

'Oh, no it isn't … but we served your purpose so well.'

Nicholas gasped:

'What do you mean?'

Hester flung herself at Nicholas like someone demented:

'Don't listen to her,' she gasped. 'She's lying and–'

Nicholas swept her aside as though recoiling from her touch.

'Haven't we had enough melodrama,' he said cuttingly.

Valerie turned to him and her voice was very quiet and firm as she went on:

'Hester and Hector Wincott had been lovers for quite a long while before she divorced you, Nicholas. But Hector had no intention, whatsoever, of being involved in any divorce action. At that time he was a very wealthy man and you were not, Nick. Fortunately, for you, you did not inherit your uncle's money until afterwards...' She looked at Hester who was now cringing, beaten. 'You schemed to get Nicholas and me to that cottage that night determined to obtain the evidence you needed; determined to marry Hector Wincott's *money*, in short. And you succeeded.'

Stephanie was watching Hester as one fascinated, for suddenly she regained her confidence; the light of cunning, then the spirit of defiance returned to her eyes as she challenged Valerie:

'And just how can you possibly know all this?' she demanded scornfully. 'Were you there? No! Of course not. This is just like all the rest of this ridiculous nonsense today. You and Stephanie are in conspiracy against me. Do you think I can't see through you, too? It will serve your purpose very well if Nicholas marries Stephanie ... that will leave Trevor–' She uttered the name scornfully – 'free for you.'

'It so happens, Mrs Wincott, that Valerie has already promised to be my wife. Only *you* could have thought of an ulterior motive such as you have just imputed.'

Hester's eyes gleamed maliciously.

'General post.' She flung Valerie a contemptuous glance. 'I'm glad you have the decency not to try to substantiate your vile story about Hector and I.'

Valerie said:

'Not only can I substantiate the story, but I can give it you in writing, if necessary. It so happens that I met Hector's daughter while I was in South Africa... You haven't forgotten Irene, by any chance – have you? Since you robbed her of her inheritance and grabbed every penny of her father's money for yourself... She knew the whole, sordid story; just as she knew that her father, horrified in the end by what he had done, died of a broken heart. And you have the effrontery to return to this country, seek Stephanie out, and imagine that you could begin your diabolical schemes again. Your meeting Nicholas that night was no coincidence; you were determined to get him back. The idea appealed to your vanity because you were – even though it did suit your purpose – piqued because he let you divorce him so easily. Then, you realized that he and Stephanie were in love with each other. That sharpened the edge of your desire. The rest was simple.'

Nicholas stood, grim, statue-like.

'My God!' His voice was hoarse. He turned to Hester. 'Now I can see through it all,' he murmured. 'I congratulate you on your incredibly good acting. Useless to pretend I suspected you: I didn't. We were incompatible; you were grossly selfish – I was aware of those things. But never – never for a second was I aware of your true character. If that makes me a fool then I am one. But I'm not the first man to be taken in by a woman like you... And, now, I suggest that you leave this district and never return to it.'

Hester looked from face to face. Hatred poured into her heart like poison. Could she have killed each one in turn, without danger to herself, gladly would she have done so. She moved to the door.

'Don't worry,' she scoffed. 'I've every intention of leaving the district. You sicken me – the whole dam' lot of you! Believe me, there are fresh fields to conquer and no one can take my *money* away from me.' She glanced at Nicholas. 'I expect you would have bored me to death in the end, anyway,' she said defiantly. Then, to Stephanie: 'You're welcome to him. I don't really know why I bothered,' she finished airily.

Stephanie was trembling and sick at heart.

Hester flashed her a last glance.

'Thanks for the hospitality... In future don't be such a fool. Never stand aside while the other woman tries to get the man, my dear. Such rotten technique.'

Stephanie flushed. Hester looked at Nicholas – and as a parting shot, murmured:

'Yes, she promised me that she would not encourage you, my dear man. I wish you joy of each other.' A snort at Trevor. 'Any man who marries an actress needs courage, or is a dam' fool.'

And with that she sailed out of the room.

Stephanie shook her head.

'I *can't* believe it,' she gasped.

Trevor murmured:

'I did warn you, my dear.'

Nicholas sighed.

'There's so much I could say–'

'It isn't worth it,' Valerie insisted quietly. 'But I had to let you know the truth, Nick. She's too dangerous and so plausible that only by killing her influence, once and for all, could we hope for happiness in this circle of ours.'

Stephanie said reflectively:

'It never occurred to me to doubt her.'

'And you gave her that promise?' Nicholas's voice was shaken.

'Yes... And I kept it,' she murmured as one having no regrets.

The sound of a car snorting its way down the road sent them to the window.

'The last of Hester Wincott,' said Valerie briefly. 'She'll get out of this country and begin again elsewhere.'

'It is beyond me,' Stephanie insisted. 'What can anyone like that get out of life.'

Trevor shook his head.

'It is more than I can fathom.'

Nicholas said slowly:

'They get out of it precisely what they put into it – which is nothing. That is why they are driven to the evils they are. Her only enemy is Hester.' Then as one dismissing the past, his hand reached out and drew Stephanie to him. 'I don't have to explain that we are to be married – do I?'

Valerie chuckled.

'I think we can take a hint!'

Stephanie smiled at her – a warm, loving smile in which was understanding, affection and trust.

'I lose someone whom I believed to be a friend,' she said simply, 'and gain one who I know *is* my friend – may I say that?'

Valerie answered gently:

'You may, my dear.' Then, lightly, to ease

the emotional tension. 'You should have seen us rushing back in the early hours of this morning! I think we were both terrified lest Hester might have got you to the altar ahead of schedule, Nick!'

Nicholas shook his head.

'I can never tell you how greatly I appreciate it – both of you.' He flicked his cigarette-case from his pocket. 'I hope I'm reinstated, Morly, as a fit member of society?'

'Definitely! I always had to try damned hard to convince myself that you *were* an outsider,' he admitted frankly.

Stephanie gave a little chuckle.

'And we humans imagine ourselves to be normal. When one thinks of the impossible things we do; the way we allow ourselves to be deceived and, then, cling to our pride by way of making ourselves thoroughly unhappy! We really should be in "The Snake Pit" – all of us.'

Valerie cried facetiously:

'We should have been – if Hester had been given her own way!'

Stephanie allowed herself to bask in the contemplation of her own happiness; to look at Nicholas and thrill with the ecstasy of realizing that, soon, he would be her husband and that the nightmare of doubt and suspicion and desperate hurt was no more. To dwell on the thought of Hester would be merely to perpetuate the memory of misery and serve no constructive purpose. A surging emotion filled her heart in those moments as the deep consciousness of a spiritual fulfilment possessed her. She felt Nicholas's hand holding hers, and a sense of security came to her as of a traveller crossing the threshold of home. For so long she had wandered in the wilderness of a seemingly uninhabited land without hope of sanctuary; while unreality, loneliness, had been the spectres walking beside her, until only by clinging to the numbness of in-difference could she endure the journey. Now, slowly, miraculously, she returned to warm, pulsating life, aware of the world around her and of the blood flowing in her veins. She *belonged* once more and that same belonging had its inception in Nicholas's love, in the promise of the future and the magic, enchanting happiness of the present.

CHAPTER XVIII

The September dusk lay softly upon the acres of Wilderness Farm; in it was reflected the crimson of the afterglow, giving to the earth a mellowness and depth of gently fold-ing shadows which crept over valleys and rested in the cradle of the Cotswolds.

Nicholas stood, with Stephanie beside him, and gazed out upon the scene as a man who had come into his heritage.

'Are you sure this was really what you wanted,' he murmured. 'To spend our honeymoon here, my darling?'

'Quite, quite sure,' she answered and, involuntarily as he spoke, she fondled the wedding ring so recently placed upon her finger at the little church at Coleshill. 'This is home, Nicholas. Later, we can steal away to the Continent but, for the moment, I want to drink in all this beauty, share it with you – your wife.'

'Of seven hours,' he added, and his voice shook with the passion of remembrance.

She rested against him as one exhausted by the emotion engulfing her.

'A last look at all this,' she whispered, 'before we shut out the world, my dearest … do you remember the first time you showed me over part of it…'

'Perfectly. I was in love with you from that moment – fight you thought I tried.'

'Splendid!' A sigh. 'I loved you and I hated you for not selling me your table.' A little laugh. 'Now I'm thankful you didn't sell it, or else I should not have the pleasure of looking at it and loving it, myself.'

A full moon was rising above the ridge of the trees as they stood drinking in the wonder of the countryside spread out before their eyes; a moon hanging low and deeply golden and diffusing the heavens around it with a soft roseate glow.

'Peace,' Stephanie whispered. And her mind, for a split second, embraced the events of the past two weeks, during which time she had made hurried preparations for the wedding. Michael's delight and simultaneous announcement that Felice was expecting a baby! A tender smile played about her mouth. Trevor and Valerie, already married and honeymooning in London and staying at the Ritz. The engagement party given at Castle Grange by Sir William and Lady Graceton for her and Nicholas ... the glory of the setting that quivered with the happiness that surrounded them, as they danced until the early hours and drove back to their respective homes, hating, grudging the convention that kept them apart, yet clinging to its precious tradition for all that, because they had found a love which could accept nothing less than the blessing the Church had to offer.

And now...

Eyes met in wordless inquiry as they stood rapt in contemplation of the scene, aware of the sweet, sharp knowledge that the lands belonged to them; that, for generations to come, the hour of their marriage would mark the beginning of the story of Wilderness Farm...

Nicholas hardly dared to breathe so great was his happiness. This was his world and, in Stephanie, he had found someone to share it; to see it with his eyes as something more than mere *land,* but rather, as a tradition, rich in all the spiritual forces and exultant in its supremacy.

'Darling!' Her voice was low, hushed and, together they turned and slowly walked into the house that was to be their home. They moved side by side up the wide staircase, feeling the warmth coming from firelit rooms below, in a soft, comforting wave and taking in the fragrance stealing from flowers that were massed everywhere, giving life and colour and artistry to the scene.

Their bedroom, large and lofty, had been furnished specially during the past weeks, with antiques beloved of them both. By day, the massive floor to ceiling windows gave a view over the entire farm and the county from Warwick to Worcestershire and Gloucestershire.

The silence was heavy as though only their heart-beats were recorded in it; as though time ceased to exist and life encircled only that moment which was *now* and so rightly theirs.

Nicholas drew her to him, gazing at her in the soft, subdued light of a standard lamp which was set to throw into relief the magnificent four-poster bed.

'Happy, my darling?'

'Too happy – can one be almost afraid of happiness when one has been so sad?'

'Perhaps... No regrets?'

'Nicholas! *Regrets!*'

'I was thinking of your decision to give up the business,' he said gravely. 'It came to me just now lest you might miss the–'

She put a hand up to his mouth to silence him.

'I couldn't bear to be away from here – and you,' she answered earnestly. 'I want to build a home, my darling; to watch all your ambitions for the farm materialize. And, above all, I want children to carry on its tradition.' She looked up at him and passion, held sensitively in check, flamed wildly between them.

Hungrily, he held her, his lips seeking hers and in that instant, he felt the weight of her body relaxing against his, the swift desire mounting between them, the ecstasy of surrender surging in a warm tide upon them as she clung to him, her parted lips offering still greater oblivion in that fierce response which gives as its demands and finds rapture in the giving, making body and soul one.

'I love you – love you.' His words came hoarsely, almost desperately.

And her answer as she felt his arms lifting her completely against him.

'And I love you – now and always.'

Moonlight poured in upon them from windows no longer curtained... The stillness was deeper; the silence broken only by their half-smothered sighs of love. For them the world died leaving only the perfection of their absolute belonging.

The publishers hope that this book has given you enjoyable reading. Large Print Books are especially designed to be as easy to see and hold as possible. If you wish a complete list of our books please ask at your local library or write directly to:

Dales Large Print Books
Magna House, Long Preston,
Skipton, North Yorkshire.
BD23 4ND